YOUNG-SOON SLUNG THE RIFLE OVER HER SHOULDER

Rushing down the alleyway until she reached a fire-escape ladder, she shoved a Dumpster into position and vaulted onto it, finding purchase on the edge.

She hefted the DZJ08 in both hands and let it go with a careful, underhand toss. It cleared the railing and landed on the bottommost deck. She leapt and grabbed for the third rung up. Immediately, she started climbing hand over hand. Her palms were calloused from years of field training and she could easily lift twice the weight of her lithe, agile frame.

This was child's play compared to what her instructors had put her through.

Upon reaching the fire escape, she retrieved the launcher, primed the weapon and hefted it onto her shoulder. Then she took careful aim. The Americans didn't know it but they were driving straight into a trap.

Now all she had to do was wait for her prey.

Other titles in this series:

DON PENDLETON'S

STONY

AMERICA'S ULTRA-COVERT INTELLIGENCE AGENCY

MAN®

PRODIGY EFFECT

A GOLD EAGLE BOOK FROM
WORLDWIDE®

TORONTO • NEW YORK • LONDON
AMSTERDAM • PARIS • SYDNEY • HAMBURG
STOCKHOLM • ATHENS • TOKYO • MILAN
MADRID • WARSAW • BUDAPEST • AUCKLAND

Recycling programs
for this product may
not exist in your area.

First edition October 2013

ISBN-13: 978-0-373-80441-2

PRODIGY EFFECT

Special thanks and acknowledgment to
Matt Kozar for his contribution to this work.

Printed in U.S.A.

PRODIGY EFFECT

CHAPTER ONE

Bering Sea

Twin F-16DM jet fighters streaked across the cold blue sky on an intercept course.

A few minutes earlier, a secured satellite transmission from Joint Base Elmendorf-Richardson had pinged the fighter patrol to advise of an incoming bogey. The origin of the object was unknown and it was transmitting no signals, despite repeated requests on all channels to identify. Both were conditions that forced the air command of the 18th Aggressor Squadron to order the intruder shot down.

Well, that was just fine with USAF Captain Don "Jockey" Seward—and his wingman, Captain Dino "Dynomutt" Fawcett.

The pilots banked in response to the order and immediately embarked on an intercept course that would bring them in contact a mere eleven miles off the coast of Alaska. Even as they proceeded toward their target, Seward and Fawcett knew the Coastal Missile Defense System-Alaska would already be online and prepared to deploy electronic counterjamming and ballistic measures to stop the missile if the interceptors failed in their mission. Fat chance. These two men were decorated USAF veterans—having seen combat in both the Gulf and Pacific—who were more than happy to oblige any time a threat to security of their country was detected. They were also itching to taste a little action.

"Looks like it's going to be an interesting morning," Seward told his wingman.

"Roger that, Jockey," Fawcett replied. "I have target marked at now 18.16 miles, 56-November, 166-Whiskey, elevation six thousand five hundred."

"Copy, and confirmed," Seward said, all business now. "Stand by to target."

A minute passed in eerie silence for the pilots, the distant buzz of radio traffic between Elmendorf-Richardson and CMDS-A taking the priority on channel. When they were within five nautical miles the order was confirmed to target the unidentified craft, with a special order to disable over destroy if at all possible. Both pilots realized in the same moment that because air command didn't really know what they were dealing with, they were hedging their bets in the hope of shooting the bogey down and dispatching a salvage operation to retrieve it intact. The waters below were cold and deep, but not so inaccessible as to make recovery impossible, and command would know the F-16DM fighters were toting some low-yield warheads in their arsenal.

As they got closer, the channel was cleared so the pilots could coordinate their efforts.

"Golf Three to Golf Four," Seward called officially, quite aware their every transmission would be monitored.

"Golf Four here."

"I have the bogey in sight. Acquiring a lock."

"Roger, Golf Three. Confirm that target is moving *very* slow. Over."

"Roger that, Golf Four."

Seward paused to consider that and wondered if he shouldn't call an abort for more data.

It wasn't a small plane, but it was moving at about the max speed of a twin-engine Sea King. Seward knew this because he owned one himself, and he'd never seen any sort of weapon that would fly at that altitude or speed. Hell, a kid with a BB gun could practically shoot the thing down. It just didn't make sense and Seward wondered if it wouldn't be more prudent to collect additional data, take a closer look before they just blew the thing out of the sky.

After wrestling with his decision a moment longer, the thrumming tone of target lock in his ears, Seward shook it off and triggered the warhead. The missile launched with incredible speed in contrast to that of its target. Two seconds passed…three…the missile hit. The low-yield warhead was designed to strike an object in the tail, the heat from the expended fuel generating a frangible-type detonation that would turn the ballistic system of any target to confetti. The missile did the job nicely, blowing out the entire propulsion system and knocking the whatever-it-was off course. The object continued another half mile before dropping into the choppy waters of the Bering and knifing beneath the surface, ultimately to settle on a shelf at a depth of approximately eight hundred feet.

UNKNOWN TO THE civilian populace and most of the military, the entire incident in the Bering Strait was routed straight to the Pentagon, where it landed simultaneously on the desks of the Secretary of the Navy and Chairman of the Joint Chiefs. The report, in turn, was added to the CIA daily brief to the President due in large part to some analysts who suggested the as-yet unidentified object might possibly be a testing prototype belonging to the North Koreans.

When the Oval Office was made aware of an immediate effort already under way by the Coast Guard and Navy to recover the object, the President cleared the Situation Room and placed a call to the one man he knew could help sort out the mess.

Harold Brognola answered that call on the first ring. "Yes, sir."

"Hal, it's already starting out to be one of those days," the President replied. "Did I wake you?"

"I hardly sleep these days, sir. The odds are probably in your favor."

"We have a situation, and I'm sending the details to you at this very moment. I want to ensure the safe recovery of the device in question, as well as implement some proactive security controls. Please see to it that your people are involved in this every step of the way."

"Of course, sir. You'll have our full cooperation."

"And, Hal…keep a low profile on this one if at all possible? There are a lot of our own involved this time. I don't want to make noise unless it becomes absolutely necessary."

"Understood, sir. I have just the men in mind for the job."

CHAPTER TWO

Carl Lyons, leader of Able Team, sighed with relief as the HH-65 Dolphin chopper landed on the deck of the Coast Guard cutter *Glacier,* a WAGB-class heavy icebreaker.

The crewman slid the door aside and tossed a casual salute as Lyons and his two teammates disembarked the SAR-class helicopter and ran in a single-file crouch across the deck. Sharp, cold winds bit at exposed skin not protected by hoods and goggles. Each man toted a personal kit that included weapons, spare ammunition and several changes of clothing. In addition to the red-orange Arctic coats with zip-in fur and neoprene liners, each man wore black BDU fatigues marked with sewed-in stencils above the left pocket that read U.S. ONI. Stony Man Farm had also arranged matching credentials identifying the trio as agents with the United States Office of Naval Intelligence—it had been the best cover under the circumstances.

While their identities would suffice enough such that nobody would ask questions, Lyons didn't really feel comfortable in the role. He hated boats, for one, and he wasn't terribly keen on a *military* cover ID since it meant he had to kowtow to the higher brass. A good number of agents within the ONI were former Navy, and as Lyons had never served in any branch of the armed forces he didn't always come off as experienced.

Not to worry too much since Rosario "Politician" Blancanales and Hermann "Gadgets" Schwarz, his Able Team colleagues, were old combat vets of the U.S. Army and knew their way around military protocols pretty well. So Lyons tried to stay out of the way—as much as he could while still maintaining his position as the team leader—in favor of leaving the more delicate work of military customs to his comrades.

An officer showed them through a door that emerged onto a very long corridor. It took them several minutes to reach an external stairwell that led to the bridge. In addition to its resupply missions for Arctic research stations, the *Glacier* also boasted capabilities as a scientific research platform. It could warehouse up to five laboratories and quarter nearly as many scientists as were necessary, although most of the time the vessel didn't serve this role. The mission to recover the ballistic device that had been shot down two days earlier had prompted the deployment of the WAGB-18 out of its home station in Washington State.

The commander of the ship greeted Able Team as they entered the bridge.

"Permission to come aboard," Blancanales said easily.

"Granted," the officer replied. "I'm Captain Boardman, and you've of course met my operations officer and your escort, Lieutenant Commander Szpusta."

Lyons introduced the members of Able Team, using their cover names. When the handshaking was dispensed with, he asked, "What's the current status of the operation, Captain?"

Boardman grunted. "Where the hell do I start? I suppose you've been briefed."

"Just barely," Schwarz remarked.

"We were kind of called up in a hurry," Blancanales added. "As I assume were you, sir."

"Weren't we all?" Boardman replied with a congenial wink. "Well, let's see… I suppose we could begin by saying that the device is wedged into a crevasse of an ice shelf at a current depth of about 230 meters. But we've hit a snag."

"What kind of snag?" Lyons asked.

"The warhead…missile, call it what you will, is wedged nose-first and we're concerned about triggering an underwater explosion if we force it out. That would muck up our operation real quick, don't you know."

"Agreed."

Boardman scratched his chin and turned to a nearby console that displayed a multicolored diagram. "This here shows a computer-simulated map of the immediate salvage area around the object, as well as the position of the tethered ROV. Frankly, we're not having a whole lot of luck with that remotely operated vehicle. We're using an MP1-class Mine Neutralization Vehicle but it's not really designed for this kind of precision work. Typically MNVs are deployed by Avenger-class mine countermeasure ships."

Blancanales's brow furrowed. "I guess I understand the need for expediency, but we were advised you were supposed to have an expert aboard assisting you with the recovery."

"True," Boardman said, "although she hasn't arrived yet. I guess she got caught up in some bad weather."

"She?" Schwarz prompted.

"Sir, if I may?" Szpusta interjected. When Boardman nodded, Szpusta continued. "We're waiting for Dr. Stavros, a chief ballistic missiles expert with the Defense

Advanced Research Projects Agency. Dr. Stavros is renowned in her field and has done many operations of this nature, apparently. Until she gets here we're at somewhat of a disadvantage."

"DARPA, eh? I see," Blancanales replied.

"Which brings me to a question of my own, gentlemen," Boardman said. "I was told to expect your arrival but, frankly, I wasn't told exactly what ONI's part is in all of this. Would you care to elaborate?"

"There's not much we can say without compromising national security," Lyons replied.

Blancanales picked it up without missing a beat. "But as it's your ship, sir, you deserve to at least know our role while we're aboard. Essentially, we're on hand to maintain security of the operation, as well as to ensure that whatever this thing is, information isn't leaked to unfriendly ears."

Boardman's eyes narrowed and his face took on just the hint of redness. He turned to an unnamed officer and said, "XO, you have the bridge," before gesturing for the three men to follow him into an adjoining briefing room. A table took up most of the space with a half dozen chairs ranged around it. Boardman waved the three warriors into the chairs before closing the door and taking a seat at what could roughly be called the head of the table.

"I pulled you in here because I didn't want what I said to be publicly disseminated." Boardman cleared his throat before continuing. "But from what I just *thought* I heard you say, it sounds as if perhaps the Navy has concerns about the discretion of one or more of the crewmembers aboard this ship."

"We don't know what the Navy's concerned about as it relates to your crew, Captain," Lyons said. "What we *do* know is that there are some concerns at very high levels that your little treasure below may have originated from North Korea."

"You can understand," Schwarz said, "that's probably not something SECNAV would want to get out to anyone under the circumstances."

Lyons concluded, "Which is why we're here. To make sure that any and all information remains secure, as well as to ensure security protocols are strictly followed by your civilian passengers."

"I have no desire to get in a pissing match with you boys," Boardman said. "But you'd best understand that I'm the captain of this vessel, and ultimately the safety of everyone aboard this ship, *including* you three, falls on my shoulders. Is that clear?"

"Crystal, sir," Blancanales said with one of his famous smiles. "And understand that we have no intention of doing anything that would undermine your authority."

"Captain, our job is simple," Lyons said. "We're to observe and assist, if you request it, and once the operation is complete and we've returned to port, we're out of here and back to Washington. You're still the boss. Fair enough?"

"Okay, I'll take your word as a gentleman on it." There was a rap at the door. "Come!"

Szpusta opened it and poked his head inside. "Sir, I apologize for the interruption but Dr. Stavros has arrived."

Boardman nodded and all four men rose before filing out of the meeting room.

Priscilla Stavros was strikingly attractive—Lyons guessed she was in her early forties. She had smoky-blue eyes and sensuous lips and wore her shiny black hair in a ponytail. Her hip-hugging ski pants accentuated her shapely thighs and calves, but any other details were obscured by a long, green fleece coat with white piping along the collar and sleeves.

"Good morning, gentlemen," she greeted, her voice warmly husky. "I'm Dr. Priscilla Stavros."

She extended her hand to Captain Boardman first, and then acknowledged the other officers in strict order of rank from senior to junior, reserving her final greetings for the three men of Able Team. When her eyes met Lyons's, and they shook hands, the Able Team leader experienced a surge in desire.

If Stavros even noticed Lyons with her cursory inspection, she made no show of it. But had he noticed just a momentary twinkle in her eye and quirk at the corner of her mouth in what might arguably be deemed a mischievous smile? Only time would tell. But for the moment Lyons knew she was here to do a job and he wouldn't do anything to risk either Able Team's mission or the security of Stavros and company.

"I think I speak for all of us when I say we're glad to see you, Dr. Stavros," Boardman said.

Stavros nodded in acknowledgment. "Your preliminary reports were transmitted to me aboard the flight. I have to apologize for the delays, but weather is one of those things we cannot control."

"At least not yet, right?" Schwarz joked.

Stavros glanced at him, flashed a smile and then returned her attention to Boardman. "There's no question you are faced with a challenge. And I completely concur that the tools you're trying to use to execute the salvage are not suited to the job at hand. But I've already taken steps to correct that issue. I have a DSRV-2 being air-lifted in. We'll need your permission for the chopper to land, Captain."

Boardman tendered a curt nod. "Granted. Lieutenant Commander Szpusta, please see that the top-deck crew chief and his men are ready to receive whatever equipment may arrive."

"Yes, sir. Although I do feel it's pertinent to point out we're not equipped to store something of that size at present. I don't know if we have time to rearrange the topside equipment currently stored."

"I'm forced to agree with the commander," Stavros said. "This is a Mystic-class Deep Submergence Rescue Vehicle that is 15 meters in length, 2.4 meters in diameter at its center and weighs more than 30 tons surfaced. That doesn't even include the adjunct equipment that must be loaded separately onto it."

"Hmm…." Boardman scratched his chin. "That *is* a problem."

"Any reason the chopper couldn't just drop this thing right into the water close enough you could attach an EVA line?" Schwarz suggested. "When you're finished with it, you can then just tow it or airlift it out."

"Excellent idea!" Boardman looked at Stavros. "Dr. Stavros, any objections?"

"None."

"Is there anything else we can assist you with?"

"I don't think so at present. Although I would like to get a look at whatever additional data you've collected in the event things have changed since I received the initial reports." Stavros turned toward the Able Team warriors. "I was also advised that the Office of Naval Intelligence would be present for the duration. Apparently, you're here to ensure the, ah, *security* of myself and staff."

"That's right, ma'am," Lyons replied.

"Seems like sort of an odd job for the ONI," Stavros said. "Are you positive there's nothing more to it?"

"Let's just say our mission is to be seen and not heard whenever possible."

"It's what our higher-ups like to call 'low profile,'" Blancanales added with a charitable grin.

"Too bad," Stavros said with a knowing smile as she inclined her head in Schwarz's direction. "Because Mr. Black already assisted by coming up with a suggestion to drop the DSRV-2 into the water directly."

Schwarz was visibly appreciative of her recognition of the contribution. Lyons felt a sour taste but then chided himself for being jealous. This wasn't a competition to see who got the girl, and he didn't believe for a second Schwarz had made his suggestion in the hope of wooing Stavros in some fashion. What the hell? They weren't in high school here—this was real life. Get hold of yourself, he thought.

"We'd best get out of the way and let you work," Lyons said, turning to Boardman. "Captain, if you don't mind, maybe we could get settled below?"

"Absolutely," he said. "I'll have the master-at-arms show you to your quarters. We still have a few hours until chow. I assume you'd prefer to dine with me and the officers?"

"Either way's fine. We're more than happy to eat with the enlisted if there's limited room at the captain's table."

Boardman nodded and with that, Able Team left the bridge and followed the petty officer to their quarters. They were quartered together, although the accommodations were cramped and spartan. The bunks were positioned alongside each other with minimal leg room between them. The trio immediately shed their cold-weather coats and then checked their weapons. Lyons had forfeited his Colt Anaconda in favor of a brand-new FNP-45, both for its compactness in concealment and durability in the harsh marine environment. Lyons missed the familiar heft of his hand-cannon but the FNP-45 was simply the best choice for this mission. Blancanales and Schwarz had brought their standard fare: Blancanales was verifying the action of a P-229 chambered in .357 SIG while Schwarz did a quick wipe-down of his 9 mm Beretta 92-A1.

When they'd completed checking and holstering their weapons, which they wore in open-carry mode, the three men sat on their bunks to talk about what they'd observed thus far.

"I don't like it," Lyons said.

"What's not to like, Ironman?" Schwarz replied, using his nickname. "This is a cushy job if you ask me. And that Dr. Stavros is a real looker. I only wish we got more details protecting such beautiful assets. Huh, Pol?"

"I hadn't noticed," Blancanales said with a glib expression.

"Oh...*sure* you didn't."

Blancanales arched an eyebrow at Lyons. "So what's eating you, amigo? Give."

"Well, I don't like Boardman's attitude, for one."

"Typical sea captain," Blancanales said with a dismissive wave of his hand. "Old school."

"I also didn't like that Stavros seemed to know everything about why we're here," Lyons said. "We know that information didn't come from the Farm. So who's she been talking to?"

"Could be anyone wagging their gums, Ironman, and I

wouldn't let it worry you that much. Just means they did us justice in as much as our cover is ONI."

"Maybe so, but much of this still doesn't make sense to me. For one, I'm not convinced this little sunken treasure is actually a weapon shot off by the North Koreans."

"Well, where do you think it came from, then?" Schwarz asked.

Lyons's eyes narrowed and he chewed his lip before answering. "I'm betting it's another country. According to the reports we saw, this thing wasn't moving very fast. Sounds like whoever shot it off *wanted* us to find it."

"But what other country could it be?" Schwarz asked.

"How about China?"

Blancanales nodded. "That's a plausible theory. Go on, you've piqued my interest."

"It just doesn't *feel* like the North Koreans to me," Lyons stressed. "They like to brag, make everything they're doing public so they can wave it in NATO's face, and in turn wave it in ours. Let's not forget that we know while all eyes have been turned on North Korea over nuclear weapons proliferation, the Chinese government's been lending coin to everybody and their dog. They've got some reason to want to have that kind of financial influence and I'm guessing it's because they don't figure anybody's going to look too closely at the dirt under sugar daddy's fingernails."

"So they fire off a low-velocity ballistic device and try to frame the North Koreans for it? Sounds a bit farfetched."

Lyons didn't take Blancanales's remark at more than face value and he didn't take any personal offense, either. It wasn't meant as some sort of affront by his friend and teammate. Blancanales was a sharp tool in the shed, and

Lyons trusted his judgment. The Able Team leader knew his theory was long on bias and short on evidence, but it didn't make any difference—something in his gut told him he was onto something.

"Let's suppose you're right for a minute," Schwarz interjected. When Blancanales gave him a quizzical look, Schwarz added quickly, "No, just hear me out. If Ironman's right and there is some merit to his theory, then we have to start digging a little deeper."

"Meaning?" Blancanales said.

"Meaning—" Schwarz stopped to put his hand to his forehead and gather his thoughts "—that we'll have to keep a very close watch on Stavros. Get the information as she gets it and make our own interpretation. After all, this *could* be an attempt by another country to frame the North Koreans. Maybe it's the North Koreans wanting us to think it's the Chinese. And *maybe* it's another country entirely."

"Could be our own," Lyons added.

Blancanales fell silent for a time and finally said, "The plan's too elaborate with too much risk of getting caught. I think that thingamajig was definitely fired by another country but we have to be careful about assuming one country over another."

"I'd agree except for one minor technical point, Pol," Schwarz said.

"And that is?"

"I noticed the dimensions of that device when Boardman showed us the data. There's no way it had a fuel capacity that could take it any considerable distance, even given the low speed. Only three countries I would think have the technology to deliver a projectile that small over that distance—China, North Korea or Japan."

"And we could almost trust a hundred percent it wasn't the Japanese," Lyons said.

"I don't trust anything or anybody at this point," Blancanales said. "The facts are we don't have enough information to make any sort of intelligent decision."

"Well, Gadgets is right about one thing. Our best bet is to stick close to this Dr. Stavros and see what she comes up with."

"I volunteer," Schwarz said, shooting up his hand like an eager kindergartner.

"We'll *all* volunteer," Lyons said. "And put your hand down, you look silly."

Schwarz stuck out his lower lip in a pout.

Lyons yawned. "We'll need to stick close to Stavros and pump her for whatever information she'll give us. I think I'm going to talk to Boardman about joining the observation crew in this minisub they're bringing."

"There may not be room for all of us," Blancanales said.

Lyons shook his head. "I'm going it alone. I want you guys up here to keep an eye on my six and watch for any trouble. If something goes wrong, I don't want my final tomb to be at the bottom of the Bering Sea."

"Going down in a submarine on your own?" Blancanales chuckled and added, "That's very brave and grown-up of you, Ironman."

"Aw…blow it out your ear."

CHAPTER THREE

Tianjin, People's Republic of China

As cold rain hammered the streets, city lights cast blurry streaks against the window of the hotel room. Jim Dumbarton peered absently through the glass even though his view was effectively obstructed. He didn't like being in China and especially not when they knew he was with the CIA. The Company hadn't put an agent inside this country with an effective cover since the end of the Cold War. When CIA agents came into China, the Chinese knew it but pretended they didn't, and the top brass at Langley pretended they didn't know the Chinese were pretending.

It was like some sick Abbott and Costello routine.

What Dumbarton *did* know, however, was that the time he spent here cooling his heels would be well worth it if they could pull off this defection. Because their Chinese counterparts knew Dumbarton and one of his British SIS affiliates, Grover Haverhill—and who the hell today named their kid Grover, Dumbarton had always wondered—they figured it was easy to keep pretty close tabs to prevent the foreign agents from trying any funny business.

But as it turned out, while Haverhill might have been a pompous British jackass in the most stereotypical way possible, he was a master at deception and disinformation. They'd cooked up a grand scheme to get Teng Cai out of the country and back to the United States before the Chinese knew what was happening. And it was all set to go down tonight, finally, which Dumbarton was counting on to buy him a comfortable seat back in the States.

Yep, this Teng Cai was his ticket out of Shangri-la for good, and Haverhill had managed to secure the deal with similar goals in mind. The Briton hated his duty post nearly as much as Dumbarton and he planned to use Teng Cai's defection as leverage for a more comfortable post.

"What's so important about this Teng Cai, anyway?" Dumbarton had asked when Haverhill first approached him with the idea.

Dumbarton had met Haverhill in the corner of a local bar where he could get the details without the risk of someone overhearing.

"Only that he's the biggest secret the Chinese military might have ever had."

"One man?" Dumbarton asked with a snort.

"Not a man, a *boy*. A fourteen-year-old genius. A prodigy quite unlike any other this country's ever produced."

Dumbarton snickered. "They should try talking to Japan. They got child prodigies walking around there by the droves."

"Yeah, well, maybe so but I'll bet they ain't bloody likely to have the kind of aptitude for military sciences that Teng Cai has. And I'll tell you something else," Haverhill disclosed, "the kid wants *out* of this place."

"What's he got to trade?"

"He's not willing to cough that up until he's out of the country," Haverhill said following a hefty swallow of Beefeater.

Dumbarton wiped absently at trickles of sweat lining the bottle of Chinese beer he'd been nursing. "Well, that sure won't fly with my people. How come your folks aren't willing to take him?"

"I can't contact anybody high enough up to have the authority to make the decision. Defections are sort of a thing of the past in my neck of the woods, mate. They don't give a bloody rat's arse about any assets that won't stay in-country."

"Makes sense," Dumbarton replied. "It's how they know they're getting anything real. Most defectors have to be set up for life, and that's a pretty expensive proposition for any government unless they know the goods they're trading are worth it. Intelligence collection has become expensive and taxpayers aren't as willing to foot the bill as they once were."

"Might help if they didn't put half of every one of your operations on the six o'clock news."

"Not my fault, pal. Keeping secrets has *always* been an art form and, well…frankly Congress is filled with a lot of negative critics these days."

"So you don't think your people will bite?"

Dumbarton swigged his beer before replying, "I didn't say that. I'm just saying that unless we know what we're getting up front, it probably won't sell. Tell you what. You see how much you can drag from this boy wonder and if you hit something juicy, I'll run it up the flagpole and see who salutes."

It only took a few days for Haverhill to do just that. When word came that Teng Cai knew about a low-altitude drone project by his government, one designed to carry nuclear payloads for tactical strikes by flying below radar at low speeds, Langley sat up and took notice in record time. It surprised Dumbarton when his superiors came back and ordered the defection become his number-one priority. He was to do whatever necessary to secure Teng Cai, protect the boy and smuggle him out of the People's Republic of China by whatever means at his disposal.

When Dumbarton gave Haverhill the good news, they immediately began to plan an operation within a window of less than thirty-six hours. The two men had wondered if they would be able to even pull it off, but Fate seemed to be on their side. Within a very short time Dumbarton would be aboard a boat that would take him via the South China Sea to rendezvous with a seaplane. From there, he would connect with an American destroyer.

The door to the hotel opened with a soft click and Dumbarton's eyes flicked toward it as his hand dived beneath his jacket to the butt of his Glock G-26.

Haverhill's familiar face peered around the doorway. "Sorry, chap, forgot to make the knock first."

"I almost blew your head off."

"Yeah, that would've ruined my day," Haverhill replied with a nervous laugh as he closed the door.

"We all set?"

"Most definitely."

"Good." Dumbarton climbed from his seat and went to the compact refrigerator. He withdrew a mini bottle of Jim Beam and a Coke. "I was starting to get worried."

Focused on pouring his drink, Dumbarton didn't hear Haverhill cross the room like a great cat stalking a herd of antelope. He didn't see the semi-auto .22-caliber pistol with attached sound suppressor Haverhill withdrew from a shoulder harness. Dumbarton didn't realize until the last moment he'd been betrayed, and that was only because he was keenly and suddenly aware of a presence behind him—a presence intent only on doing harm. The

CIA agent slipped his hand beneath his own sports coat, confident he could overcome Haverhill's treachery using tactical surprise. But Haverhill had already leveled the pistol at the back of Dumbarton's head.

HAVERHILL SQUEEZED THE TRIGGER twice. Both rounds entered through the base of the skull, traveling upward to transform parts of Dumbarton's brain to mush. The sounds of his body rocketing forward and head smacking the overhead cabinet made more noise than the reports from the pistol. Haverhill watched with a mix of displeasure and fear as Dumbarton's body collapsed to the tired, cracked linoleum.

Haverhill stared a moment, pistol dangling at his side, and then holstered the weapon and headed to the bathroom. He returned with two bath towels he formed into bulky rolls and wrapped around Dumbarton's head to prevent the little bit of blood from leaking onto the floor or carpet. He then crossed to the bed and dug beneath it until he came clear with a large plastic bag he'd placed there the day before. He had Dumbarton's legs into the bag when the door opened to admit three more men, all Chinese nationals.

Wen Xiang, the team leader, stuck his hands in the pockets of his trench coat and grinned. "I see you wasted no time. Most excellent."

"Never mind that now," Haverhill said. "Why don't you boys give me a hand with this?"

"Yes, gentlemen," Wen Xiang said with a knowing wink. "Please help our friend here."

Haverhill paid no attention to the sudden and swift movements of the men. By the time he realized he had a problem, it was too late to do anything about it. Unlike

Dumbarton there was a moment, however brief, where Haverhill actually got to see it coming. The gaping mouth of the sound suppressor blurred in Haverhill's vision just a moment before the hot flash of powder burned his eyes out.

And then Grover Haverhill's world was ended as suddenly and violently as Haverhill had ended that of James Dumbarton.

Stony Man Farm, Virginia

"WE'VE GOT BIG trouble, men," Harold Brognola said.

His announcement didn't bring much of a reaction from the men of America's most elite antiterrorist unit— they'd heard it before. Comprised of five of the toughest commandos ever assembled, Phoenix Force had fought the good fight in just about every region around the globe. And while the majority of Americans didn't even know they existed, it didn't change the fact they were better than Delta Force, better than Special Forces or Navy SEALs. They were truly the final option when the chips were down, the odds were insurmountable and the situation was grim.

"Trouble's our specialty," replied David McCarter, the leader of Phoenix Force.

A former commando of Her Majesty's SAS, McCarter thrived on action. While he'd mellowed some over the years with the added responsibilities of maintaining the safety and well-being of his team, McCarter was still ready to face off against any enemy that threatened the freedom and security of America.

"I'll let Barb lay it out for you," Brognola said.

Blue eyes twinkling, Barbara Price, Stony Man Farm's

mission controller, tucked a lock of honey-blond hair behind her ear. "Yesterday evening we received reports from one of our connections inside the CIA that their key agent in the city of Tianjin has disappeared. Not two hours after receiving that first report, officials from the People's Republic of China notified a British embassy that they had found the bodies of both a British diplomat and an unidentified American south of the city along the banks of the Hai River. The American was eventually identified as CIA undercover officer James Dumbarton. We have, as yet, not been able to solicit the British government to release the identity of their man but we're pretty sure that it might be a member of the British SIS by the name of Grover Haverhill."

"That's all real interesting, Barb," T. J. Hawkins said. "But what's that got to do with us?"

"*Santa Maria,* I'm sure she's getting to that, *compadre,*" Rafael Encizo said. "Just keep your spurs on, eh?"

Encizo had made the remark with a half smile so Hawkins didn't appear to take it personally. This kind of banter wasn't unusual, especially between the serious-minded Cuban immigrant and Hawkins, a native Texan and former member of Delta Force. The two men were as opposite in their levels of patience as they were united in their love for America.

Calvin James watched the entire exchange with amusement and then told Price in a conspiratorial whisper, "Just ignore them. It works for me."

Price smiled as she continued. "Moving forward? The Chinese Ministry of State Security isn't saying much, but from our preliminary findings these men were killed execution-style."

"Assassinations?" Gary Manning shook his head. A

former member of the Royal Canadian Mounted Police and Phoenix Force's demolitions expert, Manning had a near encyclopedic knowledge of terrorist groups all over the world. "Now that *is* strange—covert assassination of foreign espionage agents doesn't really smack of activities by any known terrorist group operating in that region."

"Agreed," Brognola said. "And in light of the recent incident off the coast of Alaska, we're wondering if the two issues aren't connected in some way."

McCarter asked, "What about Able Team? We got any additional information from them that might shed some light on the situation?"

"Nothing so far, although it's still a little early in the game," Price replied. "But the timing of these deaths, be they assassinations or otherwise, has to be more than co-incidence. We also received some intelligence a short time ago that has helped us to develop a working theory around this situation. I've asked Bear to present that to you."

To this point, Aaron "the Bear" Kurtzman had been sitting quietly, hunkered over a computer workstation to one side of the room. Now he sat straighter in his wheelchair and let his eyes scan each of the Phoenix Force warriors with a smile before he typed a code word into the computer. A massive wall screen flickered a moment before an image of a young boy, accompanied by two adults and a third man in a Chinese military uniform, materialized.

"Meet Teng Cai, gents," Kurtzman said. "This picture was taken several years ago, when Teng Cai was about eleven. Cai is nothing less than a prodigy, which is probably an understatement if ever there was one. He's a genius. A whiz kid with astounding commands of mathematical aeronautics and spatial programming paradigms."

"Who are the other people in the picture?" McCarter asked.

"The two in civilian clothes are his parents. His father is now deceased, but his mother lives in Hebei Province on the northern border of Tianjin. The man in the uniform has been identified as Air Vice-Marshal Yan Zhou of the PRCAF."

"Uh-oh," Encizo interjected. "I think I already see where this is going. A defection gone hard?"

Kurtzman replied, "Give the man one of your cigars, Hal."

"That's *exactly* our theory," Price said. "Scuttlebutt among those in the know at the Company is that Dumbarton may have been working with our as-yet unnamed British diplomat on a plan to smuggle Teng Cai out of the country. According to our records, some locals with connections to the British SIS had chartered a boat crew for a midnight run down the Hai River and out to open sea. Now we don't know their destination, but word is the deal was brokered in cash and four passengers were slated. We think those passengers included Dumbarton and his co-conspirator, plus two—most likely Teng Cai and his mother."

Manning nodded. "Sounds like a *very* good theory to me."

"We also have it on good authority that SECNAV sent an encrypted communication to a U.S. Navy destroyer at this point here," Kurtzman said, tapping another key.

A topographical map of the Philippine Sea replaced the image of Teng Cai, et al. The map displayed a red dot superimposed with latitudinal and longitudinal coordinates.

James let out a low whistle. "I spent a tour in the Philippines. If I remember my geography, that's a good seven to eight hundred miles from Tianjin. Much too great a distance for any sort of local craft."

"Not mention the risk of intercept by a variety of maritime authorities patrolling those various regions," McCarter added. "And then there're the bloody pirates and drug smugglers running about."

"We think wherever they were headed was much closer," Price said. "Maybe a larger port or perhaps even a small island where they might rendezvous with a larger boat, perhaps even a plane. The destination was kept under wraps. We can't even find out why the Navy had agreed to dispatch a destroyer to that area."

"So you're saying that even if the Company *was* working with Dumbarton on this, they're not going to tell anybody else," Hawkins said. "Damn but the politicking has run amok, as usual."

"Afraid I'm forced to agree with you on that one," McCarter replied. He let out a sigh. "So what's the game plan?"

"We think Dumbarton's British counterpart might have been playing footsies with sympathizers inside the Ministry of State Security, and they ultimately betrayed him," Price said. "There's no other plausible explanation at this point. Now we've managed to reach out to one of our contacts inside Red China, guy by the name of Hark Kwan. He's a former agent of the MSS and a hundred percent trustworthy."

"You'll pardon me for asking, but how can we be sure of that?" McCarter said.

Price grinned. "He's given up good intelligence to us on a number of previous occasions. *And*...he's worked directly with Striker in counteracting Chinese affiliates to the Russian Business Network."

The mention of Mack Bolan was all Phoenix Force needed to hear. The Executioner had waged an endless war against terror groups threatening the American way of life, to make no mention of the fact it was his devotion to duty and ideals that had provided the foundation on which Stony Man had been built. Bolan was a consummate soldier who represented everything America stood for—at least the America the men and women of Stony Man understood.

"If Striker vouches for this Kwan, that's good enough for us," Encizo said, echoing the sentiments of every individual in the room.

Price continued. "Your mission is to penetrate Tianjin, locate Teng Cai and get him out of the country."

"And what if it turns out he actually doesn't want to defect?" McCarter asked.

"Then you remove him *involuntarily*," Brognola said around an unlit cigar. The Stony Man chief pulled the soggy tip of the stogie from his mouth and said, "We're convinced that Teng Cai knows something about this device currently being recovered in the Bering Sea. In fact, we believe he had a direct influence on its development, and if not, then we're pretty sure he has other intelligence vital to national security."

"In either case, we think a faction of the Chinese government may be responsible for the demise of Jim Dumbarton," Price said. "Whether sanctioned or not, we can't just let it stand the way it is. We need you to find out what the hell's going on over there, then take swift and remedial action based on those findings."

Price looked at Brognola, who nodded and then said, "There's one more thing. We believe *if* the British SIS had been working with the Company to facilitate Teng Cai's defection, they'll likely try again. We can't risk them getting into bed with any more of the wrong people. This could result in considerable hostilities between the United States and China. If such hostilities go public, we can forget about any further cooperation from them with regards to American interests be they financial, political or otherwise. Understood?"

All of them nodded.

Price stood. "Okay, then you'd best get moving. Jack's waiting for you at Andrews."

"Good luck, men," Hal Brognola said.

CHAPTER FOUR

Carl Lyons swallowed back the bile that had formed like putty in his throat, gulping air and trying not to notice the bubbles streaming past the oval viewports of the DSRV-2.

Every so often he'd looked forward to the dive console and watched as the large red screen with yellow numbers recorded their depth during their descent. Lyons hated boats, yeah, but he hated submarines even more—this was hardly his idea of fun. But then again, what mission ever was? They had now been suspended with their portside to the shelf where the missile, or whatever the hell it was, had been wedged.

Priscilla Stavros had taken a keen notice of Lyons's growing discomfort during the dive and she now rested a hand on his forearm. "Are you all right, Mr. Norris?"

"Call me Carl," Lyons said in response to her formal use of his cover name. "And yeah, I'm fine. Why do you ask?"

"You look a little peaked," she replied.

Lyons smiled. "I think it was breakfast."

"Of course, sure." Stavros didn't look convinced but she didn't press the point. "Have you ever been in a submarine?"

"Few times."

"Ever aboard something this small?"

Lyons shook his head. "Not even close. I served most

of my tours at air stations. Never did have much use for sea duty."

"Other than the mandatory six-month float, of course."

"Right." Lyons cursed himself for nearly slipping up his cover.

Part of him wondered if Stavros was even buying their story. He still didn't know who could've slipped her information about them, even with all of the official documents and paperwork Stony Man had prepped to layer their cover identities. With perhaps the exception of some of their weapons and the electronic doodads Schwarz carried, Able Team was careful to ensure that even their equipment and luggage met the standards anyone might expect applicable to whatever cover identities they used. But Stavros was no idiot. She'd been in this game plenty, not to mention she had a borderline genius IQ according to her dossier, so it wouldn't be tough for her to spot a phony.

If she had, though, she hadn't betrayed it to Lyons or anyone else.

Stavros continued, "The first DSRV-2, the *Avalon,* was decommissioned in 2000. What many don't know is the Navy built more than one. None of them saw use so they stuck *Avalon* in a museum. The other three they stripped of the top secret equipment, refitted them with civilian variants and then sold them off to private concerns."

"I'm surprised you managed to get your hands on one so easily."

"I own my own research company," she replied. "We have lots of grants, not to mention plenty of private funding, so I got very lucky."

"I'm sure your connections helped," Lyons said. When the remark brought a frown to her face he backpedaled.

"Sorry, wasn't making any sort of implications there. Just an observation."

The etched lines at the corners of her eyes and around her lips vanished and she nodded. "Thank you. Actually, this is quite a vehicle if you take the time to understand it. For example, we're currently at a depth of about 800 meters, which is less than one-fifth the maximum depth rating. Additionally, we retrofitted this system with an umbilical attachment, so our power comes directly from the ship. These models used to operate solely off batteries, requiring them to be recharged regularly, but now they just act as backup systems in case something goes wrong with the umbilical."

Lyons took another look around and nodded. "It is impressive."

"Doc?" the DSRV pilot called back to her. "We're holding steady and ready for retrieval if you'd like to come take a look."

"Thank you." Turning back to Lyons, politely she said, "Excuse me, Carl."

He nodded and watched her ass appreciatively as she pushed out of her seat and squeezed down the narrow walkway to a console that looked like it had been especially added. Beauty and brains all wrapped into a hot package like that—Lyons wondered if she had a boyfriend but then forced his mind to other matters. Nearly 2,600 feet over his head his teammates were standing on the deck of the ship, likely freezing.

Gadgets is probably bitching Pol's ear off, Lyons thought with a smile.

Lyons turned his attention to Stavros, who had donned a headset and was now issuing instructions in a calm but firm voice. The lady was sure as hell impressive. Not only did she specialize in aeronautical weapons systems, but she also served as CEO for a company reputed for its work in maritime exploration and deep-submergence recovery. Brilliant was the only word Lyons could conjure for someone with that much brains and an entrepreneurial spirit to use them.

What he also had to remember was that she was suspect, just like everyone else on this mission.

"Turn us one-point-seven degrees Jones," Stavros told the pilot.

Lyons couldn't even feel the shift in direction, it was so miniscule, but he relied on Stavros to know what she was doing.

"Hold there. Okay, that's it…perfect! Ben, do you see that crack in the base of the shelf just beneath where our target is wedged? I think if we can get a blower in there, we should be able to force it out."

"If there's already enough of an air pocket beneath it," confirmed a voice resounding through the overhead speaker.

Lyons recognized that as Benin Koresh, Stavros's assistant. After Able Team had met him, Schwarz had immediately put in a call to Stony Man to tap their files for a profile. Born in Jerusalem and a naturalized citizen to the U.S. as a child, Koresh's credentials were no less impressive than those of Stavros's. The guy held a Ph.D. in climatology with a minor in underwater geology, and had published many famous papers on a variety of topics, as well as acquired a number of prestigious science awards for his work in climate change. He'd even spent time consulting with the Clinton administration.

"I think we don't have much choice," Stavros said.

"It's the least risky option, I'll grant you that," Koresh

replied. "I say let's go with it and see what happens. Worst-case scenario is it fails."

"Understood. Extending bracing arms now."

"You'll need one on top, the other at the tail fin, Prissy."

"Understood. Jones, move us aft exactly eight meters."

This time Lyons felt the DSRV-2 move, if ever so slightly, the weightless in the water taking most of the friction and leaving him with the sensation they were floating more in space than in deep water. In the distant, inky blackness he thought he actually saw twinkling lights, like stars, and he decided it was worth mentioning. He donned one of the headsets and keyed into the channel they were using.

"Dr. Koresh, this is Norris. Sorry to chime in here but I'm seeing what looks like a series of lights in the distance. Twinkling almost like stars. Do you know of any natural phenomenon that would cause such a thing, or should we be concerned about that?"

There was a long silence and then Lyons heard Koresh chuckle. "Oh, my gosh, at first I was taken aback. But then I remembered. It's ice!"

Lyons's brows furrowed involuntarily. "Ice?"

"Yes. You see, almost none of the light spectrum penetrates beyond the upper part of the mesopelagic zone— er...I'm sorry, that's about 150 meters. However, we do know that there are bioluminescent creatures and fungi capable of sustaining life at those depths. What you are seeing is most likely reflections of those beings manifested by the ice. Quite fascinating, eh?"

"Yeah," Lyons muttered. "Quite."

"Initializing pressure," Stavros cut in.

Lyons clammed up and listened as Stavros and Koresh talked each other through the procedure. Three-quarters of everything they said sounded like gibberish to Lyons but he didn't let that bother him. Better for him to just clam up and let them do whatever it was scientists did in these situations. He wasn't even sure when it happened but all of a sudden he heard shouts over the speakers, then saw Stavros raise her fist and whoop along with them, and he willed himself to relax. Obviously they'd gotten the job done and the device was now free for them to retrieve.

Well into their second hour of submergence, Stavros confirmed they had grapplers attached to the ballistic device and were ready to ascend. Only then did Lyons allow himself a sigh of relief as he felt the DSRV-2 begin to rise. He'd be happy to get onto the deck of the ship. It was a boat, yeah, but in comparison to being deep in the cold, dark and eerie environment of the Bering Sea with its bioluminescent beings and its twinkling ice, it would seem like a cakewalk.

As Stavros took the seat next to Lyons, he said, "Congratulations, Doctor. You did a fine job."

"Thank you," she said. "But I'm exhausted."

"I'll bet."

Stavros lowered her voice and in a very conspiratorial fashion leaned in close to him. "You're not *really* with the ONI. Are you?"

Lyons froze in his seat, unsure for only a heartbeat how to respond. "Of course I'm not. But I think you already know that."

She nodded. "I kind of figured. So you're not really here to protect me and my people?"

"No, that part is actually true," Lyons said. "Why? Think you don't need protection?"

Stavros laid her head back and closed her eyes. "No, actually, I think I'm going to. And that's what scares me."

Tianjin, People's Republic of China

AT HALF PAST two in the morning, Air Vice-Marshal Yan Zhou left his office, rushed downstairs and was escorted out the secure back entrance of the Provincial Capital Center and into his waiting staff car. Accompanying Zhou were two men who, by most Asian standards, could be termed literal giants. They wore black leather suit jackets over their shirts and ties and they carried themselves with all the decorum of trained professional bodyguards. They also wore pistols in shoulder leather, and they served as Zhou's constant companions.

While nobody in his or her right mind would even have attempted to assassinate an important and popular man like Zhou, the Chinese air force's third in command did have a few local enemies. His job often involved rubbing elbows with the dregs of the political circles within the massive bureaucracy that could only arise from the governance of nearly 1.4 billion people—some of those individuals were plain killers and criminals. Hell, even the governments of the greatest power in the world had to occasionally employ persons of this caliber for the dirtier work.

It saddened Zhou that the Ministry of State Security had to maintain certain parties devoted to the elimination of any potential threat to Chinese control. He was a military man. He didn't believe in using government forces, military or otherwise, to control its own citizens. At the same time he understood that certain situations called for more desperate measures when conventional means simply couldn't resolve the more important issues. In this case, the ends really *did* justify the means and while Zhou understood it, nobody could force him to like it.

The driver of the staff car rushed him across town. Zhou's two bodyguards sat in jump seats with their backs to the driver. A third man in front determined the route and was in place to ensure the driver followed it. Zhou watched the lights rush past as the vehicle crossed the Hai River via the Rong Wu Gao Su and continued south until entering a factory district in the Jinghai District. Eventually they arrived at their destination, an abandoned textile mill a few blocks off a reservoir.

The two bodyguards exited the car as soon as it stopped, taking a position just outside as another man entered and secured the doors behind them. Zhou turned on the overhead light, which was tinted red so that they could see each other, but given the special tint on the bulletproof windows, would not allow anyone from the outside to observe them. The car had even been equipped with special electronic devices lining the doors that created enough electronic interference to prevent audio surveillance from penetrating the vehicle.

The man who sat in front of Zhou was short with a thin, drawn face and ghostly pallor. Although Wen Xiang wasn't ill—the gaunt look simply a natural one on him—his appearance still bothered Zhou to some degree. It was like talking to a skull.

"Good evening, sir," Xiang said with an incline of his head.

"Don't 'good evening' me, Mr. Xiang. You and I have a matter of some import to discuss. I'm not happy, not a *bit* happy, with what's happened so recently."

Xiang appeared to swallow hard. Good. He wanted to remind the ministry's top assassin of his place whenever possible. The top officials in the government wouldn't have ever publicly recognized Xiang as working for them.

If caught in the act of killing someone who had been targeted for death, even if officially ordered by the government, Xiang's very existence if not his Chinese citizenship would be renounced at every level. They could leave him in the cold at any time, and there wasn't a thing Xiang could do about it.

"You assured me that you could take care of this matter quietly and quickly," Zhou continued. "You performed admirably in the latter form. But your disposal of the bodies was sloppy. There are a good number of foreign agencies asking some very uncomfortable questions. Some of them are reaching Beijing, and as you know that's never good."

"My men were sloppy," Xiang said. "I'm sorry if you've been put to any inconvenience, but the job has been done and I would think outside of whatever political inconveniences this might have caused that at least your troubles with Teng Cai have been abated."

Zhou pondered Xiang's point for a moment, wondering if the assassin was trying to be conciliatory or impudent. "If the truth of this gets to Beijing, I'm quite certain that this will turn into much more than—how did you put it…*inconvenience?*"

"I mean no disrespect, Air Vice-Marshal, but it is not truth that should concern you. Only bureaucrats and philosophers deal in the truth. My profession is concerned only with facts, and from those facts we change the facets that are not politically palatable until what we present is a truth that is. This is what I am paid for, aside from bloodying my hands where our masters don't want to."

"How dare you!"

Xiang raised a finger and for some reason Zhou couldn't find his voice. The dark, penetrating orbits that peered out from deeply inset eyes appeared to narrow like a cat's. "I was not talking about you, sir, so please spare me any indignation. I was under the impression we had a relationship that permitted candid discussion."

Zhou calmed down, realizing that the flush in his cheeks—while hot against his own skin—didn't show under the red lights. He'd nearly allowed this dog to goad him into saying something he could've regretted later. Xiang had a reputation and it was known among certain circles that murdering his benefactors wasn't above him. Zhou had the clout and political power to make Xiang uncomfortable, to be sure, but it didn't make him invincible. If Zhou stepped over his boundaries, even ones as broad as he enjoyed, Xiang could make him disappear and nobody would ask questions, even the heads of the ministry.

"I've decided to forget your impertinence in the name of maintaining a good working relationship." Zhou reached into his pocket and withdrew a slim metal cigarette case. He took one out, and then offered one to Xiang, who accepted.

The assassin lit them both with a butane lighter before saying, "Perhaps I was a bit too soon in interpreting your motives, sir."

Zhou took a deep drag and waved it away in a cloud of gray smoke. "Forget it."

"There is another matter I believe we should discuss," Xiang said. "It would seem you may not want to be so hasty when you hear what I have to tell you."

"Go on."

"Certain information has come to me from reliable channels that indicates the Americans may try again. Trouble is heating up in the Bering Sea region, not far from the coasts of Alaska."

Zhou tried to appear noncommittal. "Really? I'd not heard this news before."

"Please, Air Vice-Marshal," Xiang replied, "let's not insult each other by being unnecessarily coy. The attempted defection of Teng Cai arising around the same time as this recent activity off American shores could not be chalked up to mere coincidence. We have our own resources within the ministry, and I have considerably high clearance. You must know that my masters keep files on *everyone* who might wield considerable influence within our government, particularly over military powers. And we both know your influence is considerable."

"What's your point, Mr. Xiang?"

"I think you can infer that on your own. The facts are these. We think the Americans will try again, and we think they will try very soon. This means you'll be requiring my services once more."

Zhou's expression soured, and he produced a scoffing laugh. "What do I have to fear from these Americans?"

"Maybe nothing," Xiang replied. "And then perhaps you have everything to fear. If they're determined enough to steal Teng Cai, there won't be much you can do to stop it, even with all of your military might. This is a game that only a few of us understand, and I am a member of those few."

"And yet nothing is free, Mr. Xiang. Is it?"

Xiang inclined his head with another cruel smile, and Zhou thought he saw a flash in the assassin's eyes. "Admittedly, there are certain…let's say *commodities* that might satisfy any potential indebtedness that should arise from ensuring the continued security of your operation."

"I have my own security."

"Yes, but what do they know of the, ah, delicate situation now currently before you? Isn't it better to entrust this matter to someone who already understands the issues?"

"What is your price?" Zhou asked in an even tone, doing nothing to hide his exasperation.

"To be quite honest, I want weapons in an as-yet to be enumerated quantity. Small-arms mostly, although some ordnance may also be required. And I would require some of the cache immediately. Just a matter of good faith, if you will."

"What does someone like you need with weapons?"

"Uh-uh," Xiang countered. "I don't ask you too many questions, sir. I would ask the same courtesy in return."

Zhou considered the request a moment longer and then nodded. "Okay, let's suppose I would agree to your terms. You still haven't told me exactly what it is I'm paying for."

"First, I will make sure that your transfer of Teng Cai that you think nobody knows about will happen without incident. I will also ensure to advise you if any information pertinent to your operation, whether with Teng Cai or in the Bering Sea, comes through any channels within the ministry. Finally, I will make sure that any further attempts by outside parties to interfere with you will end in exactly the same fashion as that idiot Haverhill and his American partner."

"And in return I supply you weapons and ordnance."

"And no questions asked, of course."

Zhou nodded and extended his hand. "Very well, Mr. Xiang. I will agree to your terms. But if you or your men foul up again, our deal is terminated."

Xiang tendered another cold smile. "As you wish."

CHAPTER FIVE

They'd barely cleared the deck of the *Glacier* when trouble came and came hard. As passing rounds zinged in their ears—their origin indeterminable—Able Team went into action.

Lyons grabbed a fistful of Stavros's coat and planted her facedown on the rough surface of the boarding plank while Schwarz and Blancanales found cover behind a topside storage crate. Blancanales's eyes scanned the choppy shoreline comprised of steel-and-concrete buildings, searching desperately for some sign of the sniper's position. The rounds were coming in steadily but inconsistently, which meant they were under fire from one or more assailants concealed at a distance.

"Snipers!" Blancanales said, confirming the suspicions of all.

Schwarz turned in time to see two USCG sailors rushing toward their position, their eyes wide with befuddlement. Schwarz realized they weren't aware of the situation and shouted at them to get behind cover. His warning came a moment too late for one of the men. A high-velocity bullet scored, striking the man in the arm and spinning him wildly into his comrade. The pair tumbled to the slippery deck plates amid a steaming spray of blood from the impact. Schwarz grit his teeth but felt something warm his chest when the uninjured sailor immediately went about the task of staunching the flow of blood. The bullet had taken a good chunk of flesh from his friend but it didn't appear fatal.

Schwarz turned to Blancanales, who had his pistol out and tracking. He swept the muzzle side to side, ducking once to avoid a bullet that ripped through the top edge of the crate they were using for cover and took away a good portion in a scattering of wood splinters and pieces of metal from the strapping. Blancanales finally spotted the muzzle-flash from the shooter but it was at such a distance he couldn't do much about it.

Lyons ordered Stavros to keep her head down before charging back up the gangway and settling into cover between his friends. "What the hell's going on?"

"Don't know, Ironman, but I spotted at least one position."

"How many gunners you estimate?"

Blancanales shrugged, brow furrowed and lips pursed in thought. "Based on the frequency I'd guess two shooters…three at most."

Lyons turned to Schwarz. "Gadgets, you still got that direct communications link to the bridge?"

"Already on it," Schwarz replied. He keyed the transmitter on his wireless headset. The Able Team warriors hadn't been without them since they'd first come aboard. "This is Security Team Foxtrot to bridge. Do you copy?"

"Hinkle here. Go ahead." It was the ship's executive officer.

"We're taking sniper fire from unknown enemy," Schwarz said. "Keep your personnel clear of the deck until we further advise."

"Copy that, Foxtrot."

Lyons looked around and caught the wicked profile of a Bofors 57 mm deck gun. A little too big, not to mention they couldn't be sure civilian targets wouldn't get in the way. Lyons panned his memory for other top-deck armament and remembered seeing an M-240B 7.62 mm light machine gun mounted to the starboard side.

"I wonder if that M-240 Bravo is primed?" he asked his teammates.

Blancanales nodded. "I think it's live. At least I thought I remembered seeing one of the crew testing it earlier today."

"Cover me," Lyons said.

Blancanales and Schwarz didn't look convinced they could actually do much good covering their friend with nothing more than a couple of pistols, but they knew the present moment wasn't the time to argue the point. As Lyons broke cover, they exposed their positions just enough to get line of sight in the proximal direction of the snipers and opened up simultaneously. The reports from their sidearms resembled pop guns in comparison to the loud booms coming from the sniper rifles, but the engagement was enough to attract interest from their enemies. If nothing else, the muzzle-flashes from the rifles were doing a lot to expose their respective positions.

By the time Lyons reached the M-240B atop a swivel mount he had two of them pegged with certainty.

Lyons checked the action as he pulled back the bolt and inspected the chamber long enough to verify the weapon was hot. The bolt came forward with a satisfying clank. He jammed his shoulder against the padded stock as he wrapped his finger around the trigger and laid his face against the ice-cold metal. Right eye close to the circular rear sight, Lyons swung onto the first target area and waited for the muzzle-flash he knew would come, hoping the sniper's aim wasn't true. Well, he'd know quickly enough.

As soon as the muzzle-flash appeared, Lyons eased back the trigger and grinned with satisfaction as the weapon hammered against his muscular shoulder. Every fifth round turned out to be a tracer, and Lyons thanked whoever had been performing maintenance on the weapon for thinking ahead. Lyons couldn't really tell if his aim was on but he could definitely see the results. A crimson spray erupted from the target zone at one point.

Scratch one baddie, he thought.

The firing from the other snipers ceased, and a moment later two shadowy figures emerged from alcoves and rushed up the shoreline street of the wharf. Lyons had a flash of insight—it was Sunday and that's why the waterfront area was abandoned. The businesses and factories were all closed, thankfully, which had significantly reduced the risk of bystanders getting in the way. Lyons keyed the transmitter on his headset and advised his teammates the ambushers were on the run.

"Should we pursue?" Schwarz asked.

"Damned right!"

Lyons jumped from the mount block and landed on the deck, dropping his weight so he didn't slip. He then sprinted toward the front of the ship and spotted a large rubber roll against the stern rail, secured there by yellow marine roping. He used the roll to vault over the deck railing and landed on a small berthing dock along the starboard side. He shoulder-rolled on impact and came to his feet, gaining speed as he snapped his pistol from shoulder leather. His strength and stamina were testaments to his Ironman moniker.

Schwarz and Blancanales weren't quite so swift, opting

to descend the gangway on the port side, which caused them to fall behind. Lyons glanced once over his shoulder, realized it would take them time to catch up—if they could even manage—then remembered that they had parked their SUV rental nearby. It was good thinking and he could hardly fault them for it. He poured on the speed, his arms like windmills and legs like pistons. It was difficult to keep his wind given the cold, abrasive air but he knew letting the enemy escape was out of the question.

Just ahead, Lyons could see the pair of snipers round the corner. He was gaining—he *had* to be gaining given the lead they had. He wondered for just a moment if they weren't dealing with amateurs but he forced such thoughts from his mind. It wouldn't do to underestimate the enemy. Lyons redirected his focus to another place in his mind, a place he'd gone many times before under similar circumstances. While he'd never been able to understand this place, or even why it worked for him, it had served him well. Blancanales and Schwarz had dubbed it "berserker mode" but Lyons never cared much to identify it, fearing if he ever understood it he'd no longer be able to call on it.

Lyons rounded the corner less than a minute later. Something cold and satisfying settled in his gut as he spotted the two snipers inside a late-model sedan. They had the engine started and the driver was trying to navigate the narrow street, swinging the nose around in an attempt to make their escape. As he put the vehicle in Reverse, he stupidly tromped on the accelerator and the tires couldn't find any purchase on the patch of black ice.

Lyons kept running as he leveled his FNP-45 and squeezed the trigger repeatedly. The .45-caliber slugs peppered the sedan, several connecting with the trunk.

One round created a spiderweb pattern that started at the passenger's-side top corner and angled downward nearly half the length of the rear window. Lyons shuffle-stepped to a halt, knelt and took better aim, emptying his magazine as he went for the tires. He was rewarded with a screeching sound as one of his rounds found its mark, flattening the left rear tire with a loud pop.

The sedan finally found purchase and began to re-treat, although more slowly now that it was lame. Lyons dropped the magazine and reached to his belt for another, slamming it home and letting the slide come forward. He heard a roar behind him and turned to see Able Team's SUV fishtail as Schwarz fought to straighten the vehicle. Lyons gave them a wide berth as Schwarz tapped the brakes multiple times, the herky-jerky movements rocking Blancanales to and fro like a milkshake.

Lyons whipped open the driver's-side rear door and jumped in, barely getting the door closed after him as Schwarz gunned the SUV.

"Follow that cab!"

"Yes'm, Miss Daisy," Schwarz quipped.

The sound of rubber scraping over black ice eventually gave way to that of gravel and ice pelting the underside.

Lyons tapped Blancanales on the shoulder. "You let him drive?"

"He had the keys," Blancanales said with a shrug.

"Well, ain't that just grand."

"WE MAY NOT escape this time," Chin Nam said.

Ju Young-Soon kept her eyes on the slick street and tried not to think of how much she agreed with her part-ner. When her superior had sent them on this mission she'd been told it was one from which none of them might return. Had they known how prophetic their words? Young-Soon thought of the other man on her team now. She'd not wanted to leave Han behind, but they hadn't had a choice. Not only had she already lost a third of her team, but they'd also failed to destroy the missile proto-type or to assassinate the American scientist.

"We have no time for doubts," Young-Soon said. "We must get away so we can try again."

"Try again?" Nam scoffed. "We're outgunned. Han is dead and you are wounded! What chance do we have? We must return to Korea and face our failure."

"We will not face our failure. Now shut up and prepare to leave the vehicle when I give the signal."

"What are you going to do?"

Young-Soon looked in the rearview mirror and in a hissing tone replied, "Exactly what the Americans will expect."

She whipped the wheel to the left and turned the cor-ner, then ordered Nam to bail. He looked hesitant at first but one searing glance from her and he opened the door and rolled onto the pavement, swinging his legs to en-sure they weren't caught under the wheels of the sedan. Young-Soon watched to confirm Nam was able to find concealment from the Americans, and then put on as much speed as she dared. The sedan began to fishtail. The rear end shimmied violently as the tires eventually shredded, leaving her only the rims.

To her surprise, she'd managed to make considerable distance before she spotted the pursuit vehicle swing into view. She couldn't tell how many occupants were on board but it didn't really matter. At least she'd been able to plan for this eventuality, although she'd not considered what might happen if their vehicle was disabled, as now.

Young-Soon spotted an alleyway and turned the wheel hard right, causing the rear end to rotate around her center until it slammed against the far wall of the alley. She reached to the seat behind her and withdrew the single-shot rocket launcher. The Chinese-made DZJ08, which she'd actually managed to purchase on the American arms black market, fired an 80 mm warhead and boasted a range of up to 300 meters. Young-Soon had planned to use it to destroy the missile recovered by the Americans but only *after* they had accomplished their primary mission, the assassination of Dr. Priscilla Stavros. She'd never planned on a team of specialists being in place and offering protection for the scientist, although in retrospect she cursed herself for not at least considering it. Now things would be more difficult.

Young-Soon slung the Steyr TMP provided courtesy of their American contacts, tucked the DZJ08 under her shoulder and scrambled from the sedan. She rushed down the alleyway until she reached a fire-escape ladder. She shoved a Dumpster into position and then vaulted onto it, her tiny feet finding purchase on the edge closest to the fire escape. Young-Soon hefted the DZJ08 in both hands and let it go with a careful, underhand toss. It cleared the fire-escape railing and landed on the bottom-most deck. She leaped from the Dumpster and grabbed the third rung up. She immediately started climbing, hand-over-hand with all the dexterity of a chimp, ignoring the ice-cold metal. Her hands were callused from years of field training and she could easily lift twice the weight of her lithe, agile frame.

This was child's play compared to what her instructors had put her through.

Young-Soon finally reached the deck of the fire escape

and retrieved the launcher. She primed the weapon, hefted it onto her shoulder and took careful aim at the sedan. The Americans didn't know it but they were driving straight into a trap. Now all she had to do was wait for her prey.

"Looks like they biffed it," Lyons said.

"Careful," Blancanales replied, the stolid voice of reason. "Appearances can be deceiving. Gadgets, I'd approach with extreme caution."

"Way ahead of you, Pol," Schwarz replied as he tromped on the accelerator.

"What are you doing?" Lyons demanded. "He said approach with *caution*."

"Trust me!"

"Famous last words," Lyons muttered.

Schwarz continued accelerating but instead of slowing when he came alongside the enemy sedan he continued past and then slammed on the brakes. His teammates heard him counting under his breath before he shouted for them to get down. They ducked in their seats just a moment before the rear window of the SUV shattered and orange-hot flames licked at the cloth interior of the roof, singing much of it and leaving black marks. A nauseating gust of smoke roiled through the SUV, the odor of scorched material and vinyl nearly overpowering the trio.

Able Team went EVA with their pistols at the ready. The sedan had been turned into a blackened hulk as smaller explosions and the popping of incinerated fiberglass threatened to douse them with shards of superheated debris. They found in relative safety in front of the SUV.

Lyons reached to the back of his neck and came away with a palm replete with bits of singed hair. He shook his head in utter amazement as he looked in Schwarz's direction. "How did you know?"

"I only saw one person bail out of the vehicle. I knew you hadn't gotten the other one so I figured one of them ditched early. They wouldn't have done that unless they were planning to destroy their ride in hopes of taking us down with it."

"Well, if they're on foot now we might still be able to catch them," Lyons replied.

"Uh, probably not," Blancanales said, peering around the corner and pointing. "Look."

Lyons and Schwarz joined him in noticing that both rear tires of their SUV had melted with the heat, the rubber still bubbling against the pavement.

"Oldest damned trick in the book and we fell for it!" Lyons said, slamming his fist into his palm.

"Don't complain, Ironman," Blancanales said. "At least we're still alive."

"And more importantly, Dr. Stavros is still alive," Schwarz added.

Lyons sighed. "Yeah. I'm only worried about how much longer we can keep her that way."

Ju Young-Soon hadn't waited for the explosion, immediately tossing the disposable launcher into the Dumpster and then climbing the remaining five stories to the roof. She'd dashed to the opposite side and gone in search along the edge until she found a place where she could safely jump to the roof of the adjoining building. She'd continued that way for half a block and then located another fire escape. Within a few minutes she'd managed to put at least ten blocks between her and her enemies.

Young-Soon didn't concern herself with finding Chin

Nam—he knew both their first and second points of rendezvous. They had pre-established multiple escape routes in the event something went wrong, as well as agreed on three separate meeting places at scheduled intervals. She checked her watch and realized it would grow dark soon, something that was typical only for late December in Alaska. Young-Soon considered it a blessing her operation had been during this particular time and in this part of the country, although there were more daylight hours the farther north one traveled.

An icy wind rolled up the sidewalk she traversed, bitter enough to cut even through the neoprene stretch pants and thermal underwear she wore beneath them. At least her feet were still warm, and the graze she'd taken in her forearm had stopped bleeding—obviously very minor. It would have seemed insane to any observer that a woman like her would be out at this time of the evening but nobody else was apparently insane enough to join her, so she had the entire trip to herself. By the time she reached the first rendezvous point, a small bed-and-breakfast adjacent to a bus stop, she couldn't feel her fingers, even though she'd had them stuffed into her coat pockets.

The hood on her fleece-lined jacket had protected her ears and covered her head, although her nose burned enough that she didn't doubt she'd suffered minor frostbite. When she entered the room at the B and B, she was surprised to find Nam hadn't arrived. What could've possibly delayed him? She'd given him more than a head start and he'd had ample time to make it to the rendezvous point. Damn that bastard—if he didn't arrive soon she would have to leave again and head for the alternate location.

Thinking of setting out once more into that bitter cold

night, Young-Soon took the liberty of setting a large kettle of water on to boil. At least she would have time to consume some hot tea and feed her body. The cold and nearly two-hour walk had sapped much of her strength. She'd considered early on taking public transportation but she'd dismissed it as too risky. The Americans would most certainly have alerted local police to be looking for them.

When the kettle finally whistled, Young-Soon poured it into her prepared cup. She stripped out of her jacket and with the large mug cupped in her small hands, sat in a rickety wooden chair and began her vigil. Only thirty-eight minutes remained and she hoped Nam would make it before that time expired. If something had happened to him, as well, she would truly be alone.

It was a thought more chilling to her than the rising wind that howled outside the frosted window of her very quiet and temporary sanctuary.

CHAPTER SIX

Tianjin, People's Republic of China

A milky, red-blue dusk settled across the horizon as Jack Grimaldi set down the plane carrying Phoenix Force at Tianjin Binhai International Airport. Within five minutes they were cleared to taxi to a private commercial hangar. They had come in under the cover of a major package and documents courier, but that didn't preclude them from a search by airport security officials.

Once parked at the hangar, McCarter and Grimaldi dealt with customs officers—they insisted on thoroughly screening all of their doctored passports and credentials, as well as searching the plane from nose to tail. While this went on for nearly two hours, the remainder of the Phoenix Force took up residence inside the staff facility adjacent to the hangar. It included a fully equipped kitchen, bunk room and entertainment lounge. The commercial hangar even boasted a waitstaff and chef, and a duty-free commissary, so they ordered up some hot chow and watched football while they waited.

McCarter and Grimaldi entered the facility just minutes before a tall, thin, clean-shaven man joined them. His hair was black and slick with flecks of gray-white at the temples. He had dark eyes and an unusually square jawline for someone of Asian descent. He wore brown cotton trousers, a pale green shirt with tie and a heavy black overcoat he'd unbuttoned.

McCarter met him halfway across the large entertainment room where Phoenix Force had congregated. "Mr. Kwan?"

The man nodded with a smile—although the querulous glint in his eyes betrayed he was sizing up the Phoenix Force leader—even as he extended his hand. "Call me Hark. You must be McMasters." Kwan had an accent that was British laced with an odd Cantonese twang.

"Right." McCarter shook Kwan's hand and then went about introducing the rest of Phoenix Force by cover names without ceremony.

When the introductions were finished, Kwan looked around the sparse but comfortable room. "Well, I know we can do better than this. I've already arranged your hotel accommodations. If you'll come with me…"

"I'll be here ready and willing if you need me," Grimaldi told the Phoenix Force leader.

At a nod from McCarter, the others gathered their weekend bags and followed Kwan single-file to a dark blue late-model Nissan NV, its engine purring. McCarter breathed a sigh of relief and a glance at his friends told him he wasn't the only one impressed at Kwan's choice. The windowless cargo van could seat up to twelve passengers, so there would be more than enough room to store their gear, not to mention a suitable amount of armament if it came down to it.

As Kwan took the wheel, McCarter opened up the conversation to more immediate matters. "You've been briefed on our mission?"

Kwan nodded. "Fully. And I have to say that this isn't going to be easy."

"Why's that?" Manning asked from his position immediately behind Kwan.

"Teng Cai is watched *constantly,*" he said. "This isn't the first time something like this has been tried."

"Well, we've got a big whatchamacallit recovered from U.S. waters," Hawkins interjected. "And when other countries try to drop that kind of thing onto American soil, our people take it seriously."

"Not to mention that we're no closer to finding out who terminated one of our key intelligence assets inside Tianjin," James added.

Kwan nodded. "You mean Dumbarton—no?"

"Well, obviously you've been *really* well briefed," McCarter replied.

"It's my business to know it," Kwan said with a mild shrug. "Or it used to be. But who killed your man isn't really any mystery. My people already know it was an assassination team from the Ministry of State Security."

"And how did you come by *that* information?" Encizo asked. "We couldn't even find out who it was from Dumbarton's own people."

This produced a chuckle out of Kwan, his eyes dancing with sparks in the light of the city as he swung onto the entrance ramp for the Jinbin Expressway. "Oh, I assure you the CIA knows exactly who killed Dumbarton. But they're not going to leak it to anybody they don't feel needs to know."

Hawkins sighed. "So much for intra-agency cooperation. All horse manure."

"You know the identity of the Brit who was killed?" McCarter asked.

"Indeed. His name was Grover Haverhill."

"And I suppose he was SIS?"

"Of course."

McCarter shook his head. "That's just bloody marvelous."

"So you said there've been other attempts?" Encizo inquired.

"Quite a few, and by a variety of different intelligence agencies all over the world. They probably would've succeeded by now were it not for Zhou."

"With the Chinese Air Force," Manning recalled.

Kwan nodded as he fished a cigar from his pocket and lit up. "Zhou wields incredible influence, not only among the highest ranking officials in my government but also the Gold Star Faction."

"Which has ties to the Russian Business Network," Manning said. "A very nasty group indeed. Is that how you ended up working with Striker?"

Kwan smiled at the name they'd reserved for Mack Bolan after he'd severed all official ties with Stony Man.

"I've known Striker for over ten years. He saved my life. Twice. That's why anyone who knows or works for him will always get my cooperation."

"And we appreciate it," McCarter said.

"But to the heart of your question, yes. My affiliation with Striker came about while I was still working with the ministry. The state had known of the GSF, but because of its membership alone my superiors chose to look the other way. I don't pay deference to any particular ideology when it comes to the bureaucrats. But when that ideology threatens the citizens of China, my countrymen, I will damn sure fight to the death to preserve their safety. Certain members of the GSF took a contrary view, and that's when they tried to kill me."

"That's all fascinating," James interjected. "But what does it have to do with Teng Cai or this Yan Zhou?"

"Zhou is a card-carrying member of the GSF," Kwan replied. "And I believe that it was his idea to sucker Haverhill and Dumbarton into this faux defection. Once they'd foolishly exposed themselves, Zhou ordered their murders."

"Any idea who inside the ministry did the job?" McCarter asked.

"Unfortunately, I believe I do. Only because I recognized the handiwork. It is that of Wen Xiang, a very cunning assassin—and my old nemesis."

"Sounds like a real sweetheart," James said matter-of-factly.

"He's anything but. Gentlemen, I cannot stress this enough. Wen Xiang is a vile murderer—of this point I would contradict no one. But he is not some mindless machine and he is not insane, although his reputation precedes him as such. Wen Xiang is a highly trained and extremely dangerous individual, and I would not underestimate either his dedication to the GSF or his connections."

"We've been there before," McCarter said. "We know what we're doing."

"Perhaps," Kwan said, glancing at McCarter as he took a long drag of the cigar. The red-orange cherry lent a shimmering cast to his pale skin. Through a cloud of smoke he continued, "But it would not surprise me if Zhou already knew you were in the country. Or at least suspected that America would send someone else to follow up with Mr. Dumbarton's demise."

"So what's your plan then if you think it's that hopeless?" Manning said.

"I don't think it's hopeless. I'm merely attempting to give you all of the facts as I know them. I wish nothing more than we succeed in your mission, but the road will not be easy. Our best hope is in Teng Cai's mother. She's well-guarded and under continuous surveillance, but I have already prepared a way to overcome those obstacles. I hope you will take my lead."

"Just tell us what you need us to do, mate," McCarter said. "If your plan's good, then I can guarantee these bastards won't bloody well know what hit them."

"If you and your men are anything like Striker, I don't doubt it, Mr. McMasters."

Once they'd reached the hotel and changed into casual attire—they'd worn monkey suits on the plane to appear more "businesslike" to security officials—Kwan gathered them around a table in one of the two adjoining suites. Spread in front of them was a topographical map overlaid on a high-resolution satellite photo.

"This map details the area in Hebei Province," Kwan began.

"Where Teng Cai's mother lives," McCarter said.

Kwan nodded. "You can see here the house—" he pointed toward a large structure "—along with this line here, which is actually a perimeter fence."

"Electronic security?" Manning asked.

"The very best," Kwan replied. "Additionally, my people confirm there are two twenty-four-hour roving patrols with dogs and a well-armed security force spread inside the house. There's also a gated, manned security entrance. Cameras everywhere, and we have it on good authority the fence has heat sensors buried throughout."

"Locked up tight as a drum," Hawkins drawled.

"So how do you propose to breach that without attracting attention?" Encizo queried.

"Mr. Rodriguez," Kwan replied with a chuckle and a smile, "I didn't say we were going to attempt to get inside undetected. That was never part of my plan."

McCarter's eyebrows rose. "Then what *did* you have in mind?"

"We have at our disposal, at least for a short time, a stealth helicopter that's been made available. My plan is to drop you onto the roof. From there, you can use the architectural blueprints of the house to get inside, locate Meifeng Cai and get her out of the compound to here." He gestured to the map at a spot highlighted with a semitransparent red dot. "This will be your extraction LZ."

"Well, that's all fine and good," McCarter replied, squinting at the map. "But you're talking a hike of more than six klicks. Assuming we can even find this Meifeng, what gives you any reason to think we can fight our way through an armed force of unknown size and capabilities with our prize, break through a well-defended compound and then get to our extraction more than three miles away?"

"Exactly," James added supportively. "I mean, we knew you had confidence in us but it seems as if you're making a lot of extraordinary assumptions about our capabilities."

"Perhaps if you'd allow me to finish I can explain some of the finer details," Kwan said.

McCarter frowned. "Yeah, I suppose we're jumping to conclusions a little early. Please...go on."

"Do you all see this very long line here?" When he was met with some sporadic nods, Kwan elaborated, "We realized this is a heat signature. And you will notice it's very inconsistent except at either end, here and here. We think this is actually a subterranean corridor."

"An escape tunnel," Hawkins said.

"Right! The heat is most likely being caused by circulators pumping air into that location. You'll notice how it's most intense at the terminus."

"Which means some sort of ductwork or grating at the far end," McCarter observed. "Which means the more intense signatures you marked at either end are probably entrance and exit points."

"Exactly. If you take some basic climbing equipment just in case, we think there's a good chance you can use this tunnel to get *outside* the fence perimeter."

"We could also get trapped in there," James pointed out.

"Maybe," McCarter said, scratching his chin with consideration. "But I think Hark here is counting on the security people believing we don't know anything about the tunnel, which would most definitely give us the advantage."

"Your insight is commendable," Kwan said. "But there is one more point that I think will sweeten the pot for you. Since the idea is to extract Meifeng Cai, having all five of you go in could slow you down considerably. I'd suggest, Mr. McMasters, that you choose two of your men to perform this part of the operation while the rest help us set up diversions."

"What kind of diversions?"

"Well, I have practically unlimited equipment resources." He glanced at his watch. "In fact, I've already arranged for all of the weaponry you requested. It should be here very shortly. What I lack is dedicated manpower for a paramilitary operation such as this. I can use the chopper to drop low-altitude explosives, perhaps even take out a few key targets. I am quite adept with a rifle. But you will need sufficient time to locate Meifeng and get her into the tunnel, and that's where we need to create a diversion."

McCarter considered it for a moment, staring at the map as if somehow hoping he'd find the answers emblazoned upon it. The others waited respectfully and then McCarter said, "I think I've got it. You said that the fence had motion and heat sensors attached?"

"Correct."

"Our friends inside the compound don't bloody know we know that, any more than they know we know about the tunnel. If we position ourselves at different points along the fence perimeter and attempt to breach it, or even make it *look* like we're trying to breach, they'll have to break up whatever men they have to check it out."

"Nice thinking, David," James said.

"We could also stagger the diversions a little," Encizo said. "That would buy even more time for whoever gets lucky enough to be tasked with the inside job."

McCarter smiled. "Do I hear you volunteering, mate?"

"Inside or outside," Encizo said with a shrug. "It's all the same to me. Figuring out who to pick is why you get the big bucks."

"I'd actually thought you'd be itching to do it. And because your particular talents are suited to just this kind of operation."

"Your wish is my command," Encizo said with a grin.

"Don't suppose I could volunteer to be what's behind door number two, boss?" Hawkins ventured with a hopeful glint in his eyes.

"Sorry, but not this time," McCarter said. He jerked his

thumb at Manning and said, "I think Gary's better suited for this operation. In fact, I'd go myself but I think there's enough that could go wrong and I need to be available to make decisions and come up with alternatives. No offense, Hark."

"None taken," Kwan said. "I had planned to suggest this myself if you didn't."

McCarter nodded. "Okay, so it sounds like we've wrapped up most of the important details. Are there any questions?"

Before anybody could speak there was a rap of knuckles on the door of the hotel room. Kwan produced a pistol and gestured for McCarter to accompany him while the remaining men made themselves scarce. McCarter accompanied Kwan to the door and took a position to the left where he could flank anyone who might try to force their way through. Kwan grinned at McCarter's choice, obviously impressed that McCarter hadn't done what the more inexperienced tended, which was to conceal themselves behind the door when it was opened. That was the move of an amateur.

Kwan disengaged the hasp-style lock and opened the door a crack, peered out and then opened it wide to admit another man. The guy was dressed in the uniform of hotel staff, which was apparently bogus because he hadn't quite managed to cover the bulge beneath the red vest over his long-sleeved white shirt. Well, it didn't much matter to McCarter or his teammates because they were focused on what he wheeled inside.

It looked like a tall linen cart and, in fact, there were white towels piled along the three shelves. The "staff member" said nothing, merely nodding at Kwan and Phoenix Force before he whipped off the towels to reveal long, deep boxes beneath them. He took the boxes off the shelves, laying one on a wide loveseat and the other on the coffee table in front of it. He opened them to reveal padded filler with cut-outs for numerous MP-5s, a detached M-203 grenade launcher and pistols of varied makes and calibers.

As the men of Phoenix Force procured their weapons of choice, Manning's eyes fell on the olive-green satchel that he knew would contain myriad explosives and other ordnance. True to his prediction, he found a dozen quarter-pound sticks of C-4 with pencil detonators wrapped separately, about twenty feet of explosive cord and a handful of fuse igniters.

Kwan noticed Manning's salacious expression and said, "There's another identical bag in there with some grenades. We couldn't swing your exact specifications but we came close enough. I think you'll be pleased with our choice."

While they'd requested some HE and incendiary, Kwan had managed to come in with the next best thing. Manning opened the bag to discover nearly twenty C-16 fragmentation grenades, the Canadian version of the U.S. M-67. Manning almost couldn't resist a chuckle at the irony of it and wondered if Kwan had actually been making a joke or simply didn't realize Manning had been born in Canada. Manning knew the first explanation was the more likely, since even with Kwan's affiliation to Stony Man and Mack Bolan, there were no files kept on any of the Stony Man team members. They used forged documents and identities whenever needed, as needed, but for all practical purposes their names—in fact, their very lives—no longer existed.

"All right, mates," McCarter said. "Let's check out the goodies and get ready to go."

"We have a special berth at a government airport for the stealth bird," Kwan said. "I'll go make a call to verify they'll be ready for us when we arrive. Is ten minutes enough time?"

McCarter nodded. "We'll be ready."

CHAPTER SEVEN

Alaska

Under heavy escort by Air Force police and a detachment of Special Forces, the convoy reached the Elmendorf-Richardson installation without incident.

An armored transport vehicle took the ballistic device to a special hangar equipped with the latest in scientific instrumentation and computer hardware systems. Everything inside the hangar was MILSPEC-rated with some additional advanced gizmos purchased from the biggest contractors in the industry including Northrop Grumman, Honeywell, Teledyne and Lockheed-Martin.

Schwarz was like a kid in a candy store, rambling on and pointing with wide eyes as his teammates accompanied him on an ad hoc tour through the facility. Their clearance for access inside had been necessitated by their mission as bodyguards to Dr. Priscilla Stavros. Orders had come down directly from the Oval Office that they were to be afforded every convenience and courtesy, including full access to any work or facilities being performed or used by Stavros and her crew. They were also to be informed before any communications were permitted outside the facility—a full lockdown had essentially gone into effect.

Schwarz finally let out a low whistle. "Got to hand

it to you, Doc. This is a pretty sweet setup they've got here for you."

Stavros waved the compliment away but Lyons noted her faint smile. "Being a government contractor all of these years has had certain drawbacks. But I will admit they don't skimp on the materials end. You're looking at the latest and greatest."

"Any of this stuff capable of stopping a bullet?" Lyons growled, relying on Schwarz's electronics know-how.

"I don't think we've ever tested it," she replied. "But I suppose given most of it is very sensitive that my answer would be *no*."

Blancanales laid a meaty hand on Lyons's shoulder and squeezed. "You'll have to excuse Carl's sense of humor. I think it was meant to be a joke."

Stavros only nodded, already bent over a particularly massive LCD monitor and studying readouts. "We've placed our prize inside radiation shielding for the time being, until we can determine exactly what we're dealing with. I don't believe the device has any kind of warhead attached, but until we can verify that for certain we're taking every precaution."

"Better safe than sorry," Schwarz said.

"How long do you think it will take to determine its origin?" Lyons asked.

Stavros's eyes didn't leave the terminal. She punched a few keys on the keyboard in front of the monitor and said, "As far as determining from exactly what coordinates it was launched, I'd guess we'll have that information within about six hours. We have to consider fuel capacity, then calculate the rate of consumption based on speed.

"The first priority is to completely eliminate any risk of detonation or other accidents that may arise from handling." She pinned the three men with a serious expression that somehow looked strange on such a beautiful face. "As I said, I believe this is merely a prototype and inert of any ordnance, but I won't risk lives until we've conducted a thorough assessment of every inch. Once I know something, I'll let you know."

"I think maybe that's our cue that we ought to go evaluate the security measures," Blancanales said. He signaled Lyons and Schwarz with a raise of his eyebrows and said, "Perhaps check the perimeter, as well?"

Lyons sighed. "Fine. Let's go."

They left Stavros to her work, but once out of earshot Schwarz said, "Shouldn't someone stay behind with her?"

"It's quite obvious she didn't want us breathing down her neck," Lyons replied. "Beside, we're only a minute away if we run into any problems."

"That was one of the reasons I wanted to take a break," Blancanales told his teammates. "I'm a little concerned about our encounter at the port."

"Do tell," Schwarz said.

"If you're thinking about how good the timing was that we got hit like we did, I'm in complete agreement," Lyons said. "That grenade launcher we found was Chinese-made."

"That bothered you, too?" Blancanales said.

Lyons shoved his hands into his pockets as they strolled down an empty auxiliary corridor toward one of the hangar exits. "Yeah. It seems almost like my thought this might be the Chinese instead of the North Koreans was confirmed with that finding. But it almost seems too convenient."

"You think somebody was using that to try to point the finger at the Chinese?"

"Or throw us off the track," Lyons replied. "That would mean it actually *is* the North Koreans and they're trying to make it look like the Chinese."

"Or maybe it is the Chinese and the North Koreans know we suspect *them*," Blancanales replied.

"This is beginning to sound convoluted enough to make us go in search of strong drink."

"Uh-uh," Schwarz chided. "Alcohol's a crutch, Ironman. 'Beware the demon of intemperance,' Abraham Lincoln once said."

"Not in the mood, Gadgets."

"Forget him," Blancanales said. "We have more important considerations. The Farm's convinced that this has something to do with the possible defection of Teng Cai."

"Yeah, the boy wonder from China," Lyons said. "It would make sense, then, and it would fit my theory this is a faction of the Red Chinese behind all of this. But we know the North Koreans throw caution to the wind when they get new toys. It's possible this is a very elaborate setup and they're looking to make China take the fall."

"But what about the evidence that Teng Cai might possibly know something about this missile?" Schwarz pointed out. "You can't dismiss the facts, my friends."

"Those are the facts as we *know* them," Blancanales countered. "Nothing else. Phoenix Force will do whatever they can to get Teng Cai out of China, assuming this whole defection thing isn't a ruse."

"That's another thing that bothers me," Lyons said. "Fake a defection to what end? The only thing the attempted defection of Teng Cai has bought the Chinese so far is one dead American CIA agent and one dead diplomat, which is probably actually a cover for one of the British intelligence services. And if the Chinese did fire this thing at us, and it's inert just as Stavros said, blaming the North Koreans only escalates tensions between us and them. I don't see how that benefits the Chinese in the least."

"Maybe they're looking to buy some bargaining power," Blancanales suggested. "You know, they'll keep their eyes on what North Korea is doing for America, and in return we give *them* something."

"What could we offer them they don't already have?" Lyons asked. "We're already tens of billions in debt to them. How does this benefit them?"

Blancanales said, "Well, we know there's no love lost between China and North Korea. The North Koreans are playing footsies with nukes right at their back door. And similarities in the views between their Communist factions aside, this could be the excuse China's looking for to take a more threatening posture against them."

Lyons stopped short of the exit door and turned to face Blancanales. "You think this is all precursor to a possible Chinese invasion of North Korea?"

"Does that sound so impossible?"

"Huh," Lyons said. "I hadn't thought of it."

"Well, in the meantime," Schwarz interjected, "while we stand around theorizing the worst possible scenarios, I think it's still important we find out who ambushed us and why."

"It was a professional job," Lyons said. "They haven't been able to identify the one sniper I got yet. Hal says it's going to take time. All of the conventional means have been exhausted, so now they're digging deeper."

"Bear will come up with the answers," Blancanales said. "He always does. But there is a place we could start digging on our own."

"And where's that?"

"Our friends down at the port were very well armed. Sniper rifles, grenade launchers, body armor—they didn't just walk through the airport with that stuff. And even if the shooters were locals and not foreign agents who got in under false identities, they would've had to acquire those resources from the American arms market. And we know plenty of people in our business that do these types of things. I'm betting that local resource is right here in Anchorage."

"Will you look at this guy," Schwarz said. "He's a regular Sherlock Holmes."

"Maybe so but he's got a really good point," Lyons said. "We'll check the security and perimeter first. Then we can go shake some trees to see who falls out."

As they turned to walk out the door, Schwarz asked in a hopeful tone, "Any chance we can go find some eats before we do that shaking?"

Lyons groaned. "It troubles me you can think of food at a time like this."

"Troubles me you can't," Hermann Schwarz muttered.

CHIN NAM SHAVED it so close that Young-Soon had her coat and boots on and was headed for the door when he came through it. She noticed his pale skin even in the dim lighting from the single lamp on a desk in the corner of the main living space. Their makeshift apartment wasn't that large but at least it had a separate bedroom and a kitchenette. Nam had chosen to sleep on the floor, giving Young-Soon the room, but when she saw his color she immediately took him by the hand and led him into the bedroom.

She clicked on the bedside table light and that's when

she saw the black blood crusting the right, lower part of his shirt. "What happened?"

"I was shot," Nam said in a weak voice.

"When?"

"It must have happened when we retreated from the ambush site," he said.

"Why did you not say something to me?"

"I didn't even realize I'd been hit until after I rolled out of the car." He grimaced as she helped him out of his jacket. "I hid in the doorway until the Americans drove past and then I ran down the street and started walking. That's when I first felt the pain and realized I was bleeding."

"What took you so long?" Young-Soon demanded as she whipped out a knife and cut off his shirt in strips.

"I had to keep stopping in public restrooms or gas stations," he said. "Tried to pack the wound with gauze or hand towels…ah, ah—anything I could find."

"Lie back," she ordered.

Nam winced with a groan as he complied. Once flat on his back, Young-Soon went to work. She was an accomplished operative but also a well-trained medic. She'd served as an emergency clinic nurse in North Korea before being selected to serve in the SSD. Not that this would be easy. She had no sedatives, nothing to kill the pain, and as she slowly eased bits of the makeshift packing he'd placed around the wound, flicking away blood-crusted bits with the tip of her knife, she could see the job would take some time.

Young-Soon stayed at Nam's side, vigilant, determined to remove every bit of it until she'd exposed the wound. Once that was accomplished, Young-Soon went into the bathroom and rifled through the medicine cabinet. She found a half-full bottle of hydrogen peroxide and a basic first-aid kit. She poured a little peroxide on the knife and nodded with affirmation when it bubbled up against the blood—she wouldn't have blindly trusted the contents as listed on the bottle until testing it. She returned with the supplies in hand and went about cleaning the wound after shoving the leather-wrapped handle of a retracting truncheon into Nam's mouth.

It wouldn't do to let others guests hear him scream.

With a nod from Nam, Young-Soon poured the peroxide on the wound and let it drain, dribbling down onto a thick piece of gauze she held against his side. They couldn't risk getting anything on the bed or floor. Nam seemed to take it pretty well. When she'd finished thoroughly cleaning the wound, she retrieved a pair of tweezers from the first-aid kit. They were designed to remove splinters but were so thick and strong enough that she thought she could get the slug out.

"I have to remove the bullet," she said. "Then I will go out and find some antibiotics while you rest."

Nam nodded slowly—they both knew it wasn't going to be pretty. But it had to be done and Young-Soon was the only one to do it. They couldn't go to an American doctor, obviously, and there weren't any contacts close enough. Such a trip could well kill Chin Nam before he got to them. Nam moaned and bit into the truncheon, his jaw clenched so tightly that Young-Soon feared for a minute there he might dislocate it, perhaps even break some teeth. She'd seen this done enough, though, that she felt she could do it without incurring too much additional tissue damage.

Young-Soon followed the wound down with a tongue-depressor from the kit aiding in keeping the soft tissue and muscle fibers at bay. She then parted the wound with the knife that she'd heated on the stove, and eventually felt the tip hit something solid. She looked at Nam periodically and, at some point, realized he must have passed out. Just as well—it would be easier for her to get this done. She got the tweezers inside, cut the wound a bit deeper and eventually managed to retrieve the slug.

Young-Soon completed her grisly task by looking for any major bleeding, realized that the slug hadn't struck any major vessels, and then went about more cleaning of the wound and packing it with a bulky dressing. She cleaned up in the bathroom, scrubbing down the instruments and returning them, covered with a pillowcase, via a dinner plate from the kitchenette, which she set on the bedside table. She would need it in the event she had to go in again.

Once that was finished, Young-Soon bundled up and left the B and B. She checked the luminous face of her watch as she descended the steps and emerged onto the sidewalk. The wind had died considerably and a light snow had begun. Young-Soon considered this better fortune, since at least she wouldn't have to battle such frigid temperatures. With snow there would be a cloud cover, and with a cloud cover whatever heat remained would be trapped closer to sea level.

Her walk to a pharmacy took Young-Soon less than ten minutes, and she found it closed. Good fortune had continued to smile on her. She checked her surroundings to ensure there were no observers or traffic in sight, then made her way to the back. The rear door didn't prove much of a challenge to her intrusion skills and within four minutes she had it open. Of course, it would set off an alarm and bring the police but she would have what she needed and be gone before they arrived.

Young-Soon walked the aisles in the back room where prescription drugs were secured. They were neatly labeled and shelved by lot number, but fortunately clustered together by their classifications. She located the antibiotics, selected a couple of penicillin derivatives in both enteral and parenteral forms, and also snatched some syringes and an IV bag of saline. She managed to get clear of the pharmacy and walk two blocks to an all-night diner with a parking lot half filled with cars. The place wasn't packed but there were enough faces inside that she could blend.

Young-Soon ordered dinner for herself and an additional meal to go. She decided to take a cab back to the B and B, paying cash and ensuring to keep the lower portion of her face obscured by the edge of a scarf, keenly aware that many taxis had internal cameras installed for driver safety. It was, after all, a very dangerous world these days.

When Young-Soon arrived she found Nam awake and not looking too worse for wear. She immediately started an IV on him, injecting the full contents of one bottle of the liquid antibiotic into the bag. She then used a syringe to give him another dose of a different type via his thigh muscle.

"I've failed you," he said. "And I am sorry."

"You've not failed, Chin," she replied as she handed him his food in the takeout bag and a fork. "If anyone has failed, *I* have failed. It was my responsibility to ensure we completed our mission and I did not."

"What are you going to do?"

"I will not allow us to return having failed," she said, putting conviction into her tone. "I am going to complete the assignment as ordered. We cannot allow the Americans to inspect that device. If we do, it will surely convince them that it's our government behind this and all will be lost."

"I will help you," Nam said around a small bite of food.

She shook her head. "No! You are in *no* condition to do anything. You're too weak to help at this point, and I will need you to be stronger when it is time for us to leave. I will finish this myself."

"What of Stavros's protection detail?" Nam asked. "I don't have to remind you that they are a covert team and clearly they are skilled. I would not underestimate them so much."

"If anything, it is these Americans who underestimated us," she said with a quick smile. "I have already proven my skills are superior to their own. They were not expecting me to destroy our only means of transportation so readily, and they were nearly destroyed by my efforts. Next time they will not be so lucky."

"And what of your next step?" Nam said. "The missile is now inside a secure facility and you have no means of access, neither do you know exactly *where* it is being stored even if you did."

"This is where those Americans are going to help me. Unwittingly, of course."

Nam stopped chewing and cocked his head. "What do you have up your sleeve, Ju?"

"I am once more going to demonstrate our resolve in a fashion that will be doubly useful."

"What are you talking about?"

"Has it not occurred to you that I left behind the grenade launcher for a very important reason? I expect they will try to trace it back to those who sold it to us. When they do, I will arrange for them to come into direct contact with me."

"And once they have?"

"They will lead me straight to the device and I will destroy it, right along with Stavros and her security detail."

"A bold plan…if it works."

"It shall, Chin," Young-Soon whispered. "It *must*."

CHAPTER EIGHT

Hebei Province, People's Republic of China

Whatever Hark Kwan's former connections with the PRC's Ministry of State Security, McCarter wouldn't have argued Kwan could still pull some serious strings. The stealth chopper turned out to be nothing less than he'd described it. Like something out of a science-fiction movie, the chopper could move undetected until right on top of an enemy, the wash of the rotors and a very odd high-pitched hum the only indicators of its presence.

McCarter had voiced his concerns about approaching the compound in such a fashion but as Kwan had pointed out, the enemy wouldn't likely even suspect what they were doing until it was too late and they realized the chopper had flown over the roof. And then there was nothing, perhaps other than a visual source, to detect they had hovered there—even for the time it would take for Manning and Encizo to get boots on the ground.

"It makes more sense to drop them first," Kwan said.

McCarter nodded. "On that much we agree."

With their plan in place the chopper pilots moved into position fast and came to a steady hover over the roof of the secured compound where Zhou's elite team had supposedly quarantined Meifeng Cai.

McCarter hadn't bothered to ask what would happen to Teng Cai when Zhou no longer had the young prodigy's mother as a bargaining chip. Certainly they wouldn't kill him, but Zhou might have enough forethought to move the boy—something that would make Phoenix Force's mission much more difficult. It was difficult to arrange a defection when the location of the principal was unknown. McCarter decided they had to risk it. Kwan had said snatching Meifeng was the only option, and McCarter had no reason to question Kwan's judgment on that point.

Kwan had a headset with direct communications to the crew, and as soon as the chopper reached the drop point he turned and nodded to McCarter. McCarter keyed the microphone on his secured team communications headset and ordered their two point men to go. Manning and Encizo went out the port side of the chopper, descending with all the skill implied by their experience in training in air assault tactics. They dropped to the roof via ropes in a controlled descent and were down and clear within a matter of seconds.

McCarter waited until he saw the high-sign from Encizo and Manning, and then gestured a thumbs-up to Kwan. McCarter couldn't hear what Kwan was saying, but he smacked the release on the slide-winch to retract the rappelling ropes with one hand as he grabbed a handhold with the other even as the chopper zipped from the LZ. The stealth bird banked hard right and McCarter wished a silent farewell to his two friends even as they blended with the night, disappearing from view in a moment.

ENCIZO AND MANNING found cover behind a large vent protruding from the roof.

They shrugged out of their harnesses and stowed them in a gear bag that Encizo then slung over his shoulder. Wearing the harnesses would betray their movements with the clanking of carabiners and clips—silence and speed were their only two advantages at this point. Already, the pair could hear the sound of barking somewhere below, their handlers probably mystified by what had caused the sentry dogs to raise such a ruckus. McCarter had estimated it would take the remaining team members minutes to get into position at various points along the perimeter, so they had very little time and the numbers were ticking.

The pair checked their weapons next, both carrying MP-5 SD-6 SMGs. A silenced variant of the H&K 9 mm subgun, the SD-6 had two additional features: a retractable butt stock and a 3-round burst capability. They were perfect for this job. The two warriors nodded in readiness to each other before breaking cover and heading to the roof access, a hatch Kwan's intelligence had assumed would be locked from the inside.

It proved no problem for Gary Manning's skills with demolitions. The Canadian withdrew a prepared charge attached to a small section of specially designed detonation cord filled with a thermite chemical inlayer. Manning waved his partner back and then triggered the charge with a remote detonator. The thermite burned at more than 3,000 degrees and made short work of the handle mechanism by "cutting" through the door and completely severing the handle and lock from the access hatch.

Manning lifted back the hinged panel as Encizo swept the darkened interior ladder with the muzzle of his SMG before dropping into the hole, careful to avoid contacting the still smoldering section of the frame where the cord had done its searing work. Manning followed immediately after his friend and the pair quickly descended the ladder to the top floor. They checked the dark hallway that stretched in both directions, each covering the other's flank as they watched for any approaching enemy.

They were just ready to clear and move toward the stairwell off the hallway that would take them to the floor below—the floor where Kwan had assured them they would find Meifeng—when trouble appeared in the form of two security men toting pistols. Encizo, still on his knees, leveled the MP-5 and triggered two 3-round bursts. The impact from the slugs drove the first man into the wall and he slid to the ground dead. The second caught at least one slug in the chest and a second in the forehead with enough force to crack open his skull. He stiffened and followed his comrade to the ground.

"Nice job," Manning remarked.

Encizo tendered a half grin. "Going to cost us some time, I'll bet. Let's move."

WHAT ENCIZO AND Manning didn't know was that the roof drop wasn't what had upset the sentry dogs.

T. J. Hawkins had executed a perfect, if hasty, descent but somehow managed to come down on the *wrong* side of the fence. The Phoenix Force warrior barely had his harness clear of the rappel line when he spotted two men rushing his position, one of them tasked with trying to restrain the dog. Something in the handler's judgment told him at the last second it was better to let the canine do its job and he released the animal. It was a Doberman and, by that measure, it was big and mean and heartily intimidating.

Hawkins went flat and swung his MP-5 SD-6 into acquisition. He squeezed the trigger twice. The first round glanced past the dog's ear but the Doberman maintained its charge. The second round struck it full in the chest, tearing out part of its throat on the passage. Hawkins felt a pang of regret as the animal let out a yelp of pain. The damage to the chest muscles debilitated its front legs and it collapsed into the grass on its chin, sliding another five yards before its lifeless body ground to a halt.

Hawkins cursed himself for being so stupid even as he reacquired the two sentries. The men hesitated, obviously uncertain about what they were up against. The hesitation cost them the precious seconds they would've needed to find cover or to at least get to their bellies. Hawkins took out sentry number one with a double-tap to the belly. The man folded, hit his knees and flipped onto his side in a writhing heap. The second sentry managed to get off a volley that chewed up earth just in front of Hawkins and pelted the Phoenix Force warrior with clumps of mud and grass.

Hawkins flipped the selector switch to 3-round burst and rolled out of position just in time to avoid the steady onslaught of rounds that danced into the space he'd occupied a millisecond before. Hawkins completed his roll, steadied his cheek against the stock and triggered his subgun. The sentry's body produced a spasmodic reaction to the *pop-pop-pop* of the MP-5 as a trio of 9 mm slugs penetrated his chest. Choking blood replaced air in a torrential spray before the sentry collapsed to the ground with a dull thud.

Hawkins keyed his radio. "Hard contact, team leader. Unavoidable."

"Understood," McCarter's voice resounded. "Get clear ASAP."

MCCARTER MUTTERED A curse under his breath as he fired a glance at Calvin James, who nodded in understanding. With Hawkins blown they would have to change the game plan and hope they could still buy Encizo and Manning enough time to complete their mission. They had discussed this eventuality in theory but there hadn't been time to drill it in practice. The situation had gone hard too soon, and that would only bring more trouble— maybe *enough* trouble they'd be forced into a premature withdrawal.

McCarter leaned close to Kwan to be heard over the howl of the wind through the chopper. "We're both going over the side on this one."

"What happened?" Kwan asked.

McCarter shook his head to indicate he had no time to explain so Kwan just nodded and directed his next orders to the flight team. They had agreed that if a change in plans happened, it would be solely McCarter's call. Once they were fully deployed, Kwan knew they were to proceed directly to the extraction zone and wait the agreed amount of time.

McCarter and James geared into the rappel positions on opposite sides of the chopper. As soon as they got Kwan's signal, the pair dropped off and descended in synchronicity until they reached ground zero. Their boots hit earth simultaneously, and James cleared the harness rigging only a heartbeat faster than McCarter.

Neither man heard the chopper actually depart but only a few seconds elapsed before they heard the explosions at the sentry gate followed by a massive fireball that produced flames a good ten yards high. Tendrils of red-orange streaks and popping sparks were followed by a roil of black smoke, the result of Kwan's handiwork with the portable grenade launcher. The destruction of the main entry point to the compound was insurance, part of their plan to create a diversion and cause the security force to focus its attention where Phoenix Force wanted.

Hell, it's where we *need* it, McCarter thought.

The two whirled at the sound of approaching sentries; it was miraculous they could hear it in the aftermath of the explosion. McCarter brought his weapon to bear on a viable target first and triggered his MP-5. The SMG chattered as he touched off several short bursts. One sentry fell under the Briton's marksmanship. The man continued in forward motion as the 9 mm rounds cut his guts to ribbons, and then performed an awkward somersault before his body thumped to a halt in the slippery grass.

Two more sentries dived for whatever cover they could find, which was essentially none. At least it didn't do them much good under the unerring skill of Calvin James. He took the first one with a single shot that cored through the man's skull and transected it at an angle, ripping out part of his jaw on exit. The other sentry steadied his weapon and opened fire—a buzz of hot rounds zinged past McCarter and James, passing immediately between them as they split off at angles. The maneuver was standard, surely, but it disoriented the sentry who had probably just a minute earlier been enjoying a meal or smoke break.

McCarter didn't let the one sentry concern him, but the approach of reinforcements—six heavily armed men all wearing body armor—set him on edge. They couldn't necessarily win a fight against these heavies on their limited ammunition supply. They had packed light with the thought of swift retreat in mind. McCarter reached into his combat harness and came away with one of the Canadian-made fragmentation grenades. He rolled to one knee behind the sanctuary of a tree trunk, yanked the pin and lobbed the C-16. The throw turned out so accurate it bounced off the armored vest of one of the combatants before exploding.

Body armor and helmets were life-saving implements against ballistics, but superhot fragments propelled by the shock of impacted gases? Not so much. As the recipients of McCarter's little package realized all too soon after the grenade landed. The shock wave knocked two off their feet, and a third caught shrapnel full in the face. Another of the men who apparently had seen the grenade, had made a natural turn away from the blast source and suffered shrapnel wounds in the exposure points of the armor as a result.

The remaining pair managed to avoid any apparent injury, as they had been flankers for the team and were far enough out that simply throwing themselves to the ground spared them of injuries. McCarter and James used the distraction to pour out fresh volleys of autofire from their MP-5s but the action seemed more prophylactic than destructive. T. J. Hawkins rectified that situation quickly enough when he emerged from the concealment of a hedge to the left of the enemy and opened up with a sustained barrage of his own. Hawkins swept the muzzle along the ground, cutting into the lower backs and buttocks of the trio of sprawled sentries. None of the shots was immediately fatal, but was incentive enough that the enemy opted to surrender the fight.

Hawkins moved among the living and disarmed them with the proficiency of a professional. He'd spent many years with Delta Force, and he had been a welcome addition to Phoenix Force after the retirement of Yakov Katzenelenbogen, McCarter's predecessor. While a native Texan and occasional blowhard, for all his blustering Hawkins had proved himself a tough, resourceful teammate. And he'd become a good friend to every one of them.

In the lull of battle, McCarter and James stared at Hawkins—the ten-foot hurricane fence separated them.

"You think it's electrified?" Hawkins asked.

"Dunno," James replied. "Kwan didn't say anything about it. Just heat sensors or something."

McCarter gestured at the parade of weapons lying around. "Grab one of those assault rifles and give it a toss."

Hawkins brightened at McCarter's notion, scooped up one of the weapons and after clearing the magazine well and breach, tossed it muzzle-first toward the fence. The metal made contact with the fence and then clattered to the ground without sparks or other indicators to suggest the fence was electrified.

"Seems safe enough," Hawkins said.

He moved up to the fence and whipped out his combat knife. Using the serrated edge with its beveled heavy-gauge wire cutter built into the hilt, he snipped at the fence one agonizing link after another. While he worked, James and McCarter provided cover to his rear and flanks. They were certain no more sentries would come, most of them probably dispatched to deal with the explosion at the gate. At least it would buy Manning and Encizo additional time, and maybe even make their job easier.

Their teammates could only hope the two men got out with their prize and made it to the rendezvous point.

EVEN AS McCARTER, James and Hawkins were coping with their part of the mission outside, Manning and Encizo had their own hands full.

Their backs pressed to the wall, Encizo took the moment to study the layout interior again while Manning covered their flanks with the muzzle of his SMG. Kwan's intelligence had it on good authority Meifeng Cai resided somewhere on the second floor. The house stood more like an estate, so that meant they'd have to search half a dozen rooms or better to locate her. Once he'd checked the layout against their position, he nodded his readiness to proceed at Manning.

Encizo stepped forward first on point, keeping his back to the stairwell wall as they descended to the second floor. They didn't encounter resistance on the stairs—a good thing since they had to keep a healthy distance between each other. They made it to the second-floor landing unchallenged. Encizo peered around the corner and down the length of the hall. He turned back to Manning and pointed to his eyes before holding up a fist and extending three fingers. He then pointed his palm downward.

Three sentries, only sidearms. Probably standard house staff, so it wasn't unusual for them to be only passively armed. Still trouble, though, since the entire place would now be at the height of their security posture. The rumble of a distant explosion through the high ceilings of the hallway signaled an increase in resistance on the exterior grounds.

Hold on, guys, was all Encizo could think.

With a curt nod, the two emerged onto the hallway level and kept close to the walls as they moved into target acquisition. Encizo and Manning opened up simultaneously with their MP-5 SD-6s. The sentries were no match for the speed and stealth of their opponents and they fell immediately under the marksmanship of the Phoenix Force pair. The first hit the wall behind him hard with the impact. The other two were pummeled with enough rounds from the steady 3-round bursts that they slammed into one another. They joined their comrade on the carpeted floor a moment later.

Encizo gestured to the door on his left and Manning provided cover as Encizo opened it and engaged a high-powered flashlight through the room with a red-lens filter. It came up empty. The same happened with the two rooms to Manning's right, but in room number four, Encizo hit the jackpot. The wide eyes of an older Chinese female—streaks of gray running through her otherwise dark hair cut neat and long enough to cascade off her small shoulders—stared at the two men in horror. Her features roughly matched the old photo they had viewed in their briefing at the Farm.

Encizo tracked his flashlight across the remainder of the room but didn't find any enemies waiting to ambush them.

Manning and Encizo entered the room and crossed to the bed in a few strides. Meifeng sat bolt upright and held the blanket pulled tightly to her chest. Encizo started to open his mouth but the sudden, violent energy with which she reacted caused the words to lodge in his throat. A wicked-looking pistol—an older model but quite surely functional—appeared above the blanket and centered on his chest. Encizo moved to get out of the way just as the first shot rang out, his face close enough to feel the heat of the escaping gas from the muzzle-flash and the zing of the bullet.

Manning managed to come in on the flank and whipped the stock of his SMG in an underside arc. The edge caught Meifeng's wrist and knocked the pistol from her grasp. Encizo recovered and snatched her arm, yanking her from the bed and taking her prone to the floor. He snatched a pair of thick plastic cuffs from the cargo pants of his night-black fatigues and cinched her hands behind her.

"She's clear," he reported to Manning.

They each grabbed an arm and hauled the terrified woman to her feet.

"We're not going to hurt you," Manning said in *very* halting Chinese. He had no idea from the expression on the woman's face, which remained little more than a cross between defiance and fear, if he even had the right dialect. James had a little more experience than the rest of them in the Asian languages but not much. He switched to English. "Do you understand me?"

She winced with an almost imperceptible movement of her head that the two could only assume was affirmation.

"Let's beat feet," Encizo said.

They managed to get out of the room and down the hallway before the sound of heavy footfalls coming up the stairs reached their ears.

CHAPTER NINE

There was a total of six new arrivals and they were heavily armed.

Encizo and Manning had both planned their options in the event they encountered trouble after they had their target in hand and were in the process of escaping. They figured that any resistance they encountered in their escape would be unlikely to suspect any enemies had actually penetrated the house, so at least they would have the element of surprise on their side. The two Phoenix Force warriors used that fact to their advantage.

In the gloom, Encizo made a simple gesture that told Manning their opposition had only seen Encizo and not Manning or Meifeng. The Canadian turned her around and pushed her up the stairs ahead of him even as he heard the ratcheting of Encizo's MP-5. Encizo managed to get off several bursts to scatter the team on the first-floor landing before he yanked a C-16 from his harness, pulled the pin and tossed it down the carpeted steps.

Encizo whirled and followed up the steps two at a time, rounding the corner just before the grenade blew. Flames and heat licked at the Cuban's heels, but none of the whistling shrapnel reached his flesh. Shouts of pain and confusion were audible as the echo of the explosion died. That would buy them at least a little time. Maybe enough to get down the stairwell at the opposite end of the house.

Manning had to practically drag his captive behind

him, and at one point she started to dig in her heels. In short order, she found resistance futile against the two Americans as they simply picked up her slight form between them and moved her along so that her feet barely touched the floor. The maneuver didn't cause them to have to bear all of her weight while at the same time it forced her to either assist them or lose all control to move her own body.

Meifeng apparently finally came to realize that fighting them wouldn't bode well for her and she eventually propelled her legs to keep pace as best she could. They reached the opposite end of the second-floor hallway, and Encizo stepped over the bodies and executed a flying sidekick that took the door at the end of the hallway off its hinges. He crossed the darkened room, whipped open a recessed door in an alcove and checked to find another flight of steps that was dark and empty.

The trio made their way to the first floor and emerged onto an indoor solarium with a pool taking up most of the center space. They skirted the room by an outside wall, Encizo staying on point to navigate any potential trip hazards. He moved with unremitting speed and stealth, and Manning swore sometimes the guy was part cat with the way his eyes adjusted so quickly to changes in light.

They came upon a set of flagstone steps that descended into another area, this one populated with some rounded tables and chairs. They reached another door but found it locked. Encizo raised his MP-5 and shot off the lock. The Cuban had never been one to stand much on ceremony and this operation proved no exception. Beyond the door they found more steps that descended to the underground floor.

Manning went down first, his SMG leveled and ready

for action. As the blueprints had indicated, the security control room was off to their left, protected only by a room-length window with wire mesh that ran from about a five-foot wall to the ceiling. Four security men were inside the room and intent on monitoring the cameras and other devices, watching the action that continued to happen on the exterior. Why Yan Zhou's people had never bothered to install a full security suite for the *interior,* as well, didn't make a whole lot of sense but at this point it hardly mattered.

Manning waved Encizo ahead, indicating he and Meifeng should continue for the door on the far side of the corridor bordering the control room. He whispered, "I'm right behind you."

Encizo nodded and dashed down the corridor with their prize as Manning edged up to the door and slapped a block of C-4 against the exterior. He heard a shout from inside the control room as he planted a pencil detonator into the block of explosive and then jumped to his feet and hauled ass after them. The security team inside the control room reached the exit door at about the same time Manning caught up with Encizo and Meifeng just as they were dashing through the open metal door at the far end of the corridor. He risked a backward glance, flashed a wicked smile as he saw the men starting to exit the control room, and then slammed the metal door behind them as his thumb passed over the switch.

A massive explosion shook the door and walls of the dark, damp interior of the ventilation tunnel. Manning didn't have to look to know the resulting blast would not only have taken down the control room team but also caused considerable damage to the surrounding hall— enough to provide a blockage of debris to such a level that it would give them the time they needed to traverse the tunnel and make their escape at the far side.

"Nobody's coming through that mess anytime soon," Manning told Encizo.

Encizo nodded with a knowing wink. "Mighty fine work, amigo."

Manning checked his watch. "That little detour put us behind schedule by several minutes."

"Then we'd best make up for lost time."

With that, the two men turned and headed down the makeshift wind tunnel with their prize in tow.

ONCE HAWKINS HAD completed breaching the fence, he joined McCarter and James in a tactical retreat maneuver.

The three warriors trotted away from the perimeter and entered the nearby woods. James took point with an electronic compass that sported a backlit display. In addition to the sensitive electronic magnetometer inside the device, the compass included a military-grade dry compass, as well, in case the electronics failed or experienced a power loss. To be safe, McCarter had brought along a second one.

They were navigating in the dark and had a considerable distance to cover to reach the rendezvous point. No matter how well they'd memorized the topographical map Kwan provided—they hadn't brought the map along in case they were captured or separated from their packs— this was unfamiliar ground and they were traveling at night. Every one of the Phoenix Force team members knew how to read a map but they weren't superheroes. Even experienced navigators could become disoriented and only fools would've attempted this type of operation without using technology to help guide their efforts.

"According to this, we have about six hundred meters to go…due north," James said after orienting the compass to their present location.

"How long we plan to give them if they aren't there?" Hawkins asked.

McCarter frowned. "If they aren't there, then they're either dead or captured."

"And I heard you give them orders to move out if we didn't show at or before the specified time," James said.

"Right," McCarter said. "Not to mention they have much less of a distance to go and it's a straight line. So let's stop standing around here jabber-jawing and get cracking."

The men nodded, and James took off at a good clip with McCarter following and Hawkins on rear guard. The three kept a good distance between one another, enough they wouldn't all die at once in an ambush but not so much that each man couldn't see the one in front. Now and again, McCarter would check his six to ensure Hawkins stayed with them. The enemy force, or what was left of it, probably still had their hands full back at the compound trying to figure out what the hell had happened. McCarter wouldn't automatically assume they didn't have patrols, however, or that they might not send a force into the woods to investigate.

As they continued on their trek, he pondered all of the possibilities that Hark Kwan had presented to them earlier that day. To think they could be up against a force as large as the Gold Star Faction did nothing to brighten McCarter's hopes this would be a simple mission. Then again, Stony Man didn't typically hand out the simple missions to their elite fighting teams. Phoenix Force and

Able Team were the best of the best who got the worst of the worst.

McCarter had to admit he wouldn't have had it any other way.

When he considered it, Kwan's plan had actually worked out pretty well with McCarter's few suggested modifications. But Kwan still had his own potatoes to boil, his own interests and objectives, and McCarter reminded himself to keep that in mind. McCarter held no illusions Kwan wouldn't consider his own interests above those of Stony Man, and on that point he couldn't be *completely* trusted.

Not that McCarter wasn't sure Kwan hated the ideals of the GSF as much as they did. Communism equaled despotism, and despotism meant tyrants and dictators willing to subvert the very basic human freedoms to further their own goals. After what he'd seen and heard so far, McCarter didn't doubt for a moment that this Air Vice-Marshal Zhou wasn't exactly one of those types, willing to do whatever it took—including the murder of Americans and exploitation of a teenager—to push his own agenda.

McCarter and his men meant to ensure, whatever else may come, *that* didn't happen anymore.

The time it took to reach the intake shaft seemed like forever, although it really only took twenty minutes. Not bad for traveling nearly a half mile in the dark through dense forest, at night, in the cold, with nearly no light to guide them. It had obviously snowed a few days earlier, and the snow provided some natural reflection. Their boots crunched through it, making too much noise, but there wasn't a whole lot they could do about it since speed was the objective.

When they were within nearly spitting distance of the shaft, James held up a hand and gestured for them to stop. McCarter knew James and Hawkins would converge on his position once they were stationary, and within a moment he sensed their two bodies at his side.

"Any sign of them?" McCarter asked.

James shook his head.

"This is not good—"

McCarter moved the flat of his hand to signal a chopping motion and hissed the big Texan into silence. They could hear something that sounded like metal on metal, then a slight grunt as a human shape emerged abruptly from the shaft. A moment later they saw a second shape—this one small and petite—emerge behind the silhouette of Rafael Encizo.

McCarter and his team moved out of the wood line and joined their friends in a moment, Hawkins and James assisting Manning with his equipment and their weapons while McCarter engaged Encizo. The Briton couldn't see much but he could easily make out the gleaming white smile that split Encizo's dark complexion. The two men shook hands and then McCarter turned an appraising eye on Meifeng Cai.

"We come bearing gifts," Encizo said.

"I see that," he replied. "She speak English?"

"Either a little or a lot," Encizo said, scratching his head with a ponderous expression. "We're still not sure which."

"What kept you guys?" James inquired.

Manning gestured toward Meifeng's feet. "This one we found in bed. Nothing on her feet and there wasn't time to let her get properly dressed."

"Parts of that subterranean corridor were rough—a lot

of sharp rocks," Encizo explained. "So it took us longer since we had to carry her over those points."

"Anybody bring a spare pair of shoes?"

"I've got these," Hawkins said, withdrawing a pair of rubber wet-weather boots.

"Well, they'll be big," McCarter said with a sigh. He looked at Meifeng and added, "But at least she won't cut her feet to bloody ribbons and we won't have to carry her all the way to the LZ."

"We can cinch them to her feet using these," Manning said, pulling out a pair of thick plastic riot cuffs from the cargo pocket of his fatigues.

"Then let's get it done and get moving," McCarter replied. "Our chariot awaits us."

WHEN NEWS CAME down of Meifeng Cai's abduction, Yan Zhou wanted to reach through the phone and strangle the caller. Instead, he muttered a few expletives under his breath and slammed down the receiver. He whirled in his desk chair and stared out the sleet-spattered window of his office at the lights of the city. He didn't particularly like Tianjin, preferred Beijing like any good Chinese, but his work with his Communist allies made it a necessity to operate in this area. Teng Cai had also insisted on remaining in the area since Hebei Province was the ancestral region of his mother.

Zhou had elected to build the large compound up north as a place to keep the young prodigy and his mother where they would be secure. Now he had to wonder how wise that had been, since the men he'd assigned to security there had obviously become lax. Well, Zhou would take care of that soon enough. Someone would be held responsible for allowing the abduction of Cai's mother and be sentenced to summary execution—maybe even several would hang. And Zhou could *never* let word get out to Teng Cai, or the young genius would surely shut down his work until she was recovered. Zhou had already planned to do everything he could to facilitate her retrieval but he'd have to keep it quiet even from his masters in the Gold Star Faction.

The entire incident got Zhou wondering if someone had stumbled on to his ties to the GSF. While there were many of his superiors in Beijing who would overlook his private affiliations, even with a group that had been publicly denounced as a political terrorist entity, he couldn't let word get out just how strongly entrenched he was within their ranks or how beholden he'd become to them. Certain individuals within the Gold Star Faction had pulled strings to get Zhou into his present position as the second-highest-ranking military officer within the PRCAF. Exposing those individuals to ridicule and embarrassment—particularly since they had taken great lengths to remain anonymous—wouldn't do Zhou's career any good.

Zhou picked up the phone and called the direct line that would connect him to Wen Xiang. The assassin answered on the first ring, his voice muted as if he'd been asleep. Zhou looked at his watch and realized he probably had been.

Xiang didn't hide his irritation at being roused so early. "Yes...what is it?"

"We've encountered a problem," Zhou said, careful not to identify himself. "I'm going to move up our timetable. And you will be responsible for transferring our prize to a new location."

"What's happened?"

"I can't get into it now."

"Can't or won't?"

"I'm not in the mood for any of your scorning at this moment," Zhou said. "Now listen to me. Get him moved—do it quickly and do it *quietly*. Tell him it is for security reasons or whatever. Promise what you need to. Under no circumstances should you raise that special subject with him. You know the one I mean?"

"Of course," Xiang snapped. "Do you take me for a fool?"

Zhou opted not to rise to the bait. "How long do you think it will take?"

"We'll have it done within two hours."

"Excellent. When that's completed, I have a very important mission for you. Call me when you've finished and I will give additional instructions."

"You do understand this, ah, new mission is outside the original terms of our agreement."

"You'll be compensated," Zhou replied tiredly. "The usual rates?"

"Of course," Xiang said with a harsh chuckle. "We're not greedy."

"Yes," Zhou said and he hung up.

He hated Wen Xiang but realized the man was a necessary evil and quite proficient with these types of operations. Zhou looked forward to the day he could offload that burden from around his neck for good. However, at present Xiang presented a resource that Zhou could ill afford to lose. He would deal with Xiang on his own terms and in his own good time, but that time wasn't now. First, he had to let Xiang off the leash once more to locate and retrieve Meifeng Cai. And to send a message to whoever had taken her that opposing the Gold Star Faction was futile and foolish.

CHAPTER TEN

Carl Lyons sat in a borrowed government sedan across from a three-story residential building on the southeastern edge of the city. It was neither the nicest part of town nor the dregs—just a quiet middle-class area with quiet middle-class residents. That wasn't the strictest truth but Lyons didn't figure he had to convince anyone of it. A scum-sucking bastard occupied one of those condominiums, and as far as Lyons knew the rest of the building occupants were model citizens.

The target's name was Se-Hong Yu, a known runner of black market arms to the highest bidder. His dossier being the only one to pop up in Stony Man's vast database, the remainder being either listed as currently missing in action from the area or deceased. Lyons decided to go with Yu and see where it led him. After all, Yu was known to be active at present and Lyons didn't have time to go shaking down every person in Anchorage with a Korean name.

"If your Korean friends were supplied weapons from a local market pipeline, Yu is most likely your guy," Kurtzman had told him.

Schwarz and Blancanales had soured at the idea of Lyons going it alone on this one, but the Able Team leader had squashed their protests. Okay, so maybe it wasn't the brightest move but the mission to protect Priscilla Stavros while sniffing out any potential security leaks came first. Fact was Schwarz and Blancanales were the two best suited toward those ends and like it or not, they all knew it. Still, going it alone was a risk. Lyons didn't mind, though—the Able Team leader was quite adept at taking risks.

Se-Hong Yu's second-floor condo faced the street. Lyons had been sitting in the increasing cold of the vehicle freezing his gonads off for the past two hours, clearing away the frost that formed on the windows in crystal patches from his breath and body heat, watching the windows intently. He didn't dare crank the engine and fire up the heater. The exhaust would attract attention, even in the dim streetlights. An idling vehicle would definitely be out of place so early in the morning, especially running at sporadic intervals but never going anywhere.

Lyons had learned how to stake out an area as a cop with the LAPD. It had been ages since he'd turned in his badge for the opportunity to join Stony Man, but some things just stuck—police work tended to be one of them. His experience as a cop coupled with his training and veteran status in Able Team had given him an even wider pool of skills from which to draw. Now it looked like that would pay off once again.

Through the spiderweb patterns in the fresh patina of frost on the side window, Lyons saw a short man emerge from the building. He rubbed his bare knuckles against the window frost just enough to expose a bird's-eye view and squinted to see if he could make out the features. It was difficult at that distance, and especially since the guy wore a hooded jacket and oversize earmuffs. Lyons watched him walk at a fast clip down the sidewalk toward a parking garage adjacent to the building. The man looked over his shoulder a few times but didn't appear to spot Lyons.

Well, it wouldn't hurt to drive past for a closer look—worst case, it wouldn't be Se-Hong Yu.

Lyons waited until the man rounded the corner that dipped into the covered garage and then cranked the engine and put the defrosters on full blast. He muttered a complaint as he rubbed his meaty fist at the mass of frost enough to clear his line of sight so he could navigate safely, then put the car in gear and performed a smooth U-turn. Lyons crawled up the street, stalling as much as possible before he finally turned into the garage and descended the ramp.

As he rounded a corner of the garage at its far end, a heavy early model Cadillac roared toward him. The warrior let out a curse as he tromped the accelerator and whipped the wheel to the left to avoid a head-on collision. The engine of the sedan would've been no match for the front end of the massive battle wagon rushing him. Fortunately, Lyons got out of the way enough to suffer only a glancing blow of the right rear corner panel, the Cadillac weaving at the last moment so that its right side only partially ripped away the rear bumper of Lyons's vehicle. Lyons dropped the gearshift into Reverse and backed into a J-turn to pursue even as the Cadillac's rear end disappeared around the corner. He accelerated smoothly so as not to burn rubber against the pavement. No reason to wear the tires prematurely—there would be plenty of time for that later.

As Lyons nearly vaulted the ramp and bounced onto the street he looked both ways to see the Cadillac had already managed to make headway down the deserted road. He swung to his left and gave chase, watching helplessly as the Cadillac continued to widen the gap. Big or not, the engine in that Caddy could easily outmatch Lyons's car, not to mention the driver probably knew the roads well. He couldn't be sure it was Yu behind the wheel, but chances were pretty good it was. The guy had probably been watching Lyons watch *him* the whole time. Lyons tried to consider where he'd gone wrong and then kicked himself when he realized he'd not thought Yu would be on heightened alert once he'd heard of what had gone down at the docks. While the Navy had managed to keep most inquiries at bay, there were other information channels besides the press.

Lyons increased speed until he had the pedal to the floor. The sun had just begun to peek over the horizon, signaling the start of a very long period of daylight, but that was still minutes away and this part of the city was still quite dim. Lyons pressed his lips tightly and white-knuckled the steering wheel, determined to catch up and bring the chase to an end as quickly as possible.

As he blew through the red light at an intersection, he caught just the flash of a white vehicle with familiar markings in his periphery. He checked his rearview mirror and a heartbeat later an Anchorage police cruiser whipped into view in a colorfully patriotic array of reds, whites and blues.

"Oh, sure," Lyons mumbled. "Managed to spot *me* speeding instead of the bad guy."

What frustrated him more was that he'd now attracted the attention of one police cruiser, which would inevitably call for more police cruisers, and pretty soon he'd have an entire parade of cops on his tail. Not to mention they were more experienced driving on these kinds of roads in this climate. Lyons weighed his options and decided he couldn't afford to let up. He'd throw caution to the wind and cops be damned, unless it got to the point where it might endanger innocent civilians. Brognola would have his *ass* if that happened.

Lyons poured on all the speed the sedan could muster and quickly realized he was gaining on the Cadillac. That puzzled him at first until he saw a pair of police cruisers farther up the street blocking the intersection in a V-shape. Lyons shook his head at such lunacy. This wasn't the damned movies—hard-core criminals like Yu wouldn't stop for a mere police roadblock. But he would if his wheels no longer worked.... What happened in the next moment seemed to pass a blur. Smoke spewed from the tires. The Cadillac started to fishtail and then the monstrosity of American engineering flipped onto its right side and came to a grinding halt in a display of sparks and smoke.

I'll be damned, Lyons thought. Spike strips.

Lyons pumped his brakes as he rolled up to the scene, bringing his sedan to a slippery halt in time to see a figure pop through the driver's-side window. From that vantage point, Lyons could make out the Asian features. Yep. Definitely Se-Hong Yu. The Korean gunrunner dipped his left hand into his long black trench coat and came away with a smooth oblong object. Lyons knew the menacing shape instantly. He glanced to his left and saw several uniforms approaching on the run with their pistols pointed at Yu. The cops weren't even considering him as part of the equation. They'd been after Yu the entire time and he'd just managed to walk smack-dab into the net they'd thrown over the area! It didn't make any sense. Had they been watching him? Yu *had* seemed to be leaving in a hurry and now he was faced with nearly a half dozen of Anchorage's finest with more probably on the way.

What the cops obviously hadn't seen yet was the grenade, probably too amped up on adrenaline to understand they weren't up against some common thug. Yu yanked the pin and tossed it at the cops before turning to drop for cover behind the wrecked Cadillac. Lyons cursed, slammed the gearshift into Drive and tromped the accelerator as he aimed the noise toward where the grenade had rolled into the middle of the street.

The cops turned in surprise at his sudden maneuver, but Lyons realized, even as he bore down on the grenade, that he was now at some risk himself. Even if he managed to save the cops he'd end up getting himself blown to smithereens. As he'd hoped, the cops dived for any kind of cover they could find when they saw him driving toward them. Lyons made sure of his direction and then opened the door and bailed out the side, rolling deep to ensure he didn't get run over by his own wheels. The grenade went off just as the front of the vehicle rolled over it. While the explosion was powerful, the sedan did a neat job of containing it with the engine block taking the majority of the blast effect and all the shrapnel. It also shredded the tires and cracked the axle, bringing an effective halt to the sedan so that Lyons, in course, hadn't ended up trading one deadly object for another.

Lyons gained his feet with the grace of a panther and liberated his FNP-45, charging toward the Cadillac and paying no attention to the approaching squad car. He rounded the far corner of the vehicle but Yu wasn't there. Lyons glanced in every direction and finally spotted a flash of the tail of a trench coat as Yu rounded the corner of a nearby alley. Lyons gave chase, willing his powerful legs to propel his equally powerful frame as fast as they would. He thought of the last time he'd pursued an enemy into an alley and how that had nearly ended, but this time Yu was on foot and probably only lightly armed.

Maybe he had another grenade, but Lyons wasn't betting on it. If he had, Yu would most likely have used it as backup to the first. Lyons did the last thing his enemy would've expected, charging around the corner like a banshee out of hell instead of stopping short and checking it first with caution. Yu didn't even see him. He was busily kicking at a flimsy wooden door that seemed more intent on splintering than actually giving way. Probably a crossbar holding it place.

Lyons eventually reached Yu. He holstered his pistol and then executed a flying tackle, keeping his forearms above shoulder level so as not to smash them between Yu's body and the brick wall. The smaller man was no match for Lyons's weight or strength, and his chest struck the wall with crushing force. The impact bounced them both back and Lyons twisted at the last moment so that he came down on top of Yu. The man squealed a flurry of insults and curses in Korean but Lyons stopped even those short by delivering a rock-hard hammer punch to the bone behind Yu's right ear. Yu let out a surprised shout before lapsing into unconsciousness.

Lyons made sure Yu wasn't playing possum before he dragged himself to his feet, breathing heavily. He was still in excellent shape but he wondered sometimes if he wasn't getting a bit too old for this kind of thing. A thought came to him and he reached into his coat and withdrew the forged credentials stowed there just a moment before an army of cops rounded the corner with weapons aimed straight at him.

"Hold it right there!" one young, fresh-faced officer ordered. "Police!"

No shit, Lyons thought. He raised the badge and ID card over his head and shouted, "U.S. federal agent—hold your fire, damn it!"

DESPITE HIS BEST attempts to avoid any contact with law enforcement, Lyons knew exactly how the drill would go and it played out just as he'd predicted.

Nearly four hours went by while the police shipped Yu off in an ambulance, hauled Lyons in, took his statement and then made half a dozen phone calls to verify he was who he claimed to be while Lyons got only one. He decided to make that one to Blancanales and Schwarz to check on things while letting the detectives talk with Brognola. Lyons knew that getting the word directly from a top administrator in the Justice Department—Brognola's official cover whenever he had to liaise with other law-enforcement agencies—would get him more respect and better treatment than trying to reach out to those channels himself.

While he'd been a little miffed by having to surrender his firearm temporarily, Lyons knew that most federal agents would have followed the line given them without argument. While congeniality had never been his strong suit, Lyons figured it wouldn't help his case to point out that by rolling his car over the grenade, he'd saved their sorry asses. But his good will and cooperation bought him some consideration all the same, and within an hour after arriving at the station they'd returned his firearm to him and transferred him from an interrogation room to a conference area that had comfortable chairs, a snack machine and a phone.

While he waited for the lead investigator to join him, Lyons slurped down some of the lukewarm mud that passed for coffee and half a sandwich from the machine. One of the officers who came in, a guy Lyons recognized as belonging to the trio that had originally tried to arrest Yu, saw what Lyons was eating and offered him a slice of pizza. Lyons accepted it gratefully and the pair made small talk until two men entered.

The tallest of the pair wore a suit and tie. He had gray eyes, thinning brown hair and a salt-and-pepper mustache that looked way out of place on his pasty complexion. The other, squat, muscular and completely bald, sported a uniform with sergeant stripes, and accompanied the plainclothes a few steps behind. The sergeant dismissed the officer, who in turn nodded to Lyons before he stepped out and closed the door.

The guy in the suit took a seat while the sergeant sidled around Lyons's chair and copped a chunk of the table on which to lean, folding his arms and casting a critical eye at the Able Team leader. The table creaked under his weight but held.

"Agent Norris, I'm Captain Cronaugher and this—" he jerked a thumb at the uniformed man "—is Sergeant Moore."

Lyons nodded.

"We're sorry to have detained you this long and I hope you were treated accordingly given your status and rank as a federal officer." The guy didn't wait for Lyons to reply, which meant he didn't really give a damn if Lyons had been treated well or not. "You can understand that we were somewhat surprised when you suddenly appeared out of nowhere in pursuit of a known Korean gunrunner."

"Why should it be a surprise, Cronaugher?" Lyons

interjected. "Surely you know about the noise that went down last evening. You can't really expect me to believe you're surprised we'd be looking into a guy like Yu. What has me curious is why the hell it's taken you people so long to get your claws into this guy?"

Cronaugher's face reddened some but he kept his cool.

Moore, however, wasn't so taken off guard by Lyons's tact. "What's that supposed to mean, Norris?"

Lyons pinned Moore with his hard blue eyes. "Don't get your shorts in a bunch, Sergeant. My point is that we suspect Yu supplied a few North Korean intelligence agents with black-market arms. Arms they used to try to assassinate a U.S. military scientist. And my intelligence contacts tell me Yu's been operating here for some time. He didn't just fall off a rice boat into Anchorage yesterday."

"You got any proof?" Cronaugher asked.

"What happened at the port is all the proof I need," Lyons replied. He sighed and sat forward, thumping his fist on the table. "Look, let's cut all the shit. You've verified my identity and now you know what's what. I can't tell you anything more than I already have since it's classified and I don't think either of you has a security clearance. And since I'm free to go, now, I'd appreciate someone giving me a lift over to the hospital so I can question Yu."

"We can't allow that," Moore cut in. "He's in our custody."

Lyons sat back and shook his head, putting an edge in his voice. "Don't think so, boys. I'm the one who apprehended him. Remember? Oh, that was right after I saved three or four of your officers from getting blown into fish chum, which of course explains why I no longer have any transportation."

Cronaugher and Moore looked at one another before Cronaugher let out a deep sigh. He returned his attention to Lyons. "Okay, Norris, have it your way. But I'll have to call the chief and get it cleared."

"Call whoever you want, Captain. But make it quick. I want to get to Yu and question him before the people he supplied get to him first."

"You think these mysterious Korean agents will try to hit him?"

Lyons frowned as he replied, "You can bet on it."

CHAPTER ELEVEN

Once Nam's condition stabilized some and she'd allowed him to rest, Ju Young-Soon took a shuttle bus to a car rental place near the Anchorage airport and procured a late-model SUV. She returned to the B and B, left more than enough to cover the cost of their stay with a neatly printed note of thanks. It took some effort to get Nam awake, dressed and down to the SUV but soon she'd transferred him to their alternate location—a discount motel on the south side of the city.

With Nam secured, she departed the motel and drove back to the airport and checked into a somewhat nicer hotel a few blocks from it. Young-Soon checked in under an assumed name. She'd brought only her equipment bag with a spare change of clothes and a collection of firearms supplied by Se-Hong Yu. Once settled in her room, Young-Soon went back to the lobby, found a bank of pay phones near the restrooms and made a call to a number she'd memorized.

"Yes?" the voice answered.

"Any word?" she asked, careful not to identify herself by name. The man on the other end would know her voice.

"Yes," he replied. "It happened pretty suddenly and apparently emergency services were called. I don't think those strangers you encountered knew that. They got in each other's way."

"Did Mother come through the surgery okay?"

"Yes." The caller gave her the name of one of the major medical centers in the city. "Do you want me to send some flowers on your behalf?"

"No," Young-Soon replied. "I'll take care of that personally."

She hung up the phone and returned to her room. After showering, she pulled her long black hair tight against her scalp and pinned it there with wide, flat clips. Then she donned a short-length wig of ash-blond before dressing in denim pants, a white blouse and a leather jacket. Young-Soon applied a generous but not overindulgent amount of medium base, then a powder blush and finally a deep pink lipstick. She couldn't do anything about her dark eyes but some hair dye did a good job of lightening her eyebrows.

Following a close inspection in the mirror and a satisfied hum she could pass muster without attracting attention, Young-Soon slung her weapons bag over her shoulder and took a back stairway to the underground parking garage. She located her SUV, climbed behind the wheel and punched the address into the GPS navigation system.

Setting this information into the system was a risk, of course, but she didn't have much choice. She didn't know Anchorage at all, and she hadn't wanted to take the time to buy a city map or to make an inquiry online via a public computer.

Young-Soon considered her options as she drove toward the medical center. There were two basic ways of approaching this. One would be to simply inquire about Yu's condition and see if she could gain entrance as a friend or lover, maybe even a fiancée. Chances were good from the information she had, though, the cops had Yu in a security wing, probably guarded and restricted from receiving *any* visitors. That left her with only one other choice. She'd have to gain access to attire as a nurse or orderly or, if possible, a doctor. The latter would probably get her access to just about anything.

If Young-Soon had been religious, she'd have thanked Buddha that no one in a medical center of that size would pay much attention to her. Many doctors in a variety of specialties would have privileges at the hospital, so the sight of an unfamiliar face wouldn't raise alarms and especially not if she came through the E.R. The problem wouldn't be getting in or even playing her role as much as getting the correct attire to begin with. She pushed down a sense of apprehension as the navigation system advised her she was within a few blocks. Now wasn't the time to lose her cool. She would simply have to adapt to the situation as it unfolded for her. That's what she'd been trained to do and that's what her government paid her for.

As she pulled into the patient parking area near the E.R. entrance, Ju Young-Soon mentally prepared herself for a rendezvous with Fate.

CARL LYONS GOT about the greeting he would've expected on his arrival at the Anchorage Municipal Medical Center. He wondered if Cronaugher or Moore had advised the three-man "protection" detail stationed in the small security wing of the hospital to detain, delay and otherwise harass him in every way possible. They didn't impede him when he showed them his credentials and advised he'd been authorized to interrogate Yu, but they treated him with something less than cool detachment. One guy even gave him the sour eye.

Asshole, Lyons thought as he pushed through the door to Yu's room.

Se-Hong Yu was not only awake but he looked to be in pretty good shape considering his encounter with Lyons. As soon as the Korean gunrunner saw Lyons his eyes grew wide and he tried to disentangle his body from the cords and other alarms.

Lyons considered his options and tried for a calm tact. He raised his arms. "Whoa there, Yu. Take it easy."

"Fuck you!" the guy said in a squeaky, heavily accented voice. "You can't touch me."

"I'm not going to touch you," Lyons said. "I'll stand right here. I just want to ask you some questions."

"Fuck you," he repeated, as if somehow he thought that was all he needed to say. "I say nothing."

"You'd better say *something,* Yu," Lyons reminded him. "Otherwise, you'll have to do your talking to the cops."

"I want a lawyer."

"As it stands right now, you got no rights to a lawyer. You're in the country illegally and you've recently made the terrorist watch-list. That means about the only thing you're entitled to is a one-way trip to some faraway prison where nobody will ever hear from or see you again."

"Fuck you."

Lyons favored Yu with a wan smile. "I see your vocabulary is extensive."

"You give me lawyer."

"I'll give you a broken arm if you don't shut your mouth," Lyons replied through gritted teeth. "Wise up, Yu. You're about as deep as you can get. So here's the deal. Yesterday morning several Korean nationals attacked a U.S. Coast Guard ship, not to mention a number of the servicemen aboard it. That's an act of war. We traced the arms used in the attack back to you as the supplier. I've been authorized to summarily take charge of you and transport you to a secure facility."

Lyons paused nonchalantly to inspect his nails. "That is, of course, unless you'd like to tell me who it was you sold those weapons to. Then we might be able to forget the charge of terrorism and let you take your chances with the local police authorities. These local agencies have never been that great at punishing criminals. The United States government, however, has become increasingly renowned for how it deals with those individuals suspected of terrorism. You have, of course, heard of places like Guantanamo Bay."

While he might have tried to remain cavalier, something caused Yu to blanch.

Lyons offered him another frosty smile. "But of *course* you have. So now you know your predicament. You have a choice here, Yu—a chance to come out of this with all of your fingers and toes intact. And perhaps a bit of your dignity. Being you're in the country illegally, you'll probably spend eighteen months in a local jail and they'll turn you over to Immigration and Customs Enforcement agents and deport you back to Korea. Since none of the cops you tossed that grenade at were killed, your luck may just hold up."

"I don't have to talk to you," Yu said. "I still have rights. I take my chances with the cops."

"Oh, I see. Well, then, it might interest you to know that they're planning to charge you with at least a half dozen counts of aggravated assault against police officers, and a whole battery of other counts. That's for starters. But if you cooperate, I might—notice I said *might*—help you if your information pans out."

It was Yu's turn to smile at Lyons and he accompanied the leer with a scoffing laugh. "I talk to you or cops, I'm dead."

"You don't talk to me, you're dead."

"I'm already going to die."

"You mean the ones you're working with," Lyons interjected. "You're saying these people are going to come here and try to kill you."

Yu nodded. "Yes, they will come here to kill me. Or they will kill me in prison, or if I'm sent back to Korea, as you say, they will kill me then. No matter what I do, I am dead."

The realization of what Se-Hong Yu told him rang alarm bells in Lyons's gut. It was all clear to him in a moment. Yu had somehow learned of the failed hit at the docks, which was why he'd left in such a hurry earlier that morning when Lyons chased him. He wasn't fleeing from Lyons or the cops—he'd known his Korean friends would come back and kill him anyway to keep him quiet.

Lyons's cold blue eyes narrowed. "You were running from the buyers because they knew *you* knew their real plans. Somehow you figured out they would come back to kill you no matter what. Tie up any loose ends."

"This is inevitable," Yu replied quietly. "So now you know why I say to fuck off, because I will not help you. I will not die with dishonor."

"You won't die at all, Yu," Lyons said. "Because I'm going to get you moved out of here. Right now."

"YOU'RE NOT ON the list," Officer Marc Hamm said for the third time.

The beautiful young nurse with the blond hair, her firm curves showing in the dark red scrubs, smiled at him. "But I already told you, I don't *know* anything about a list. This is my usual shift. You can ask anybody working in there."

"Look, nurse, I'm sorry but your name isn't on this list," Hamm replied. "And if you're not on the list, I can't admit you. Period. You'll have to go speak with the hospital administration."

"But I'll be late!" she cooed. "Please, can't you just let me in long enough to talk to the shift supervisor?"

"What's going on?" another voice asked.

Hamm turned to look at Corporal Jo Ujarak, a native Alaskan and the detail supervisor. Hamm had gone through the academy with Ujarak and they'd been up for promotion at the same time, but Ujarak had beat Hamm out by just a margin—Hamm had always harbored a notion it was because Ujarak was a native and it had something to do with Equal Opportunity Employment, but he'd never spoken of it openly. In reality, the two were pretty good friends and Hamm had learned to accept the fact Ujarak had been the better candidate and that one day he'd come into his own.

"Well, this nurse here… What did you say your name was?"

Unfortunately, Hamm would never achieve the hoped-for promotion because when his attention had focused on Ujarak, he'd failed to notice the nurse reach into the gym bag on her shoulder and produce a pistol. In fact, neither Hamm nor Ujarak realized anything was wrong until the nurse leveled the pistol at Hamm's head and blew it off with a single shot to the temple.

Ujarak sucked in a breath and reached for her own sidearm but she didn't clear it in time—the fact she held the speed record on the range made little difference. She took her own shot at a point just below the chin, the bullet entering the soft palate and traveling upward to crack through the base of her skull with enough force to slam her against the wall. But the nurse had already snatched the key card off the pocket flap of Hamm's uniform.

She passed beyond their makeshift checkpoint and was now moving toward the swinging doors into the security wing with purposeful strides.

LYONS NO SOONER had his cell phone out and started dialing the number to Stony Man when he heard the unmistakable reports of a gun. He glanced in Yu's direction—the smug expression the gunrunner held just a moment before had turned to fear—before trading his phone for his pistol. Lyons checked the action on the FNP-45, ensured a round was chambered, and then opened the door and peered out. The hall looked deserted except for a short nurse with blond hair marching down the hallway, a pistol held tight and low against her side, glancing at each room number as she passed them.

Lyons was about to duck out of view when he saw two of the cops lying in the hallway beyond the automatic doors just before they swung closed behind the nurse. He didn't know where the third had gone, maybe lunch, but it didn't really matter because he didn't doubt the intentions of this new arrival. A nurse rushed out from a room and started to speak to the woman in an interrogative tone. Lyons clenched his teeth, bringing his pistol into a point where he could draw a bead and fire, but his potential target acted with a speed and surety that could only have come from long, arduous training in the martial arts. Rather than shoot the nurse, the woman executed a perfect side-kick that caught the nurse square in the solar plexus and drove her into the wall, knocking her unconscious as she crumpled to the linoleum.

Lyons ducked into the room and secured the door with a soft click of the latch. No locks on this one, not that it would've done much good. While the armed woman was ash-blond, she sported the approximate build and height of one of the figures that had fled the dock—Lyons was *certain* of it. He eased into the proper part of the room and noticed Yu trying to detach his arm from the IV and rip the sticky monitoring pads off his chest and side.

"Stop!" Lyons whispered tightly. "You want to live?"

Yu nodded with furious affirmation, eyes wide, all sense of the earlier bravado now gone.

"Then keep quiet and don't make a sound. Pretend you're sleeping and you might come through this in one piece."

Lyons walked over to Yu's bedside, reached over the guy's head and killed the overhead light. Only shafts of daylight passed through the half-closed blinds spanning the window. Lyons returned to the door and wheeled into the bathroom perpendicular to the entrance. He got inside and noted that the space between the sink and the wall was cramped but with enough clearance where he could wait. The warrior eased into the space and holstered his pistol so both hands would be free.

He barely got his weight centered when he heard the click of the latch and the unmistakable hush of the door as it swung inward. He'd seen what his opponent could do in a physical confrontation, which meant he stood only about a fifty percent chance of taking her by surprise before she managed to put several rounds into Yu.

Well, if he didn't get to her before Yu died, them was the breaks.

Lyons waited until he saw her shadow cast lengthwise against the floor from the light of the window. He then stepped out and executed a modified sleeper hold, cautious to keep the full breadth of his vital front torso to the woman's back. Knowing she was still armed and could easily reach back with the pistol and blow his brains out, Lyons immediately threw his weight against the outer wall and ensured the first point of contact would be the woman's right shoulder. The blow did as he'd hoped, sending a jolt of muscle-numbing lightning down the woman's arm. Lyons heard the definite clatter as the pistol hit the floor.

Lyons tried to increase the pressure but he'd unfortunately miscalculated his opponent's response time. She'd managed to wriggle her lithe frame into a neutral position by turning her neck completely to the left and dropping her weight. An explosive pain rocketed through the nerve bundle at the forward aspect of the crease in his groin. Lyons bit back the pain, willing his mind to ignore the blow, but it proved enough of a distraction that he lost enough of the critical pressure in the sleeper hold that he knew instantly he'd never regain.

The woman spun the other way and managed to get a second elbow into his floating rib. He didn't feel it crack but he was certain she'd bruised it enough that he'd be feeling it later. Lyons tried to maintain the sleeper hold—what he had left of it wasn't anything to write home about—tensing the muscles of his right arm against the woman's throat. Unfortunately, she'd managed to get her neck turned enough that he no longer had the vital spot crooked appropriately. She was able to deliver a stomp to the instep that didn't really go far only because the sole of her foot, not the heel, was no match against the padded tongue of his combat boot.

Lyons recalled his training where an instructor had discussed the points where releasing a failing hold on an opponent was preferable to getting the shit beat out of you. He knew he'd reached that point. Lyons released his hold and then did something that the woman, no matter what her training and discipline, would never have expected. Lyons grabbed the back of her collar, rolled onto his back and used his weight to slam her to the floor.

While Lyons would have never christened himself an expert in ground-fighting, it was immediately apparent to him that his opponent wasn't really trained in this arena, either. She'd obviously been taught not to let a larger, stronger, more experienced opponent get her off her feet because her only response to this sudden turn in fortunes was to attempt to wriggle out of his grip. Lyons immediately seized the advantage and swung his right leg around so his crotch butted against the woman's right armpit. He then hooked his right ankle under his left and applied a classic jujitsu arm bar, pulling on the fulcrum of the elbow while levering the arm with his weight.

The woman shouted in pain and then uttered a word in Korean that Lyons couldn't be certain but was relatively confident signified her surrender. A moment passed before the door swung open and several Anchorage cops rushed into the room followed by Cronaugher.

Lyons released his hold once the uniforms managed to snap cuffs onto the woman's wrists. Breathing heavily, he accepted Cronaugher's hand in assisting him to his feet and wiped at the large drops of sweat beading over his forehead and threatening to run into his eyes.

Cronaugher cast an eye at the woman, eyebrow high,

and then cocked his head in Lyons's direction. "Hell, Norris, you just don't know how to stay out of trouble."

"It's my lot in life," Lyons grumbled.

CHAPTER TWELVE

Tianjin, People's Republic of China

Teng Cai had never believed in any one political ideology. Even in his own country he was an outcast, destined to be different not because he was a genius but merely because he'd never known what it was like to be anything but the prodigy he was. It was all a matter of construct and a "normal" life had never been a construct he could grasp.

"From practically the moment you were born, we knew you'd been destined for something far greater than us," Cai's father had once told him. "Far greater than even yourself."

Cai had always wondered about his old man; wondered exactly what happened to him and why he'd died so young. Cai even wondered if the young, strapping air force officer who had inserted himself into their lives practically the day after Chung Cai died might have had something to do with his father's death. Teng Cai had *never* trusted Yan Zhou, although he'd known that to utter such a thought even in the alleged privacy of their own home would've been an unforgivable indiscretion that would visit terrible consequences on Cai's mother. From the earliest time he could remember, Cai's talents had been wielded, even manipulated, by Zhou in the name of furthering the government. Teng Cai had realized the consequences of that manipulation from the moment he'd agreed to acquiesce and turn his studies toward developing the most powerful aerial war machines ever conceived.

They called him a child genius, a prodigy unparalleled in perhaps all of history. Cai doubted it. These things were nothing more than vain attempts to heap praise and accolades on him so he continued to do their bidding. He'd also heard the rumors of how Zhou and his cronies had suckered foreign intelligence agencies into believing he wanted to defect, and then killed anyone who came sniffing around the rumors.

Then of course there was the Gold Star Faction. How the great Air Vice-Marshal Yan Zhou could think that Cai wouldn't know anything about that was beyond his comprehension. Cai probably knew more about the political machinations of the country, and most certainly the internal politics of the PRCAF, than Zhou *ever* would.

Yes, that's how smart they consider me, Cai thought. They think I'm ignorant of their goals.

Power. It was what Zhou wanted. It was what the GSF wanted. And it was certainly what they had tried to demonstrate by robbing Cai of his intellect. Teng Cai had never told anyone, even his mother, that he wished to invent things that weren't necessarily for war but for peace. He could imagine being satisfied with developing aircraft and spaceships that could travel at speeds never before imagined. Supersonic aircraft and fighter jets, or satellite-based weapons systems under control of a world leader that could balance the power between all nations.

Instead, they fought among themselves with backroom deals and political backbiting, all activities designed to further expand the wealth of the wealthy and steal from the poor and hungry. Okay, so maybe he hadn't suffered any. He was tall for his race, well-fed and afforded the biggest luxuries available. He had round-the-clock security and fully equipped laboratories. He had both a work and personal staff at his disposal, and more money than he could spend in two lifetimes. He'd paid for it, yes, but at least his mother was being taken care of.

Teng Cai put his eyes to the high-powered microscope once more and checked the EPROM gates on the chip. This tiny little device, a sensitive electronic confluence of billions of resistors crafted into a thin substrate of semiconducting material, would dictate the navigation, targeting and propulsion-guidance systems of the next generation of signal-seeking missiles. The manufacturing had not been easy, since it had to appear as if it'd come from North Korea. What would not be apparent without a significant microscopic examination was the large-scale integration architecture in the chip.

It was the signature design that made it unique; a design Cai had first conceived of at eleven and had practically developed using computer blueprints by twelve. Now, just two short years later and only a couple of weeks from his fifteenth birthday, Cai had realized his dream in a practical way. Even if this technology were to fall into the hands of their enemies, or even their allies, it would be indistinguishable without significant research.

Teng Cai smiled at the thought that *he* was the government's biggest secret, and his prowess and genius were only ill-fated rumors to the rest of the world. No more than a handful of the highest-ranking members of myriad intelligence organizations even knew his name, and even fewer knew where he was located. Cai had to admit that, if nothing else, his masters let him work uninterrupted and ran political interference with anyone who became too interested in Cai or his work.

Of course, there were interruptions from Zhou's people, who had practically unlimited access to him. One of those was a man named Wen Xiang. Cai disliked everything about Xiang. First off, it was no secret he was little more than a gun-for-hire and assassin on the outs with certain influences within the Ministry of State Security. There were also rumors he'd murdered dozens of noncombatants out of hand, that he liked killing and that he'd even taken private contracts in other countries completely unrelated to the interests of the PRC.

So the sight of Xiang's sudden arrival did nothing to bolster Cai's mood, not to mention the assassin had a good half dozen men with him, which meant he'd come once more to relocate Cai and all of his equipment. Ah! And on the eve of getting everything completed so he could take some time off, as Yan Zhou had promised. Blast these bastards! Didn't they *care* that he'd given them his very best? Did his loyalty and diligence count for nothing? Cai bristled a moment upon seeing Xiang but he didn't react in any other fashion.

"Good evening, *Dr.* Cai," Xiang said with a cool smile that implied Cai would find it anything but that.

"Mr. Xiang," Cai replied.

"I have unfortunate news from Air Vice-Marshal Zhou."

"Is news from Yan Zhou ever *fortunate?*"

"Take caution in your tone, Cai," Xiang said, purposefully dropping the young prodigy's formal title.

While he'd attempted to be cordial, Wen Xiang had never made it a secret he disliked Cai as much as the scientist disliked him. However, for their purposes here Cai had been instructed to cooperate fully with Xiang and if there were any disputes he was to raise them with Zhou and never, under any circumstances, directly confront the assassin. Zhou knew, just as Cai did, that to show disrespect to Xiang would likely result in an end to Xiang's services.

"Wen Xiang is loyal, but it is only to the purse strings," Zhou had once told Cai after a particularly nasty discord between Cai and Xiang. "And as he is more of a freelancer than an actual employee of the government, it would not be wise to discredit him in any way."

Cai had never understood why Zhou tolerated Xiang's indiscretions, or further allowed Xiang to abuse his somewhat limited influence and authority, but he did understand the unique relationship Xiang had with the government and his affiliations with the GSF. If Cai understood this relationship correctly, Xiang could terminate his contract with Zhou at any time and disavow his allegiances to members within the Ministry of State Security. In that instance, Xiang could then go as far as to take a contract to eliminate Cai—or anyone else with whom he disagreed—which would have disastrous consequences for the PRC and GSF, as well as Zhou personally.

"I did not mean any disrespect," Cai said. "I'm frustrated because I'm close to completing my work and I assume you're here because we must transfer to yet another location. This could put me hours behind— perhaps *days!*"

Xiang made a show of inspecting his fingernails. "I attempted to talk the vice-marshal out of doing this but he wouldn't hear of it. There is a security consideration that I'm very much afraid outweighs any frustrations you might harbor. You are to be transferred to the alternate location. Immediately."

Cai nodded with a deep sigh. "Very well, Mr. Xiang. You will permit me to call Zhou and verify this?"

Xiang shook his head. "He is out of communication at this point. He advised he will meet you there. Let's go."

Cai shook his head and began to fire a disagreeable retort but then thought better of it and bit back any argument. He would follow the program to the letter, so Zhou would have nothing to use against him. Zhou had demonstrated his willingness on more than one occasion to withdraw Cai's requests for time to rest or spend with his mother, and he wouldn't risk that now—not when he was so close to completing what would be his greatest achievement. In fact, he hoped this accomplishment would secure the trust of other Party members, those higher ranking and significantly more influential than Zhou, and win him his independence. He desired nothing more than to get out from under Zhou's thumb and thereby command his own destiny.

Cai shut down all of the instrumentation at the table and began to pack up his equipment.

Xiang folded his arms. "We would be happy to pack that equipment for you."

Cai shook his head. "This device cannot leave my side under any circumstances. *That* would be a breach of security for which I will not take responsibility. It will only take a few minutes. Meanwhile, I have two bags packed in my quarters that your men could transfer to whatever vehicle you may have waiting."

Xiang appeared momentarily irritated but then turned and nodded to one of the men, who grabbed a second, and the two disappeared to retrieve the luggage. The remaining men lingered nearby, none coming too close to the highly sensitive electronics. It was on this point Cai had insisted from the beginning. He was the scientist and expert, and neither Xiang's hired guns nor any other unauthorized person was to put his dirty paws on Teng Cai's work if the teenage scientist didn't want them to. Xiang might have been in charge of security, but such sensitive lab equipment or materials were under Cai's purview and violators would pay a heavy penalty for attempting to subvert those measures.

It was the one thing over which Teng Cai could have dominion and he had no intention of letting that go.

Within ten minutes he had the equipment packed, and they were headed outside to the waiting SUV. Dark clouds, their edges trimmed by a sliver of a moon, stretched low across the otherwise dark sky. A damp chill cut through Cai's overcoat to his bones and he bit back the involuntary chatter of teeth. He preferred warmer weather. He'd even asked Zhou to provide him with an alternate location in the South Pacific where he could work during the winter months but, of course, the vice-marshal had refused for security concerns.

No matter—Cai wouldn't be in this environment long enough for it to concern him. In fact, he couldn't understand why he'd let it bother him. Obviously, he'd been letting the stress of the work get to him. He needed to rest, to enjoy the company of his mother without the concerns of the day or the next breakthrough to pull his mind away. At the same time, he knew his mind didn't work well when he didn't have a problem to solve or some hurdle to overcome. This was the nature of the work.

As Cai climbed into the backseat of the SUV, Xiang took up position in the front and another pair of his hired team took the seats on either side of Cai, sandwiching him between their beefy frames. He began to object but again thought better of it and remained silent. He would bide his time.

Soon, he thought. Soon I will be free of all of this.

DAVID MCCARTER SAT at the long table of polished mahogany and stared at Meifeng Cai, but the woman had adamantly refused to meet his gaze. It made no difference to the Briton since they couldn't communicate with her anyway—they'd ultimately decided to relegate Hark Kwan to that task. He was her own kind, as Manning had pointed out during a private postmission debrief among Phoenix Force, so it would be better to let Kwan take point anyway. McCarter hadn't been able to argue with that logic. He'd instructed his teammates to find other things to occupy their time with while they interrogated the woman. Two men alone with Meifeng, one who didn't even speak her language, would be much less intimidating than seven or more hanging around staring holes into her.

Kwan had originally suggested talking to her alone and then relaying it all after the fact, but McCarter disagreed with that tactic. He needed to hear it as they talked in case something came up and McCarter wanted to have Kwan translate a specific question for him. Most of the time, however, McCarter had resigned himself to just keeping his mouth shut and listening carefully to everything that Kwan interpreted. It wasn't until they were about five minutes into the interrogation that McCarter got a big surprise when Kwan looked at him and revealed Meifeng Cai spoke English.

"Good English?" McCarter inquired, looking expectantly at the woman.

"As good as yours, American," Meifeng replied.

McCarter leaned back in his chair and folded his arms. "Well, you speak English just fine if you ain't a bit bloody snarky about it. Good, then I can just cut to the chase. Your friend Zhou is a real piece of work. Not only is he responsible for suckering a number of foreign intelligence agents into believing that your son wanted to defect from China, we also believe he arranged the murder of your husband."

"And if you're not careful he'll eventually arrange to have you eliminated, too," Kwan interjected. At a sharp look from her, he added, "Once he realizes you are no longer of any use to him in manipulating your son."

"Yan Zhou has treated Teng quite well," Meifeng said. She looked at McCarter. "And *me,* personally."

"How long do you think that's going to last when your son decides to stop producing newer technologies for him?" Kwan asked.

McCarter said, "Once your son gets tired of being a puppet for the military and decides he no longer wants to contribute, you'll either become a pawn to keep Teng in check or they'll just simply turn both of you into fish bait."

"I will never betray my country, American," Meifeng said. "And neither will Teng."

McCarter produced a deep sigh before he sat back and folded his arms. "We understand that you haven't seen your son in over three months. Is that true?"

"I don't have to tell you anything, American."

"No, you don't. So maybe you should just listen for now. Did you know the reason you haven't seen Teng in all this time is that he's working on a *new* project for your country's air force? And did you further know that whenever anyone's gotten close to helping reunite him with you, Yan Zhou has arranged to have him moved to another location so nobody, including you, can find him?"

"Yes, Yan Zhou has purposefully been keeping your son from you," Kwan added. "You might also not be aware that he's enlisted the help of a rogue assassin from the ministry to do the moving."

A visible intake of breath seemed to catch in Meifeng's throat. Her eyes narrowed. "You lie!"

Kwan shook his head. "No lie. I have no *reason* to lie to you, unlike the man in whom you hold such high esteem."

"Madam Cai," McCarter said, "Vice Air-Marshal Zhou is only interested in one thing—furthering his own station among the political powers of government. The same political powers that call themselves the Gold Star Faction. Ever heard of them?"

When Meifeng shook her head, Kwan said, "Oh, they are a great bunch. The current higher echelons of our government are infested with these terrorist vermin. They aren't concerned with the spread of democracy in this country. All that concerns them is keeping the population under control, subservient to their aims. If you think for a moment that they or Zhou care about you and your son, you're sadly mistaken!"

Kwan thumped his fist on the table and the reverberation echoed through the room. The sudden outbreak even caused McCarter to stir in spite of himself. Kwan continued. "These men have come here from the United States at some personal risk to themselves and their own people to uncover Vice Air-Marshal Zhou's plans."

"They took me from my home!" Meifeng protested, although the tone in her voice betrayed the fact she was less convinced of Zhou's motives than a minute ago.

"That prison you call a home was guarded by an enforcement arm of the GSF," McCarter pointed out.

"How do you know this? Why should I believe you?"

"Because I've encountered them before," Kwan told her. "Who do you think it was that gave this man his information? I once served proudly with the ministry myself. I was willing to believe any lies they told me until I opened my eyes and realized it was *they* who were the true enemies of our nation. I know this from personal experience because these men killed my wife and my children when I discovered their plots and refused to continue service."

"Then you are a traitor, Mr. Kwan."

The exchange surprised McCarter—how had Meifeng even known who Kwan was? To his understanding, Kwan had never met the woman before today. Was there a past relationship Kwan hadn't chosen to disclose to Phoenix Force? Was there more going on here than McCarter realized? Whatever was going on, McCarter needed to find out and he needed to do it quickly. They couldn't afford to get snow-balled on this one.

"No, madam," Kwan replied in a tight whisper. "It is Yan Zhou who is the traitor. And if you continue to turn a blind eye to what's happening, the GSF will destroy your family just as they did mine. They started with killing your husband, whether you choose to believe it or not. They certainly care *nothing* for you. Our only chance is to find Teng before it's too late."

For a long time the only sound in the room was a ticking clock on the wall—the silence weighed on McCarter's shoulders as he was certain it did Meifeng Cai.

Finally, he looked her in the eyes and in a quiet, even cadence asked, "Will you help us?"

CHAPTER THIRTEEN

Once they got their answer, McCarter convened a meeting with Kwan out of earshot from anyone. "All right, Kwan, you want to explain what just happened in there?"

Kwan feigned ignorance. "What are you talking about?"

"Don't bugger up on me. You know damned well what I'm talking about. That woman knows you personally, and I want to know *how* she knows you."

"Oh, that."

"Yeah, that!"

"Don't get yourself worked up, friend. I'm not playing at two games here if that's what you think."

"In fact, it is," McCarter said.

Kwan didn't miss a beat as he noted, "Although I have to admit I'm impressed you caught on to it."

"I didn't just fall off the rice truck."

"Bad pun."

"Kill the banter and talk to me, or I swear on Her Majesty's eyes I'll cut you out of this thing right here and now."

Kwan took a deep breath, looked at the floor and then shook his head. He waved McCarter to one of the plush seats in the sitting room of their hotel suite and then took a seat opposite and propped his feet on the coffee table between them. "Meifeng's husband, Chung Cai...I knew him when I was a first assigned as a junior officer in the ministry. He worked for the government same as me, although he was a low-level political analyst for a lesser house. Yes, believe it or not, they still operate on the idea of dynastic rule within some parts of government. It's an arcane tradition, to be sure, but a reality even in our modern era."

"So you probably have firsthand knowledge of his death?"

Kwan shrugged and splayed his hands. "I can't be sure of anything anymore. I've been out of the circle for too long to understand. There's been a lot of political shifting in the past ten years, so most of what I get now is secondhand. And even that could hardly be deemed reliable these days, what with the GSF. However, there's one thing of which I'm certain and that is Zhou murdered Chung Cai."

McCarter nodded and replied, "And he'll do the same bloody thing to young Teng if we don't find the kid soon. What about Meifeng? Do you believe she'll help us?"

"Madam Cai's a lot of things but a liar isn't one of them. If she says she'll tell us where he is *and* assuming she knows his location, she'll keep her end of the bargain."

"Fine. That only leaves us with how to get both of them out of here without bringing down half the Chinese military on our arse. Or at least Zhou's personal enforcers. Just how competent is this Wen Xiang?"

"He's one of the best my country's ever produced. I wouldn't underestimate him. If we manage to locate Teng and he's willing to come along without ratting us out to Zhou, Xiang will do anything he can to stop us. He doesn't play by any rules. With backing from the Gold Star Faction he will have considerable resources at his disposal. Our best bet will be once we've reunited Teng with his mother, you get both of them out of the country as fast as possible."

McCarter lent his ally a knowing smile. "I take it you have a plan?"

"I do."

BY THE TIME Kwan finished laying it out to McCarter, who in turn relayed his idea to the rest of Phoenix Force, Mei-feng had disclosed her son's location. When she pointed it out to them on a map of the city, Kwan stood for a time in contemplation and scratched his chin.

The men of Phoenix Force were ranged around the table and looking somewhat dismayed at Kwan's obvious show of doubt. They were in uncharted territory here, and forced to rely almost solely on Kwan's expertise. Not that they worried the guy didn't know his stuff. Kwan had operated secretly out of Tianjin for the past decade and somehow managed to evade capture by both legitimate government officials and cronies of the GSF. He'd long been at odds with Xiang personally, as well, but assured McCarter he wouldn't let his personal vendetta with the assassin get in the way of this mission.

"This isn't going to be easy," Kwan finally remarked.

"We're used to hard," Hawkins drawled.

"What are your main concerns?" Manning asked.

Kwan looked at the floor as if perhaps the answer could be there—or maybe he was simply praying to whatever gods he thought might be listening. "This particular area is the factory district of the city. Notice how it runs right here along the Hai River?"

"You're worried about the confined paths of ingress?" Encizo ventured.

"Not our inward path so much, Mr. Rodriguez. I'm more concerned about getting *out*."

"A suggestion?" James said, raising his hand like a hesitant schoolboy.

McCarter acknowledged him with a nod. "Shoot."

"Well, we can suppose security would be expecting most anybody to come in by the road," James said. "I highly doubt they'd even consider someone might try a riverfront access."

"Don't be so sure," Kwan said.

McCarter added, "You're right—we can't make any assumptions. But what my teammate is saying makes sense if you look at it from another point of view."

"Go on," Kwan said.

"Well, it's a foregone conclusion the enemy doesn't know anything about that gadget Madam Cai uses to keep track of her son's whereabouts. And being Teng designed the bloody thing, I think we can be confident it's reliable and accurate. That said, our people have the resources to tack onto that signal and give us real-time updates on his location to within a meter. If we put together an amphibious assault, and assuming you can get us the right equipment, a couple of our people could keep the guards busy while the rest of us locate Teng and extract him from right under their noses."

"And pull him out the same way we come in," Kwan concluded. "Via the river."

James nodded. "That's pretty much what I was thinking."

Kwan seemed to consider this for a time. "Okay, suppose you can make it happen. What do you plan to do with him once you have him?"

"Once we get him downriver, you guys could have a

vehicle waiting for us," Encizo suggested. "We can double back to the airport and be airborne before anybody knows we've gone."

"What about Meifeng?" Kwan asked.

"We have our pilot waiting there," Hawkins said with a shrug. "I don't see any reason why he can't sit on her while we commit this operation."

"Hmm…it sounds as if this might work," Kwan said. "And there's a chance we could provide support again from the air, as we did before. It's not foolproof but it just might work."

"What sort of response can we expect from local authorities once the fireworks start?" Encizo asked.

"Good question to ask, mate," McCarter said.

Kwan sighed. "Sometimes there are unintended casualties. I would assume if Zhou tries to involve police that you will do what you must to accomplish your objectives."

McCarter fired a harsh look at the Chinese agent. "We have an SOP, Hark. We don't kill cops."

"And that's nonnegotiable," Hawkins added.

"I understand," Kwan replied with a nod. "And I can respect that, believe me. But what you may not understand is that I have no such luxuries, especially given the fact I will have to cover your escape. If the GSF suspects that you're fleeing the country with Teng and Meifeng, they won't hesitate to employ military means to shoot down your aircraft. And given what I know of your people, they will utterly disavow any knowledge of your operations here or even that you existed."

"What does that have to do with not killing cops?" James asked.

Kwan seemed at first to almost glare at him but then something in his expression resumed its usual inscrutability. "I'm merely suggesting that in order to pull this off, we'll have to find a way to make Zhou and Xiang's men think you're still in the country even though you've already left. By the time they figure it out, you should be safely in international airspace. They would not dare attempt to destroy you once you've made it out of their territorial jurisdictions."

Hawkins snorted. "Don't bet on it, partner. As you just pointed out, they wouldn't even claim to know us— anything that happens to us outside American airspace would be written off as some sort of accident, if it ever got out at all."

"He's right," McCarter said. "At this point, we don't even exist and if we get taken out we won't have *ever* existed where our government's concerned."

"This is sad but true," Kwan admitted.

"Welcome to Special Operations," Manning muttered.

"Hey now," McCarter interjected to break the taut silence that followed for a minute. "Let's not stack our boots in a shallow grave yet, mates! We need to hammer out the details of this plan and put all the contingencies into place. We'll get only one shot at this and we need to make it good."

The men all nodded their heads in assent and then began to plan the assault to rescue Teng Cai.

Joint Base Elmendorf-Richardson, Alaska

DR. PRISCILLA STAVROS hunched over the tall lab table adjoining the inspection hangar and peered into the electronic microscope. Without taking her eyes from the lenses, she said, "The communication patterns superimposed on the substrate layer of this chip are unlike any I've ever seen before in my entire career."

Hermann Schwarz looked up, his attention to that point riveted on a technical manual, and peered at the beautiful scientist. He felt a stirring in his groin but forced himself to keep his mind on the task at hand. His job was to protect this woman, not lust after her, and he wouldn't betray the mission entrusted to him by his friends and Stony Man for adolescent kicks. Maybe after it was over he would consider pursuing a different kind of relationship with her, but for the time being he'd keep his mind off Dr. Stavros's many delectable qualities.

"That unique, huh?"

Stavros looked up from the microscope to peer absently at Schwarz a moment, and he realized she'd probably been talking more to herself than to him. Of course, being he was the only one in the lab the past hour or so—Blancanales had left them alone to go perform another sweep with the security team and to place a call to Lyons to see how things were going in the city—Schwarz assumed Stavros had been talking to him. He realized from the look on her face, however, she hadn't really been engaging him in conversation as much as verbalizing her findings to her consciousness, as well as the voice-activated digital recorder near her workstation.

Stavros blinked and then shut off the recorder. "I beg your pardon?"

Schwarz smiled. "No, I beg *your* pardon. I thought maybe you were talking to me."

"I'm sorry," Stavros replied with a smile that would've made him forgive her had she been apologizing for jamming a pitchfork into his chest. "I often talk to myself. Old habit."

"No worries. I do it myself. So, out of curiosity, what did you find?"

Stavros shook her head. "To tell the truth, I've not quite seen anything like it. The gateway paths of the EPROM on this chip are nothing short of brilliant."

"Yes, but do they tell you anything we can potentially use to determine their origin?"

"It will take me considerable time to generate anything definite—at least from the aspect of formulating an opinion I can back up with facts. However, there's one thing I can tell you for sure and that is this missile was *not* manufactured in North Korea."

"How can you be so sure?"

Stavros frowned. "Really, Agent Black... Do you remember when the North Koreans attempted to launch their first missile?"

"Yeah, and it ended up in the drink."

"Precisely. Now we *could* argue logically that they've probably made advancements since that time. But despite that I could never believe they would have the ability to pull off something like this. This kind of programming and large-architecture complexity could only have come from a nation with the means and resources to employ the very best and the brightest."

"And maybe a half dozen nations in today's world economy would have those kinds of resources," Schwarz concluded.

"Exactly," Stavros said. "I cannot yet say with any certainty the origin of manufacture of either the missile or this chip, in particular. But what I *can* tell you without any reservation is that this chip, which I believe contains the entirety of a guidance and weapons configuration embedded upon it, was not manufactured by the North Koreans. No way in a thousand years would they have the resources to pull off something this complex."

Schwarz folded his arms and considered her report. "Okay, so that leaves us with only a few other likely candidates. Could be the Chinese, the Russians or the Japanese."

Stavros started at that last suggestion. "You think the Japanese would dare try something like this?"

"If they were trying to discredit the North Koreans."

"That doesn't make any sense," Stavros said. "As long as we're friendly with the Chinese government, the Japanese would consider that a means of stabilizing the power in all of the Pacific-Asiatic regions."

"It does, but we have to consider rising tensions between China and Japan over the East China Sea and rich oil deposits there."

"The oil deposits *rumored* to be there," she reminded the Able Team warrior. "And let's not forget that for either country to alienate the other would cause potential repercussions from America. There are still certain lines the Chinese and Japanese won't cross with America, even despite the fact they have their financial hooks into the meatiest parts of our collective ass."

Schwarz inclined his head. "Very eloquent, Priscilla— you are indeed succinct."

"Oh, go on!" she said with the smoothness of a dove's coo and a mock wave of humility. She became serious, though, just as quickly and added, "I think the most likely suspects are the Chinese. They could definitely pull off something like this. In fact, I've been hearing certain rumors within defense contractor circles that there may be a new rise of Communist solidarity in China. One that hasn't been seen since the start of World War II, quite possibly."

Schwarz scratched his chin and mumbled to himself, "Sounds like maybe Carl was right."

"Excuse me?"

"Oh, just thinking about something Norris pointed out the other day not long after we first got aboard the *Glacier.* You know…you could be onto something after all. But before you take your theory to the Pentagon, they'll want proof positive."

The phone buzzing for attention at Schwarz's belt interrupted their conversation. He checked the ID, saw the encrypted code signaling it was Blancanales, and excused himself from the room to take the call in the adjoining hallway. It wasn't so much a problem discussing business in front of Stavros but she had more important things to occupy her time—Schwarz didn't want to distract her.

Professional courtesy, he told himself. "Yes, Pol."

"I just got off the horn with Ironman," Blancanales said. "You're not going to believe what sort of trouble he's gotten himself into the past four hours."

"Why am I not surprised?" Schwarz muttered. "I told you it was a big mistake letting him stay out past curfew, dear."

"Noted," Blancanales said in his typically good-natured way. Banter between the men was a mainstay of their relationship, and only on rare occasions would one or the other refuse to play along.

"So what ant's nest did he kick over this time?" Schwarz inquired.

"Well, you already know that he found Se-Hong Yu," Blancanales said. "The guy finally copped to supplying weapons off the black market to the North Koreans. The same weapons they used to attempt that hit when we rolled into the docks."

"Gee, wish you could see my shocked face."

"Well, someone tried to punch Yu's ticket and Ironman happened to be in his room when it all went down. Two cops are dead, sadly, but Ironman managed to take her alive."

"Her? The assassin was female?"

"Roger that."

"Ironman swore that one of the two that fled the scene that day was a woman. Looks as if he was right."

"Yeah, except that's not the strangest part."

"Well, quit your dawdling and get to the point," Schwarz said. "I'm a very busy man, you know."

"The woman is a North Korean agent," Blancanales replied. "Apparently, the government sent her our way to kill Stavros and destroy the missile. But the really strange part is she didn't hesitate to explain any of it, or to identify who she was when Ironman questioned her."

"He ought to be careful," Schwarz interjected. "She's up to no good—that much is for sure."

"I couldn't agree more. As I pointed out to him and the Farm, this one we should most definitely watch, and be wary of any information she divulges. Since we have no way to verify it."

"That's just what I was thinking," Schwarz confirmed.

"Well, whatever happens next will probably be decided once he gets back here with her and we have a chance to delve deeper into her story."

"What? He's bringing her *here?* That's crazy!"

"Apparently, she has information that can positively disprove North Korea's culpability in this plot."

"That'd be a neat trick."

"Agreed."

"That still doesn't explain why he's bringing her here."

Blancanales sighed. "She says she'll only show it to the lead scientist on the project because apparently nobody else but someone with firsthand knowledge of such technologies would be able to positively authenticate her proof."

"I don't like this," Schwarz said. "Feels like we're just bringing the wolf right into the sheep's pen."

"I've been through all that with him," Blancanales replied. "And I even made my feelings known to Hal and Barb. They still insist on letting Ironman proceed with this whole crazy idea."

"So when are they scheduled to arrive here?"

"Within a half hour."

"Cripes," Schwarz muttered. "That doesn't give us much time to get a security SOP together."

"Well, we've already been promised a heavy detail from the provost marshal's office, not to mention an executive waiver of liability directly from the Oval Office if it goes sideways for any reason. Hal wanted to make sure the Farm wasn't held responsible since we were actually recommending they *not* do this."

Schwarz let out a snort. "Lot of good that'll do us if she comes in here with some sort of microscopic tracking beacon and a stealth drone blows all of us up on spec."

"Aw, now you're just making things up."

"I hope so," Hermann Schwarz replied.

CHAPTER FOURTEEN

Ju Young-Soon, wedged between two agents from the FBI in the back of an unmarked government sedan, stared ahead and said nothing for the entire trip from Anchorage to the U.S. military installation. She had to admit to herself that this was certainly one of the most desperate ploys she'd ever attempted. Nothing in her experiences had prepared her for this. She'd been trained to evade capture at all costs and, if captured, to resist interrogation and most forms of torture their enemies were known to employ. She'd never thought she'd be taken alive in her attempts to eliminate their coconspirator, Se-Hong Yu, to prevent him from revealing their plans.

Young-Soon knew her days were now numbered. She no longer cared for her own life but she didn't wish to see the destruction of her country or an increase in tensions between her people and the Americans. She didn't hate the United States. In fact, she had no real feelings toward the U.S. one way or the other—she'd learned to be dispassionate in her role as a spy. Young-Soon acted out of duty and nothing more. To introduce feelings into her job could only lead to disaster, quite possibly even her death, at which point she wouldn't be of much good to anyone—especially her own people.

Young-Soon stared at the back of the blond American's head. For this man she had some dislike, but she had to admit this was more from her own embarrassment at having let him best her in a physical contest than at the fact he was an American. Her reasons for deciding to disclose what they knew about the Red Chinese and their attempts to deceive the United States into thinking it was North Korea testing their nuclear strike capabilities against American shores had only occurred to her at the last minute.

Chances were they thought she was merely stalling the inevitable, although she admitted to herself not knowing exactly *what* that was. With one of her men dead and the other currently in no condition to help her, this was her last resort. She didn't intend to let the opportunity slip through her hands if she could bring a peaceful resolution to the conflict. Of course, her decision to do this—while it might save her life or grant her immunity from prosecution notwithstanding—would put her at odds forever with her own country. They would view suicide as having been the more honorable thing to do. Yet, when had she been afforded such an opportunity? No, there had to be a way to work this out, if not for the sake of peace then at least for the betterment of a country that would now, in all likelihood, reject her forever.

The ride from the Anchorage police headquarters to Joint Base Elmendorf-Richardson took about twenty minutes. As they passed through the security checkpoints, the statistics ran through her mind. Units included a number of air groups and fighter squadrons including the 11th Air Force, 673rd Air Base Wing and 477th Fighter Group. The base also served as headquarters to the Alaskan NORAD Region and included a number of supporting units from both the American Air Force and Army.

Young-Soon's handlers had also briefed her on the fact that the American recovery team would most likely take their prize to the excellent R & D facilities secreted at the base. While they didn't have much in the way of specifics, Young-Soon had been at this game long enough to know the base would contain such facilities. They would send their very best scientists to study the missile, among them one Dr. Priscilla Stavros, aged thirty-eight, who was well ahead of most other of her peers in the area of air-combat systems research. If anyone could crack the mystery, it would be this Stavros woman, and Young-Soon had opted to play her cards in the hope of making direct contact with her.

It took them almost another forty-five minutes to get all of the proper clearances necessary for bringing a political prisoner and foreign agent onto the base, during which time she had to agree to be photographed, fingerprinted and have her vital information cataloged into their systems. Young-Soon had not, of course, been carrying anything but her forged passport and other credentials on her person but she knew they wouldn't believe any of the information there. Since she had decided on this course of action, Young-Soon opted to tell the truth about her real identity. What the hell did it matter now? She wouldn't be going back to North Korea; that much was certain.

Once the processing had been completed, the agents and blond American—a squad of MPs accompanying their sedan both front and rear—transported her to a nondescript hangar deep within the base. It stood nestled among mountainous foothills on all sides. The blue-white outline of recent snow stretched down the hills like icy fingers, gleaming starkly in the long Alaskan sunlight filtered by a hazy gray mist. The chill of the air bit at her exposed skin as they escorted her from the car to a steel access door at the side of the building. Two MPs then briskly ushered the four into a small room with a table and chairs at the center and a whiteboard at one end. A projector hung from the ceiling.

Even within the room the cold nipped at her nose, but Young-Soon held her silence. She refused to move, to fidget or to shiver—she wouldn't give the grim-faced federal agents or stoic MPs standing guard at the door the satisfaction of knowing she was the least bit uncomfortable. Let these arrogant men chew on that fact for a while. At a nod from Norris, the two agents followed him outside along with one of the MPs. The second was directed to stay inside the room, taking station at the door, with his hands in easy reach of his sidearm. Young-Soon had done her best not to let her eyes come to rest on the weapon at any time. The MP knew it was there and so did she, and that was about all the attention she gave it. To show any interest would have put them more ill-at-ease, and untrained men with firearms tended to have itchy trigger fingers when they felt uneasy.

No, she wouldn't do anything so stupid—it would've been utterly pointless anyway. She was committed and there was no escape. She would remain strong and resolute.

CARL LYONS RETURNED to the interrogation room with a cup of coffee for the North Korean agent. Blancanales and Schwarz followed him inside and took seats at the table. The trio had already agreed Blancanales would take point on the interview.

"Ju Young-Soon, my name is Special Agent Rosarez. I'm with the Office of Naval Intelligence." Blancanales waved at his two companions. "These are agents Norris and Black. We've brought you something to drink."

Young-Soon shook her head, but Lyons set the coffee cup on the table near her arm anyway. He then stepped back and leaned against the wall, his arms folded and one foot propped flat against it.

"What about something to eat? Are you hungry?" Blancanales asked.

She shook her head again but Blancanales glossed over that. He nodded at Schwarz, who rose, opened the door and muttered something to one of the MPs just outside the door.

"First, you must understand that neither I nor my associates here intend to do you any harm," Blancanales continued. "If you wish to talk to us, it has to be completely voluntary since we have neither the time nor the inclination to employ harsher means of questioning you. However, you must also understand that if you choose *not* to talk to us voluntarily and share whatever information you might have, you forfeit any protections or deals we might be able to arrange with our government. In that case, your actions will be deemed acts of terrorism and you'll be turned over immediately to agents with the Department of Homeland Security. They will, in all probability, transfer you to the prison at Guantanamo Bay. Do you understand?"

"I understand," Young-Soon replied. "But I will only speak to your lead scientist, Dr. Stavros, regarding what I know about the prototype missile you recovered."

"What makes you think we've recovered anything?"

Young-Soon couldn't help but snort in derision. "And you warn me not to play the fool. Who do you think it was that attempted to destroy the missile? And we had an agreement, I and your Mr. Norris there, that I would only divulge the information to Dr. Stavros."

"You're not in a position to dictate terms," Lyons growled.

Young-Soon's smile was sweet—almost. "On the contrary. I think I'm in an *excellent* position to dictate terms. You may judge me an enemy of your country and a terrorist, but there is no threat you can employ that will cause me to waver. I have already gone beyond my original mission parameters and am likely no longer welcome to return to my own country."

She put her gaze back on Blancanales. "So you see, Agent Rosarez, I really have nothing left to lose at this point. I don't fear death and I don't fear you. Therefore, if you are unwilling to let me speak with your scientist, then I have nothing more to say."

"She's on her way," Schwarz noted. "Just hold on to your panties."

Blancanales gave his friend a sideways glance, sighed and then returned his attention to the Korean woman. "You'll have an opportunity to present your proof soon enough, ma'am. Right now, I'm more interested in what you have to say about the Chinese government and what they have to do with this. And why you honestly expect us to believe they would go to such extraordinary lengths to discredit your country."

"You have to admit that's a pretty fair question, lady," Lyons added. "A destabilization of relations between North Korea and the U.S. would only serve to make the region more dangerous to China. You're parked in their backyard, so how would it benefit them to increase tensions in the Asian-Pacific theater?"

"The People's Republic of China is hardly concerned by a small country like ours," Young-Soon replied. "Due to the unified goals of reinstituting Communism across all of Asia, an ideal supported both publicly and by private concerns, there have been certain benefits by my country to ally themselves with the Chinese. Unfortunately, they do not see what I've come to see."

"And that is?" Schwarz prompted.

Something haunting flashed across Young-Soon's expression as she replied, "That such alliances bear with them a heavy price. If Communism is to spread once more, it will be the Chinese government that wants to control it—just as they've attempted to subvert the economies of dozens of countries, yours included, to increase their holdings. I was sent here to stop them from doing this but I have failed."

She paused a moment to look directly at Lyons. "And since I was unable to silence our supplier before he could talk, these are the only means left to my disposal to bring a solution to our problem."

"So let me get this straight," Lyons said. "You try to assassinate one of our scientists and destroy a missile that has all the signature markings of North Korean manufacture, a missile we know to be capable of supporting a nuclear payload by the way, test-fired at American shores. Failing that, you tried to cover it up by killing a known North Korean dealer of black market arms. You also murdered two police officers, which isn't going to score any points in your favor."

"And now," Blancanales said, "if I'm understanding you correctly, you're proposing we work *with* you to uncover this alleged deception by Communist factions within the PRC government."

"That is exactly what I'm suggesting, yes," Young-Soon said quietly.

"In return for what?" Lyons asked.

"Amnesty."

"Ha! That ain't going to happen, lady, no matter what information you might have. All you've bought yourself here is a delay in the hanging."

A sharp rap at the door interrupted any further discussion, and a moment later the door swung inward to admit Priscilla Stavros. Lyons started to open his mouth to protest they weren't ready for her yet, but something in her eyes caused him to rethink it. Schwarz had already informed him of Stavros's discovery about the architecture of the guidance and navigation chip she'd examined, and her conclusions that the missile had definitely not been manufactured in North Korea.

It was Lyons who'd ordered everyone to keep quiet about that little point until they'd heard what Young-Soon had to say. Now that Stavros had confirmed it, and it seemed to fall in line with what Young-Soon had already disclosed, the Able Team warriors had found themselves caught between a rock and hard place. Lyons already pretty much knew what Brognola would say when they called to give their full report of what had transpired to this point. And given what he knew, Phoenix Force's current mission in China left little doubt there was a strong connection between their missions now.

When the door had closed, Stavros took a seat and pinned Young-Soon with a studious gaze. "I'm Dr. Stavros. I understand you wanted to speak with me regarding the missile we recovered from your country."

"My country did not build that missile," Young-Soon said with a frosty expression. "And we did not fire it at you."

"I know."

That seemed to bring Young-Soon up short—she obviously hadn't planned for Stavros to be so direct with her.

"Anything else you want to contribute that might be helpful to my investigation?" Stavros asked. "Such as who *might* be responsible for the manufacture of this weapon?"

Young-Soon was still hesitant but her mood quickly went haughty. "Only rumors but…yes, there is a possibility this weapon was developed by scientists within the People's Republic of China."

"Do tell," Stavros directed. "Go on."

"There have been intelligence briefs in certain political circles of my government that—" Young-Soon stopped suddenly, perhaps losing her nerve. Then she took a deep breath and plunged forward in a rush of words. "Well, my superiors are convinced the Chinese air force is building smart missiles with nuclear capabilities. Missiles with virtually undetectable profiles that can fly at incredible speeds and distances, and hit select sites with pinpoint accuracy."

"Drones, you mean," Schwarz said. He looked at Stavros and shook his head. "Surely there isn't anything new or surprising about stealth drones."

"These ballistic devices are said to be able to deliver more than just nuclear payloads and conventional ordnance," Young-Soon continued. "There is also the thought that because of these advanced guidance systems they could be utilized to deliver manpower and equipment to a specified target."

Stavros's eyes narrowed. "The missile we recovered is barely large enough to carry one man, let alone multiple persons."

"Come now, Dr. Stavros," Young-Soon replied with a wispy smile. "You must know that missile was a prototype. Even our engineers and analysts were able to determine that much from the shoddy intelligence we collected. The Chinese air force has the ability to build much larger structures capable of housing multiple soldiers. Imagine special operators that could be deployed to a precise LZ at the speed of sound with high accuracy. You have seen the guidance and navigation systems firsthand. You must know their capabilities from your examination. And it's no secret small special operations units of six to twelve men can create significant results if they are dedicated enough to their mission. We all know that the Chinese have the resources and military expertise to train such covert action teams."

Schwarz shook his head and let out a low whistle. "I have to admit the applications for this kind of technology are practically limitless. It's nothing short of nightmarish!"

"Agreed," Blancanales said, although he remained a bit less impassioned than his cohort. "Imagine being able to launch missiles carrying men and equipment that can penetrate our airspace undetected, reach operational LZs in no time and deposit covert operations teams within our own borders before we could respond. That would give the Chinese a significant military advantage over every other country in the world."

"We may have an even greater problem," Stavros said. "But this is best left for a separate discussion."

She stood and looked at Young-Soon, started to open her mouth, but then just settled for inclining her head in respectful acknowledgment before leaving the room. It was her cue she needed to talk to the rest of them in private, so Able Team filed out after her with instructions to the MPs to attend to Young-Soon's needs until they returned. The three men took to pursuing Stavros, the only clue to her departure the sharp reports from her heels as she headed down a parallel hall at a good clip. They found themselves having to rush their pace to catch up to her.

As they entered the laboratory, Schwarz said, "What was all that about?"

Stavros looked around to ensure they were alone and then turned on them. Something had paled her normally Grecian complexion. "Sorry I beat such a hasty exit, but after what we just heard in there I'm convinced things are more serious than even your new friend may be aware."

"How serious?" Lyons asked.

"I think this missile is a prototype, yes, but there's no question in my mind the chip is *not*."

"And exactly what does that mean?"

Stavros rendered a deep sigh. "The guidance and tracking architecture on that chip is too complex to have risked letting it fall into the wrong hands. I found it puzzling that some of the systems on the missile were still active even though it had been submerged. It was powered by special, high-capacity batteries. It took some doing to deactivate those before I felt we could safely remove the chip. I think, now, it was a mistake to bring it here."

"Uh-oh," Schwarz interjected. "I hope you're not going to say what I *think* you're going to say."

Stavros nodded. "The systems have homing beacon capabilities, as well. I suspect whoever designed and deployed it has been tracking our every movement. I also think they fed that information back to the hit team that tried to blow us all up at the docks."

Lyons had opted not to disclose Ju Young-Soon's exact identity to Stavros, or to reveal the role she played in the assassination attempt out of concern it might prejudice

Stavros's opinion of what Young-Soon had to tell them. He could now see that had been the right call.

"I don't know what their reasons would be for tracking it here," Stavros said. "But there's a good chance they know it's here and they would have very good reasons for taking this kind of risk. As far as I can tell, they might even have deployed fully capable versions of this prototype already, and our IBEWS might not ever pick them up."

That thought set their collective teeth on edge. If these new missiles really could spoof NORAD's Incoming Ballistic Early Warning Systems, it might pose a significant threat to American security by any measure.

In a quiet and worried tone, Lyons said, "We'd better call the boss."

CHAPTER FIFTEEN

When Chin Nam awoke for about the fifth time since losing consciousness, he was sure the fever had at last left him. Pain still coursed through parts of his body until it set some of his very nerve endings on fire. For a time he wished to return to his fever-induced delirium.

As the fog cleared from his consciousness and reality took hold, Nam considered his predicament. He turned his head slowly toward the windows and saw the brightness of midday bleed around the edges of the curtains drawn closed. This wasn't the place he last remembered being in. Yes, they had been at the bed-and-breakfast, and he did remember the bitter chill of an early morning ride in a vehicle. Where had they gotten the vehicle? He willed his mind to focus and then he remembered that it must've been rented by Ju Young-Soon. She had finally decided to move them, and probably not too soon. Then where had she gone? Nam vaguely recalled her mentioning something about taking care of the one loose end that could compromise them. That meant Se-Hong Yu—she should've returned hours ago from that.

How long have I actually been unconscious?

A steady thump at the door interrupted his train of thought and gave him pause. Nam stared long at the door, waiting through an unknown span of time. Another series of thumps told him the knocker was persistent, almost as if he knew the place was occupied beyond any doubt. Nam could feel the sudden hammer of his heart in his chest. He looked out on the window and felt his gut sink when he saw he was five stories up. Too far to jump—that much was certain now.

Nam remembered his pack and searched furiously, finding it by the time the third hammering series at the door resounded—this time with much more insistence behind it—so he could locate and pull his loaded pistol from the pack. Nam padded quietly to the door, his bare feet a whisper on the carpet, and softly replied, "Yes?"

"Open up," a heavily accented voice replied. "It's me."

"And who is 'me' supposed to be?"

"It's me, Wee Hum Han."

Nam's face twisted with an involuntary scowl. He knew why Han had arrived—the guy was a fixer. Their handlers would only send in somebody like Han if either the mission had gotten screwed up or… Nam felt a catch in his throat. Cleanup crews like this would only step in under two circumstances: original mission operatives were all dead or the mission leader was dead and time had run out or was in very short resource. So that's why Ju Young-Soon hadn't returned.

Nam tucked the pistol into the waistband of his pants at the small of his back and then unbolted and unchained the door to permit the entry of Wee Hum Han and two other men Nam didn't recognize. Once they were inside he resecured the door and then turned to face them. This team was known as a *dong maeng seung moo won,* or an alliance crew. Their job was to make sure that any mission that had been compromised either be completed or that all evidence of the mission be removed if the first task became impossible. Nam also knew on occasion that cleanup involved assassinating the original members of the team, but that was only if they had been captured or were incapacitated in some way, and that was very rare indeed. Training agents was very expensive, and the North Korean government didn't have unlimited resources. They would go to great lengths to protect and salvage any intelligence assets.

Han looked around the room and then smiled, although Nam didn't see anything ingratiating about it. He subconsciously put his hand in a position where he could pull the pistol much more quickly.

"Where's Ju Young-Soon?" Han asked.

Nam thought at first about saying he didn't know but then decided for a different ploy. He wouldn't give Han any reason to become concerned before absolutely necessary. He went casually to the bedside table and withdrew a pack of cigarettes. Something inward smiled as he thought of how Young-Soon had tried to remember to provide him with every amenity before leaving. He swore right then that if she were dead, he would use every resource at his disposal to find whoever killed her and finish them.

"She's gone to complete the mission," Nam said, keeping his tone as casual as possible.

Wee Hum Han didn't look convinced. "Alone? What did she think she could possibly hope to accomplish alone?"

Through a cloud of smoke, Nam replied, "Our other man is dead and I was wounded—on the verge of death myself had it not been for her quick thinking. With both of us out of commission she had no *choice* but to go alone."

"She had a choice. She could have called for our assistance."

"And give our superiors reason to believe she had failed?" Nam shook his head. "What kind of fool do you take her for? While there's still breath in her, you know as well as I that Ju Young-Soon would never give up quite so easily."

"It seems you may have allowed your overconfidence in her to cloud your own judgment." When Han said this, something hard was etched into his features.

"What are you talking about?"

"Why do you think I was called in? It seems that Young-Soon has not only failed to assassinate the American scientist and destroy the prototype, but she has failed to kill Se-Hong Yu and allowed herself to be captured. My team was put on full alert less than two hours ago. Strictly speaking, she has failed miserably in her mission and we must now clean up the mess."

The pistol in Han's grip seemed to appear out of nowhere. Nam tried to keep the newfound lump of fear bottled deep in his gut, to draw from it as a source of strength. Even as he stared at the barrel he'd been half expecting something like this.

"You don't seem surprised," Han finally said.

"Not getting the reaction you'd expected? Perhaps even...*hoped* for?"

"How did you know?"

Nam took a calm drag from his cigarette. "You were always a bit too vested in your work, Wee. I would have thought a man with your dedication to Korea would look more forward to killing our common enemies than your own people, but instead you've defied such wisdom for your own wicked purposes. You've always been devious—I'm not sure what turned you into such a coward. Perhaps it was a bad upbringing?"

An engorged vein made an appearance in Han's left temple, and Nam could see his grip tighten on the pistol.

Nam found himself half-surprised when Han didn't simply blow his head off right there and then. It was in that moment he realized that he'd probably been given orders to keep Chin Nam alive until he could get whatever information might be critical to completing the mission. After all, he might be the only survivor now that there was a chance Young-Soon was dead. Nam realized his only chance of perhaps finding her alive and still succeeding in the plan was to drag this out as long as possible. Yes, he had to make Han believe he still had something to barter with.

"If you want to kill me then just go ahead and get it over with," Chin Nam said in as cool a voice as possible. "After all, my other teammates are now dead and, as you say, you have orders to complete our mission. Surely you don't need me and I refuse to return to my country in shame. Killing me would be a great favor."

Something changed in Han's expression, something that told Nam his ruse had succeeded. Han lowered the pistol and squeezed his eyes shut as a smile played across his lips. Or was it a smile? Maybe it was merely an expression of mocking, a delighted sneer of sorts that made Han feel as if he now had the upper hand in this contest of wills.

"Why, no," he replied as he slid the pistol back into its place beneath his jacket. "I would not think of killing you, my friend. You are still alive and, while injured, you still have vital information. It is entirely possible you can still complete your mission. And because you are a fellow countryman, a patriot with honor, I am inclined to *help* you complete the mission rather than kill you. This way you will always remember who it was that came to your aid when you were defeated—you will *live* with that knowledge of who it was who saved you in your hour of need."

Excellent, Nam thought. His ego is even larger than I'd hoped.

"It appears that I have no choice, then," Nam said. "Since you will not kill me and I have no way to finish this mission on my own, I will have to accept your help."

"Yes, you will. And I'm confident that it shall be a most bitter pill for you to swallow."

"And this angers you?"

"On the contrary," Wee Hum Han replied. "I could not be more delighted."

Nor I, thought Chin Nam.

Stony Man Farm, Virginia

"SO YOU THINK there may be a North Korean paramilitary unit operating within Alaska?" Hal Brognola asked via the secure satellite connection.

"No, we think there's a Chinese paramilitary unit operating within Alaska," Carl Lyons replied, staring at the video monitor. "I mean, well, there *is* a spy network of North Koreans here but that party's pretty much been broken up."

"Okay, now I'm officially confused."

Barbara Price cleared her throat, shifting her eyes to Brognola as she said to Lyons, "Why don't you start over with this, Carl? We're sort of all operating here on very little sleep."

Lyons sighed, trying not to look annoyed as he gathered his thoughts. "Okay. You know that in the course of my locating Yu we triggered some unintended consequences, namely this Ju Young-Soon killing two Anchorage police officers and trying to assassinate Yu so he wouldn't talk. Not to mention she left some good bruises on me before I could bring her down. When she saw the cops were ready to hang her from the nearest tree, she struck a deal with us in trade for information."

"Right," Price said. "And you think she stipulated the conditions of only giving this intelligence to Dr. Stavros so she could get into federal custody and as far away from the Anchorage authorities as possible."

"She said as much," Lyons replied matter-of-factly. "I was skeptical at first, until she told us a story so far out we were forced to believe her. Matters were only complicated when Stavros actually *confirmed* Young-Soon's story about the Chinese attempting to deceive us."

"Okay, I'm up to speed on all that," Brognola said with some minor irritation in his voice. "What I *don't* understand is to what end? It doesn't benefit the Chinese government one lick to attempt to deceive the United States into something that could well destabilize the situation in Asia. There's already enough turmoil over there—why compound it?"

"Aha!" Schwarz blurted, his face unseen. "Scooch over, Ironman, and gimme some face time here."

Lyons did so reluctantly and Schwarz's sharp features now filled the video screen at the Farm.

"Hello, Gadgets," Price greeted him.

"Salutations, dear lady. We posed the exact same questions to Young-Soon and she didn't have many answers. That was until she mentioned the government's desire to spread Communism, to implement a neo-Red order, of sorts. That's when I remembered you telling us about Phoenix Force's mission to pull that Chinese whiz kid out of Tianjin. That can't be a coincidence."

"We absolutely concur with you on that point," Price said. "There's no doubt these two issues are related. But that still doesn't provide us proof of collusion by Chinese government officials to undertake covert operations within the United States."

The camera swiveled back to Lyons's face. "That's because it's not the Chinese government pulling the strings—it's officials within the government who work for the GSF."

"Oh, damn," Brognola muttered. "It never even occurred to me until just now. The GSF is backing Yan Zhou's projects so they can get terrorist resources inside America. The neo-Communist regime has gone completely high-tech on us!"

"Exactly," Lyons replied. "They don't have to do a thing to cover their trail because they think we're going to blame the North Koreans. And even if we discovered it was the Chinese, the parties in power would deny it because they really *don't* know anything like this is going on. Not everybody in power in China is sympathetic to the GSF. In fact, I'd bet most of the Chinese populace doesn't have a clue exactly who it is pulling the strings in their hierarchy."

"It's unfathomable!" Brognola said.

"Maybe not, Hal," Price countered. "If you think about it, we have a supposedly transparent government right here and we don't always know everything the people in power are doing. Look at how corruptible some are in certain circles. Stony Man can't be everywhere at once—no government agency can."

Brognola sighed. "I'll grant you that one. And when you're right, you're right. Okay, so what do you want to do, Ironman?"

Lyons clucked his tongue, his eyes glazing slightly in contemplation "Well, we're still processing all of this on our end but we've discussed it and…" He paused to look at his teammates for affirmation before pressing on. "We think if the Gold Star Faction's prodigy has already perfected this technology, they'll attempt to test it in a more practical sense. To that end, Stavros has started working on a way to detect the signals from this guidance system."

"So you think attempting to stop them at the source would be possible?" Price asked.

"Ah, probably not, Barb," Schwarz said. "This is going to take some time. Even with my help, which Dr. Stavros has agreed to accept, there're layers of ciphered encryption in these programs. We have to hack through that and I don't know how long that will take—if we can do it at all."

"So what's your other option?"

Blancanales chimed in at this point. "If Phoenix can find this boy wizard in the next twenty-four hours and get him back here, that would certainly solve our having to devise a decryption process."

"They're working on it," Brognola said, "but I don't know that we can guarantee anything yet. We finally managed to solicit the cooperation of the boy's mother, and we have a probable location."

Price said, "What they couldn't tell us is what it's going to take to get to Teng Cai, and then subsequently to extract him and his mother in one piece. And we know with certainty that they're a package deal. It sounded as if Zhou has considerable resources at his disposal, which is *not* going to make their job any easier."

"Understood," Blancanales replied.

"We'll keep working it hard at this end," Lyons said. "At least we know it won't be boring."

"Uh-oh," Price replied. "I'm not sure I like the sound of that."

Lyons shrugged and splayed his hands in a gesture of mock helplessness. "Not much we can do about it, ma'am. Young-Soon's pretty much informed us that her government will assume she's either dead or captured at this point, as her team's been incommunicado since their ambush at the docks failed. It was a three-man team and she claims to be the lone survivor. There's no doubt the North Koreans will send a cleanup crew to try finishing the job."

Price glanced at Brognola. "That would be standard operating procedure for Korean intelligence."

"It would be suicide for their people to attempt to destroy the missile or to make another assassination attempt against Dr. Stavros. The security there is just too tight."

"Nonetheless, she says they'll try," Lyons said. "And frankly, I don't think it's wise for us to just sit on our hands and wait for them to come to us. I believe it's time we leave protecting Stavros to MPs and take Young-Soon with us on a scouting trip."

"That's risky," Brognola said.

"To make no mention of the fact it's not very bright," Price said. "How do you know she won't try to escape?"

"Because we've already informed her that we'll shoot her dead if she does," Lyons said. "I was quite explicit on that point. And besides, she's already pointed out that she has nowhere to go. She decided to talk to us, and up to this point she's been pretty forthright."

"Nothing to lose," Price observed with a short nod.

"Right."

"I don't know, Lyons," Brognola said. "I don't like it one bit."

"We don't have many choices here, chief," Lyons replied. "And quite frankly I'm *not* going to just sit around here and wait for them to try again. It's time to take these bastards down and take them down hard. If we wait, we could wind up with more dead cops up here. Or dead soldiers. I don't want that blood on my hands, and I don't think you do, either."

"All right," Brognola finally agreed after a long minute of silent contemplation. "But you keep Young-Soon on a *very* short leash. And if she steps out of line even once, don't hesitate to do the needful."

"Oh, you can bet on that."

"In the meantime," Price said, "we'll do what we can to get an update on Phoenix Force's current status and transmit whatever information we glean via secure channels."

"Let's put an end to this as soon as we can," Brognola said. "It won't do us a lick of good getting Teng Cai out of China and to your location if the GSF manages to hatch their plans before then. Our understanding from the contact working with Phoenix Force is that the mercenary group currently operating under Zhou's oversight is comprised of some very nasty customers."

"Yeah, but it would seem they forgot one teensy-weensy detail," Schwarz said.

"What's that?" Price asked.

"Phoenix boasts a complement of its own nasty customers."

"Amen to that," Harold Brognola replied.

CHAPTER SIXTEEN

Tianjin, People's Republic of China

The gentle lapping of water against the assault rafts was the only sound in the eerie silence. Biting cold cut through the combat suits of the three men who'd blackened their faces with camo paint. A cloud bank stretched across the expanse overhead, obliterating any light from the moon or stars—David McCarter considered it a stroke of good fortune. Their mission would be difficult enough and he figured Phoenix Force could use every advantage at its disposal. They were headed into unfamiliar territory against a force of unknown size, with the location of their target the only constant.

So what else is new? McCarter thought.

Their plan was replete with unknowns, but Phoenix Force had done more with less and McCarter knew his teammates were equal to the task. His biggest concern still fell to potential contact with law enforcement, and that had him on edge. Despite Hark Kwan's position, McCarter would not engage brothers on the same side and for good reason—this wasn't their fight. Zhou and his masters in the GSF had done nothing to prevent this situation, and now Phoenix Force had been forced into a course of action McCarter had hoped to avoid. Then again, this is why they collected their pay. What was the

SEALs mantra—The Only Easy Day Was Yesterday? McCarter hoped they'd all be able to say that tomorrow.

The Briton keyed the transmitter on his throat mike. "Sierra One to Sierra Three, how do you read?"

A slight delay before Manning responded with, "Five-by-five, Sierra One."

"You in position? Over."

"Roger."

"Acknowledged. Hold there and wait for our signal. Out."

Even as he switched off, moving the transceiver switch to inactive and putting the team into temporary communications blackout, a predetermined course of SOP for assaults such as this, McCarter felt the assault raft bump against one of the pier supports. The landing stretched far above their heads, the outlines of the moorings barely visible in the encroaching darkness and cold mist that rolled suddenly into the area. The dock was designed for a much larger craft, but it would serve their purpose. They'd come with the right equipment for the job, having chosen this spot for the very reason they could conceal themselves in the blackness of the dock underside if an eagle-eyed sentry were to come upon them as they made their assault.

Without a word, McCarter pointed at Encizo and jerked his thumb in an upward motion. The Cuban replied with a nod before raising a short, squat device to his shoulder and aiming it over the top. The thing had the profile of a mini-shotgun but in fact the titanium alloy tines that protruded from its muzzle implied a much different purpose. There was an almost null report from the device when Encizo aimed at a point almost directly above his head and squeezed the trigger-style release. The grappler performed a graceful arc and the clawlike hook of the head landed on target. As it reached its zenith, Encizo grabbed a ratchet-style handle along the side and began to crank like a fisherman reeling in the big catch—the grappler made a crazy twist around one of the moorings and then the tines bit into the heavy wood.

Encizo pulled on the dense, fibrous cord of the ascension line with all his weight and nodded assuredly at his teammates it would hold. T. J. Hawkins went first, biceps visibly taut through the skintight material of his black-suit as he pulled his muscular form easily up the heavy-duty cord. He made the top of the pier, swung his legs over and landed catlike on the thick, wooden planks of the dock. McCarter followed in similar fashion at a signal from Hawkins, having a bit more trouble than his younger companion although no worse for the climb. Two hours minimum every day of physical training kept all of them in peak condition, so for the most part this was a stroll in the park, although Hawkins had some advantage given his experiences as a mountain climber.

Once Encizo had finished his ascent with Hawkins and McCarter on guard, the three moved in staggered formation along the dock. They kept a reasonable gap between them, Encizo on point, not so much they lost sight of one another but enough to prevent being taken down as a unit by any ambush the enemy might throw at them. The trio made it off the dock and had nearly covered the distance to the outcropping of wharflike buildings where Teng Cai was sequestered when they encountered their first bit of trouble.

It appeared in the form of two sentries who stood watch at a rear door. One of them smoked a cigarette, the odor reaching McCarter's nostrils even before Encizo spotted them. A nearby row of 55-gallon drums provided enough concealment for Phoenix Force and they assembled on that point, utterly obscured from their enemies' line of sight but still in such a position they could assess the situation.

None of the three men spoke, knowing that in the quiet, cold darkness a whisper could carry a surprising distance. McCarter made a quick assessment, then pointed to Encizo and pulled his hand back, palm down flat. Encizo nodded and passed his MP-5 to Hawkins before he reached for the rather wicked-looking shape slung across his broad shoulders. Weighing just less than 8.5 pounds with an overall length of about 3 feet, the Barnett Ghost 400 Crossbow could deliver a bolt at nearly 400 feet per second with more than 150 foot-pounds of energy. It also boasted a 3×32 power scope with IR enhancements straight from the workbench of John Kissinger, the Farm's weaponsmith, and antivibration insulators that reduced noise to the level of a toy dart gun.

Encizo expertly put the weapon into firing mode and then reached to a hip holster containing a half dozen of the 22-inch bolt arrows. He withdrew two, loaded the first and then duck-walked to a stable firing position alongside a nearby crate. He laid the second bolt in easy reach before engaging the IR switch on the scope. Encizo put his cheek to the stock. He took a deep breath as he sighted on the first target and after a small hesitation triggered the crossbow. The bolt crossed the expanse, the only sound carrying on the air the dull rasp of the cross-through firing mechanism following projectile deployment, and punched cleanly through the target's neck. Hot blood spurted as the broad-point tips of the arrowhead tore a gaping wound through the sentry's neck.

Encizo took only a heartbeat to confirm he'd hit the target before he redrew and loaded the second bolt. The survivor's movements betrayed his panic as the cigarette in his mouth dropped to the ground at his feet. At first he seemed hesitant as he stooped to determine what had happened to his partner. Encizo could make out the look of shock in the man's face even as he sighted on the target. In the terrifying moment that followed, the sentry looked around wildly as he scrambled to clear his pistol from beneath his jacket. He never cleared it. Encizo's second arrow went through the man's jacket and hand before continuing to penetrate his heart. He wobbled unsteadily before toppling onto his back, his legs flexing with convulsive movement.

McCarter and Hawkins immediately broke concealment and hot-footed the twenty-some yards to where the sentries lay. Quite a bit of blood still pumped from the neck wound of the first casualty, but the wide-open eyes peering sightlessly in shock confirmed he was dead. The other sentry's body still twitched but Hawkins didn't let it faze him, confident it was the result of misfiring neurons that prompted his movements and not any real point of suffering. Had he thought otherwise, the Phoenix Force warrior would've ended the movements with a silenced contact shot. They located a disposal point among some refuse and pallets nearby.

McCarter and Hawkins worked together to first remove one body and then the other, covering them with a tarp while Encizo masked their efforts. They had concealed the corpses in under two minutes and returned to the point near the door the sentries had been guarding. McCarter noted Encizo already studying the door. The Cuban turned and looked at him with some confusion and a bit of pleading apparent in his eyes as he jabbed a finger at the key lock, the only source of entry.

McCarter couldn't help but grin as he held up a key, the glimmer of a distant light catching it in just a momentary flash. Encizo smiled back and opened his palm to receive it. He shoved it into the lock and turned slowly but steadily—the key rotated freely and a moment later the latch gave with a barely audible click of the release. The door popped out abruptly, apparently on a spring-style hinge, but was stopped an inch or two by the toe of Encizo's combat boot. Encizo passed the key back to McCarter and then opened the door enough to poke his head through the opening.

Gloom and deep shadows greeted him as Encizo scanned the interior, the silence utterly eerie. They had considered the possibility given their recent extraction of Meifeng Cai that the GSF would be waiting for a similar operation here. It was quite possible they were walking into a trap, but Phoenix Force had agreed it was worth the risk. The prize was too high for them not to exploit any opportunity that came their way. The key objective in the mission would be to ensure in the course of retrieving the young prodigy they didn't get him killed in the process. A dead prize was no prize at all in this particular instance.

Encizo waited a full minute before deciding it was safe for them to proceed. He had an extra responsibility as designated point man for this mission and he took it seriously. If he got killed in the process of saving his teammates, that was the risk that came from being the guy out front, but he wouldn't roll the dice on the blood of his friends. Their deaths would haunt his conscience forever. Diligence with a dollop of caution would keep all of them alive and Rafael Encizo was an undisputed expert in such things.

The makeshift foyer beyond the door widened onto a corridor. They eased up the long, darkened hallway—keeping to the shadows of the walls in staggered formation—with a closed door visible at the far end. Shafts of light glowed from the frame, casting a blue-yellow sheen on the floor and walls. In the stillness of the corridor they heard the echoes from a steady drip of water. In a building of this dimension and age, old pipes had probably been run through the walls to insulate them from the chilling winter months.

Encizo stopped a few yards from the door and glanced over his shoulder at McCarter. The Phoenix Force leader checked the homing device Kurtzman had tapped into, and then looked at Encizo and held up five fingers. Okay, they were within forty yards of Cai's position. The teenage scientist was probably quartered in an office or lab not too far beyond this door. The trio hoped that Cai was the only one there and that Wen Xiang's people had minimal security on him. Encizo nodded, then sidled to the door and eased it open.

TENG CAI DRUMMED his fingers on the long, narrow tabletop in his lab with elation. Finished at last! The last of the programming had been burned into the substrate layers of the guidance system. Now they could deploy a missile of full size and the chip would take care of everything. Everything! From guidance and navigation to targeting, the EPROM and integrated circuits would communicate with each other at speeds formerly conceived as unachievable. Cai could hardly believe it. What most competing scientists had been unable to do over many years he had managed to bring to fruition in less than eighteen months.

Finally, he would get his deserved rest and be able to lift his country to a new height of success.

Cai sat upright, his lower back aching from being hunched over the microelectronic viewer, and stretched. He rubbed at the aches and wondered how he would ever function later in life. He needed to get more exercise. It was fine to work his brain with powerful exercises, things he believed would keep him from suffering mental ailments in his later years, but he knew taking care of his physical health was equally important. A strong body and strong mind fed one another—of this much Cai was certain.

Cai climbed off the chair and stooped to rub some of the circulation into his legs. His toes tingled, the result of too much pressure on the sciatic nerve. It was time to request some better furnishings. Of all the locations they'd furnished for his work, this was the one Cai despised most. It was dark and dank in most places, this building in particular, and nestled among the other wharf buildings that made up the factory district fed by the South Grand Canal. Although the Hai River and the others that made up its confluence was a mainstay of water power and commercialism in Tianjin, Cai still didn't like it. He preferred the quieter country, such as where his mother resided in the woods surrounding the home Yan Zhou had built for them in Hebei Province.

A sudden wispy sound greeted Cai's ears and he stopped massaging to straighten and peer to his left. His eyes strained through the thick lenses of his glasses in an attempt to breach the shadows beyond. He felt a stab of panic in his gut as the three men who entered the room appeared like black specters materializing into this plane of existence from another world, one filled with blackness. They wore skintight combat suits from which dangled the tools of destruction. They smelled of violence and death.

"Who are you?" Teng Cai challenged, fighting back the lump that formed in his throat and threatened to choke off his voice.

"Not important," said one of the men. He had brown hair and a British accent, and there was no mistaking the air of command. This was the team leader. "The important thing is we found *you*."

Cai shoved his hands into the pocket of his stylish, hand-tailored trousers. One of the men, Hispanic-looking with dark hair, seemed to tense for just a moment at the movement but he kept the SMG he toted pointed toward the floor. In fact, Cai noticed that none of them was pointing a weapon at him and so he relaxed.

"I would suppose, then, it's safe to assume you do not work for Mr. Xiang," Cai replied.

"That would be a pretty safe assumption," the Briton said as he walked purposefully toward Cai. "Now it's time for you to come with us."

This actually caused Cai to chuckle. "I don't think so. You see, gentlemen, it would be nothing less than suicide for me to accompany you voluntarily. You undoubtedly are under the impression that I'm a commodity, perhaps willing to sell my services to the highest bidder. Frankly, this is a very mistaken assumption that has been made by others of your cut and ultimately such machinations have come to naught."

"Jeebus, this kid sounds like an encyclopedia," the third man said.

American-born, this one, Cai thought. Probably from the Southwest region given his dialect.

Cai said, "It seems that while you have gone to great effort to get inside here, you've given really little thought to how you plan to get out. Even now, you've let me put my hands in my pockets. Foolish, really, since I have a personal alarm in my pocket and have already triggered it. Within thirty seconds there'll be less than a dozen armed guards coming through every exterior door in this room."

"Nice try," the leader said. "But while you may be some sort of boy wunderkind, I doubt you're very comfortable around types like Wen Xiang. And even if you were, you wouldn't trigger any such alarm because that means your work might risk damage. You might even get killed in the crossfire."

"Yeah," the swarthy, muscular one added. "Not to mention we've already spoken to your mother about the security they have around you. It's funny she didn't mention anything about a personal alarm."

Cai froze in place, his fingers growing icy as he felt a sudden rush of blood to his head. In that moment he forgot everything else, desiring only to know that his mother was safe—that she hadn't been abducted or even killed by the enemies of Cai's country. While Teng Cai had no political convictions, he did maintain one policy. Anybody who arrayed themselves against his family was his enemy—it didn't matter what their nationality or ideology. This was another one of those constants in Teng Cai's world, a factor on which he would never compromise.

"What do you know of my mother?"

"Quite a bit," the leader said. "Who do think told us how we could find you? You think we located you this easily on an educated guess? Now, we don't have any more time to bloody explain this. You have a choice—you can come with us voluntarily or involuntarily. Which is it going to be?"

Cai's gaze shifted involuntarily to another corner of the lab and when he returned eye contact with the leader he saw that all three of them had followed his gaze right to the familiar-looking object mounted there.

"Shit!" the American Southwesterner said. "They got remote eyes on this place!"

Cai realized the men had not expected cameras to be part of the setup. While they were on stationary mounts and unable to pan to where the three commandos stood, the monitors had surely deduced by now that Cai was talking with someone. The young scientist knew he had no more than a minute to decide into whose hands he would trust his fate. Worse yet, who did he trust with the fate of his mother? She was everything to him—his entire world. Yan Zhou had used that fact against him and now Cai realized his next decision would determine whether she lived or died.

"There is no way you could have located me so easily unless you spoke the truth," Cai finally conceded. With a nod he said, "I will go with you."

"Smart move," the team leader replied. "Looks like today is your lucky day."

CHAPTER SEVENTEEN

Whether McCarter had correctly called Teng Cai's bluff or not, it hardly mattered to the enemy. The three warriors were barely through the door of the lab with their subject when the sounds of approaching gunners echoed through the hall. They managed to make it about halfway along the corridor toward the exit when an explosion reverberated behind them and a bright orange ball filled the doorway, charring the edges as anything flammable in the area immediately burst into flame. Thick, dark smoke roiled down the hall and threatened to overtake the prone quartet in a miasma of choking sulfur and combustibles.

"Phosphorous!" Encizo shouted as they got to their feet.

"Or thermite mix," Hawkins added.

"It's gone hard," McCarter said. "You gents get young Mr. Cai here to the raft and I'll see what I can do to slow them down."

"Fine," Hawkins replied. "But you better not dawdle, Hoss."

"Oh, don't worry about me. I'll be right on your arses—you can bloody bank on that."

Hawkins nodded before grabbing Cai's shoulder and steering him away from the pending conflict. As soon as they were through the door, McCarter whirled and knelt. He double-checked the action on his MP-5 and then reached for the lone C-16 he'd liberated from Gary

Manning's satchel. Each man on the penetration team had been allotted one grenade with the idea that any more wouldn't do them much good where they were operating, not to mention explosives weren't exactly practical when making an escape via a rubber assault raft.

McCarter primed the grenade as soon as he heard the first sounds of boots approaching the entrance. His enemies would be much more likely concerned about avoiding the thermite than they would countermeasures involving HE. McCarter was banking on it, in fact, and his theory proved correct when four Chinese terrorists with weapons carefully picked their way into the hallway. It was dark and the smoke still obscured much of the corridor, so they didn't immediately spot the grenade McCarter rolled casually toward them. Just as it came into view, McCarter opened up on full-auto burn and then turned and high-tailed out of the danger zone. He didn't have to look back to see the resulting damage executed by the grenade.

The concussive blast and painful screams of the GSF soldiers told the tale most adequately.

McCarter burst through the door, the chill air somewhat a relief against his sweaty forehead. He spotted his teammates directly ahead as they charged up the dock. As they reached it, McCarter heard the chatter of automatic weapons to his left. He risked a backward glance and spotted a jeep bearing down on his position. Two men stood in the back of the open-air vehicle, triggering their assault rifles with a ferocity that left McCarter with no doubt of their intent. In his haste, the Phoenix Force leader tripped over the edge of a pallet and despite his best efforts could not keep his feet. The subsequent fall to his belly ended up saving his life as a nasty flurry of copper-jacketed rounds buzzed inches above his head.

McCarter bit back the pain and surprise of the impact and whirled onto his back, swinging the MP-5 into acquisition between his legs. He felt a pang of regret cut through his belly, convinced he wouldn't be able to avoid the rapidly approaching vehicle in time. At the last moment McCarter shouted with involuntary surprise as the enemy vehicle bearing down on him suddenly erupted into a gas ball, swerved clear of him and turned on its side. The fiery remains of the chassis and frame ground to a halt. The sole occupant not killed instantly in the blast came to his feet, awash in flames, his scream of agony audible even above the noise.

McCarter triggered his MP-5 and put two mercy rounds into the human torch before getting stiffly to his feet. It was then he heard the unmistakable high-pitched whir and ghostly reports from the engines of Kwan's stealth chopper. The big, bold son of a bitch had come through and McCarter couldn't wait to slap the guy on the back and thank him for saving his life. It was the second favor they owed Kwan and he could only understand even more why the Executioner had come to befriend the former Chinese spy.

McCarter broke into a steady jog toward the dock, confident they wouldn't encounter any further resistance. He muttered a curse when he realized such an assumption could get him killed as a fresh torrent of autofire burned the air around him. He looked in the direction of the firing and saw the muzzle-flashes as a good half dozen men approached the pier in a leapfrog maneuver. Wherever they had received their training, the men of the GSF were anything but typical fanatics. These were trained professionals through and through.

McCarter slung the MP-5 over his shoulder and quickly descended the cord to the waiting raft. Hawkins already had Cai secured in the center of the boat, lying on one side and pressed as flat as he could manage. Hawkins had taken up a forward observation position and Encizo had the motor started. As soon as McCarter's boots touched bottom, he ordered the Cuban to make distance.

Encizo didn't need to be told twice, kicking the motor into high gear and turning the steering control to swing them out from the pier without abandoning the natural cover provided by the riverbank. The nose of the engine rose as their speed increased, but Hawkins's weight kept some part of it at bay so the raft stayed in good trim as they made their escape. McCarter looked back to see their enemies had made it to the edge of the dock and were firing on them, but they were far enough downriver the chances of being hit had rapidly dwindled.

Hawkins looked back and grinned broadly, the black smear of the camo paint lending an almost minstrel-show quality to his face. "Yee-haw! We are home free, boys!"

Encizo nodded at a growing shape headed toward them, its lights winking and a spotlight sweeping the river immediately ahead of them. "I don't think we're out of the woods yet, sonny!"

All eyes locked on the ominous shape, a helicopter of some type. McCarter knew it wasn't Kwan's stealth chopper. Kwan would've hit the GSF troops and then made his way out of the area as soon as possible—he couldn't spend too much time in the air without his use of the chopper being discovered by police or even military. Once they knew the vehicle wasn't official, they wouldn't hesitate to blow it out of the sky. Judging the slow speed of the approaching craft and the lighting, McCarter guessed it was a police chopper.

"Bloody hell, it's the cops!"

"This isn't good..." Hawkins's voice trailed off.

Abruptly, the chopper suddenly increased speed and started heading directly toward them.

"You think they've spotted us?" Encizo asked.

"Not yet, but I'm sure our friends in the GSF are giving them an earful right about now."

"We might not be left with any choice if they discover we—"

McCarter shook his head. "No. No way will we violate SOP. I will *not* shoot at the cops."

"But maybe we could just—" Hawkins began.

"Negative, no! Case closed." McCarter pinned Encizo with a hard gaze as he activated the transceiver. "Run us aground over there, near that shallow part of the bank."

Encizo looked puzzled at first but then nodded. They wouldn't expect the boat to be that close to the shoreline when the last report they received was of an assault raft tearing down the center of the Hai River as fast as she could go. They cops would sweep the central part of the river first, and then swing back and search the shores later. They would have to slow considerably to do that, as well, which McCarter hoped would buy them enough time to connect with Manning and James waiting in the Nissan NV Hark Kwan had loaned them.

Encizo cut the motor far enough offshore they could drift swiftly to the banks without running aground first. When the outline of the shore appeared, he lifted the motor from the water on its pivoting mount—no use risking damage to the thing. If they weren't able to rendezvous with their teammates, it wouldn't do to be stuck at the shore with no means of making distance should things go hot again.

As soon as the raft bumped aground, Hawkins vaulted over the bow and grabbed the rope at the end to keep the raft in position until the rest of them could disembark. McCarter unloaded next and then reached back to give Teng Cai a hand. The young man was wheezing a bit, and McCarter realized he hadn't brought any sort of jacket.

"You've got to be freezing, pal," McCarter said.

As Encizo scrambled to the front, McCarter shed his butt pack and unrolled a thermal blanket. They had brought along survival equipment just in case they upended and were forced to swim to shore. He unfolded the thermal blanket and wrapped it twice around Cai's shoulders. The teenager nodded grateful acknowledgment and muttered a thanks that turned out largely intelligible through the chattering of his teeth.

"Great," Hawkins muttered. "We save the kid from the bad guys and then let him die of pneumonia. Wouldn't that go over well back home?"

"I would appreciate not being referred to as if I were a child, sir," Cai snapped.

Encizo couldn't refrain from chuckling. He looked at Hawkins and said, "Well, I guess he told you straight."

"Can it," McCarter said as he called for attention into the transceiver.

James's voice came back this time. "Sierra Three, here."

"We had to ditch our ride short of the agreed LZ," McCarter said. "There's a bird in the air looking for us. Probably boys in blue."

"Understood. Make for shore and we'll get en route to your location," James replied.

"Copy. Sierra Leader, out." McCarter grinned at his companions and said, "Let's move, boys. Our chariot cometh."

"Now he's breaking into the King James English," Hawkins said. "Ain't that just grand?"

McCarter gave his friend the finger. "Ah, blow it out your arse."

"I THINK WE have trouble," Gary Manning announced.

He sat behind the wheel of the Nissan NV at a traffic light, his eyes focused on the rearview mirror.

McCarter was on shotgun and checked his side mirror to see the faint swirl of police lights closing the distance at a pretty good clip. He said, "Just take it easy. Might not even be for us. Maybe it's an ambulance."

"And so we should just sit here and wait to find out?" James said from the seat directly behind McCarter. "That doesn't sound like an inspiring plan."

"If we jump the gun before we know it's time, we're only attracting attention we don't really want," McCarter replied easily. "But your concerns are noted."

It seemed to the five men and their teenage charge as if all of the air had been sucked out of the interior, each one lost in his thoughts and unconsciously holding his breath. The sirens and lights grew closer, and the traffic slid aside obediently to allow the emergency vehicles to pass. The first in line appeared to be an ambulance and they all seemed to release their breaths at once as it passed. Immediately following that was a police vehicle, which entered the intersection and continued past them at a good clip.

The light turned green and Manning slowly depressed the accelerator, confident the trouble hadn't been related to them. He told McCarter, "Guess you were right."

Then the police squad car screeched to a halt and performed a skid, its tail swinging into a full 180-degree turn so that it now faced them.

"Uh-oh," Encizo said from the backseat. "Spoke too soon."

"Think they're just blocking traffic?" James suggested.

The squad car lurched from where it had stopped and proceeded in their direction, answering James's question before anyone else could verbalize a response.

"Go there!" McCarter ordered, pointing to the right just as Manning entered the intersection.

The Canadian responded with admirable speed, his actions that of the consummate professional used to repeatedly acting in response to sudden changes on the battleground. The only difference this time was their battleground had become the crammed streets of downtown Tianjin, and chances were good they would lose their running room pretty fast. They wouldn't do battle with the cops, sure, but more gut-wrenching was the idea they would have to try to elude them with bystanders all around. Fortunately, the morning rush hour hadn't begun and they still had darkness as an ally. Manning hoped it was enough.

"Damn and double damn," Manning muttered as he weaved his way through the two lanes around some slower-moving vehicles.

Fortunately, Manning could make some distance now, perhaps lose their pursuers on a side street. He considered for a moment they had overreacted but he quickly dispelled the thought when he noted the appearance of the flashing lights. It appeared the police were gaining on them, and Manning wondered how long it would take before the Chinese police boxed them in. As a former police officer himself with the RCMP, Manning recalled the old saying "You can't outrun a radio." Well, he was sure as hell going to give it the old college try.

Manning increased speed and then instructed the occupants to hold on before making a sharp left turn. He held his breath for a time but released it when he saw plenty of road ahead. He wished for much more familiar streets—Washington, D.C. or Montreal would be nice—where he didn't have to worry about running out of road. He'd been put to a considerable disadvantage because he didn't know the area and the cops did. Well, there wasn't any point in letting it bother him. He would adapt and improvise, and hope to hell the gods of fortune were on *his* side this morning.

Manning made another left just as he caught the flashing lights round the corner before the buildings obscured his view. He gunned the engine, attempting to coax more power from the V-8. Despite the heavy engine he knew they stood little chance of outrunning the squad. They had neither the acceleration speed nor maneuvering capabilities in the massive cargo van that had been converted to carry passengers.

"What we could really use right now is some of those special gadgets that Q gives James Bond," Hawkins pointed out.

"Boy, are you living in another world," James replied.

"I don't have any idea where we're going," Manning said. He called back to Teng Cai. "Hey there, Cai, you think you might be able to help us out with that?"

Cai's tight-lipped face appeared in the rearview mirror long enough for him to assess the road through the windshield. He shook his head to indicate he had nothing to offer and then ducked out of view. Well, that was great—boy genius who couldn't come up with so much as a little insight as to how they might get out of this mess. Apparently, he either didn't realize that if they were caught he would go back to working for the GSF or he just didn't care. He could always tell them they had taken him involuntarily.

"Okay, I'm open to any suggestions," Manning pleaded. "Anybody? Anybody at all?"

"More trouble," McCarter said, gesturing with his finger just above and ahead of them.

The helicopter they had encountered while on the river dipped into view and stopped to hover maybe a hundred feet above them. The forward spotlights on the craft suddenly came alive and practically blinded Manning.

The Canadian threw up one hand to shield his eyes, then saw the street ahead and assumed it was the one they'd been traveling on at the start. He considered turning right and continuing for the airport but he worried they'd get wise to that plan and cut them off. If he maintained a random course it would be more difficult for the cops to predict where they were going. Manning reached the intersection and blew the red light—nobody broadsided them and some of his passengers let out audible sounds of relief in varying degrees.

Then the road ahead came alive with sparks and Manning knew immediately they were under fire. "The cops are shooting at us?"

It was Cai who replied, "Those are not police officers. The firing pattern is from the chopper—I recognize it. That is a PRCAF Harbin Z-9. A military chopper.

I would imagine, however, that those are not military pilots aboard. Most likely they are attached to the unit of special forces under the command of Air Vice-Marshal Yan Zhou."

"Well, then, if they're not cops—" Hawkins began.

"They're fair game," McCarter finished.

"So we can get busy?" James asked.

"Bloody hell, yeah!"

With that, James unclipped his seat belt and reached for the M-16 A4 rifle at his feet. He checked the action and then, as he reached to open the sliding side door, told Manning, "Back off our speed, ace."

Manning complied and when he had it down to about thirty-five he waved at James, who whipped the side door back, leaned out and leveled his assault rifle at the hovering chopper. He could barely make out the lines of the chopper, its nonreflective fuselage little more than a silhouette in the harsh glare of the spotlight, so James used that bright circle as his point of reference. James acquired his desired target and squeezed the trigger, holding down slightly as he delivered a full-auto burst at the chopper. A moment later the spotlight winked out and the chopper veered sharply out of the line of fire.

"Nice shooting!" Encizo exclaimed.

"Well, we might've ditched our GSF flier for the moment," Hawkins remarked as he glanced out the back window of the Nissan, "but we still have that squad car on our tail and they're coming in hot."

Before anyone could reply to that bit of news, the chopper reappeared where it had been, but now only its running lights were visible. It had turned off the flashing strobe and it was at too great a distance to give even a marksman like James a decent firing solution. McCarter also verbalized his fear of shooting the thing out of the sky only to turn it into a fiery missile that might crash into buildings and kill innocent bystanders.

"Whoa now," Encizo said. "Something's happening here."

Without warning, the chopper made a sudden and erratic dip before heading straight toward their position, flying at very low altitude and cruising at a high rate of speed.

"I think we're in big trouble," Gary Manning said.

CHAPTER EIGHTEEN

A bright flash emanated from the chopper just a heart-beat before the approaching squad car disappeared in a fireball. The men of Phoenix Force could hardly believe their eyes at first, but in short order it became apparent the GSF didn't really care about police casualties—they would care even less about civilian casualties. That brought grim thoughts to McCarter and he realized if they were going to pull out of this one alive and avoid injuries or death to innocent bystanders, they would have to abandon the Nissan.

"Bail!" he ordered.

They had already determined James and Hawkins would be responsible for Teng Cai if they successfully extracted the young man, so McCarter wouldn't worry. Phoenix Force was long on experience. Each man knew his job, duties assigned by respective talents, and this fact had always served them well. They operated as a unit and they did it smoothly. It was one of the things that made them a fighting force to be reckoned with.

The men obeyed and McCarter gestured for them to take shelter in what looked like an abandoned building less than fifty yards up the sidewalk. More rounds chewed the ground at their feet, ricochets sparking their trail and sending deadly heated fragments from the 30 mm shells in every direction. It was nothing short of a small miracle the six reached their haven unscathed and McCarter couldn't help but wonder if that wasn't by design. He found the plate-glass door with its heavy metal frame locked fast, but a quick shot from his Browning Hi-Power into the lock rectified that problem.

McCarter opened the door and waved his arm to usher Cai and his teammates inside. As the last of them went through the open door, McCarter risked an upward glance and saw the unmistakable shape of human figures as they descended from the chopper. McCarter did a quick count—four in all, and they looked heavily armed. McCarter glanced over his shoulder to view the smoking hulk of the squad, its remains awash with flames, and pressed his lips tightly. No survivors in *that* one.

McCarter followed his team into the dark building, stepping through the foyer and continuing beyond it to an even darker main room. The odor of dust and disuse assailed his nostrils. It wasn't much to look at. Most of the furniture that had probably once occupied the space had been removed and a patina of dirt covered the floor. There were a few chairs encircling a low, central table in one section that had probably been a waiting area of some type, but the rest of the high-ceilinged room was devoid of anything they might use for cover.

"I think we're going to have company in short order," McCarter said.

Manning looked around and shook his head. "Not much we can use here for protection."

"Yeah, I was just thinking that myself."

"I thought I spotted some elevators over there," Encizo said. "But I'd guess they aren't working."

"Should we see if we can locate some stairs?" Manning asked.

McCarter nodded. "You two go."

Encizo and Manning obeyed while McCarter assisted Hawkins and James with getting Teng Cai over to the waiting area. The furniture wouldn't be much for cover or concealment but it would afford them moderate protection if they were forced to make their stand on the ground floor. McCarter checked the luminous dial on his watch and estimated they had a minute or less before the GSF commandos made their entry.

"Over here!" Manning called.

The four left the cover of the chairs and followed the flashing laser pointer Manning used as a makeshift beacon. They assembled on him and Encizo joined them a moment later. "Found a door to some stairs. No basement but they do provide access to the upper floors."

"Good," McCarter replied. "It will be a lot easier to defend the high ground. You move out and we'll stay behind to provide rear guard."

Encizo looked around the cavernous first floor and finally expressed incredulity. "Here? You're not serious."

"I am," McCarter replied, his lips pressed together. Looking at Hawkins, he said, "Give me your grens."

"There's no cover here," James noted. "You couldn't mount any sort of decent defense."

"No time to discuss this, mates," McCarter said flatly. Nodding at Manning, he told them, "We will stay behind and you three get our friend here to the upper floors. High as you can go."

Hawkins, James and Encizo looked among themselves with a moment of uncertainty while Cai stood behind them with passive indifference. Finally, they turned and ushered Cai through the stairwell door.

As soon as they were out of sight, Manning turned and looked at McCarter. "You know they're right, David. We have no defendable position here. That flimsy furniture over there isn't going to help us any."

"I never expected it to." McCarter whirled and trotted away with a gesture for Manning to follow. As the Canadian fell into cadence beside him, McCarter continued, "We'll defend from the elevator bank. It's plenty dark there yet it provides a perfect view of the entrance. Not to mention we can use the recesses to provide full concealment. It will be too dark for them to tell exactly what we're doing or where we're at, making it almost impossible to pinpoint us."

Manning nodded in full agreement now. "That's pretty ingenious. And you're totally right—we can hold them off a while if we stagger our fields of fire. But I'm curious about one thing."

"What's that?"

"Why did you pick me to stay behind with you?"

McCarter's smile took on extra emphasis in the darkness. "You're holding the little bag of tricks, mate. And I've learned always stick close to the guy with explosives when the odds are down."

"Ah…great. And here I thought maybe you were growing sweet on me."

As soon as the stealth chopper landed, Hark Kwan grabbed another man and they left the airport in a pair of nondescript SUVs. Kwan still had a full support network of friends and contacts he'd made over the years he'd been with the MSS. A lot of people owed him favors, too, and those with whom he'd traded out were more than happy to continue working with him for a few extra bucks.

After all, government pay in a predominantly socialist economy model wasn't exactly a fortune. While many government employees received a generous subsistence that included decent, comfortable quarters and per diem for things like meals and transportation, most could hardly have claimed they lived in what could pass as luxury. Workers were often grouped together in sectors to encourage closed social circles based on particular sectors or specialties. The very thought of such "work communes" may have been nothing less than abhorrent to his American friends, but Kwan knew it had become a way of living and surviving in his society.

Something Kwan hadn't opted to divulge to the Americans was his long-term desire to leave China. He wasn't sure where he wanted to settle. Definitely not in the United States or any other similar democratic republic—a good number of those were rapidly becoming obsolete in favor of the new Socialist or Communist orders. While that might have been Yan Zhou's ultimate dream, it wasn't Kwan's and he didn't know how much longer he could fight the tide. He hoped for something better in his homeland but he couldn't help but wonder if he was fighting a losing battle.

Kwan put any further consideration of such things from his mind—he needed to focus on the *now*. He knew his allies had somehow made contact with law enforcement and he'd just received word of an explosion in the section near the Ingchu District, a former textiles and clothes manufacturing district that had long been closed down. Most of the buildings in that area were old and condemned, so there was little in the way of bystander traffic. At least he didn't have that to worry about. But even as he and the second driver made their way toward the Ingchu District, Kwan could hear the police radio come alive with traffic.

There had also been talk of a military-grade chopper matching the description of a Harbin Z-9 seen near the area. That was probably what his American friends originally mistook for a police helicopter. It was their desire to avoid any conflict with police that had prompted Kwan to order their stealth copter out of the area rather than stick around and risk a direct encounter with police forces—now he wished he'd kept them airborne and just out of sight. Not that it would've done them much good. There were most definitely disadvantages to operating an advanced aircraft like that where eyes could see. While he was convinced they'd managed to avoid detection this time, Kwan had known the risks of using such a tool within the civilian sector. Operating against the house where they'd held Meifeng Cai had been a different situation entirely since the location had been utterly isolated by design. Well, he could at least get these vehicles into the area without too much trouble and if necessary use them to facilitate the escape of his friends.

Hark Kwan only hoped it wouldn't be too late.

WHEN THE TROUBLE came through the door, it did so in such a fashion McCarter and Manning hadn't expected.

The count of the opposition was roughly three times that of the original group McCarter'd seen descending from the chopper. Manning estimated at least a dozen guns, possibly more, an estimate difficult to obtain given the speed with which they spread out to enfold the place. Neither of the Phoenix Force warriors waited for an invitation to engage the opposition. These definitely weren't cops—their outlines suggested an array of varying assault-grade weapons.

Manning held the MP-5 close to his shoulder, controlled his breathing with the steady rhythm he'd been trained to employ in such circumstances and squeezed the trigger. His first 3-round burst rewarded him with a two-for-one deal. The first GSF terrorist flipped onto his back as he emitted a grotesque coughing sound. The second one died immediately after his comrade with a round that seemed to remove part of his head, although Manning couldn't be entirely certain of that given the virtually pitch-black interior.

McCarter got the next one with a single shot to the chest, the impact driving the man back into a fourth terrorist.

More than a half minute into the fray since the dozen or so here had made their entry and they'd only taken out a fourth. These weren't such great odds, and Manning had begun to wonder if this had really been the best place to make their stand. He recanted the thought when the remaining terrorists opened up with a full-auto burn and sprayed the area with enough rounds to chop a grizzly bear to hamburger. The Phoenix Force duo managed to avoid being hit given their cover in the alcoves provided by the elevators.

As some of the firing abated, Manning remembered his ordnance and dipped a hand into the satchel to retrieve one of the C-16s. He primed the grenade and crouched, then bobbed into view long enough to lob the gren in the general direction of the muzzle-flashes. Before the first one exploded, he'd immediately primed and delivered a second one. The grenades blew at about the same time, a happy but unintended consequence, and in the light provided by the blasts Manning figured he'd knocked at least four more of their enemies out of commission.

"Hell," Manning said as the echoes of the explosions

died out and he returned to cover. "Just about down to a fair fight now."

"Like I said, stick with the explosives expert."

HAWKINS, JAMES AND Encizo had reached the third floor with Teng Cai in tow before they heard the first sounds of firing almost directly below them, followed shortly thereafter by the floor-rattling effects of the grenades.

Encizo gestured for his friends to head for an exit door at the far end of the hallway while he pointed to the nearest office, an indication he wanted to check out any potential threats to the exterior of the building. The pair nodded in agreement before Encizo whirled, entered the room and crossed to the nearest window. It was the first in a series of windows and as Encizo got close he realized the glass had already been smashed out. Careful to avoid the few jagged shards protruding from the frame, Encizo stuck his head through the window and spotted a large panel truck with at least half a dozen terrorists milling around it.

Encizo looked in the opposite direction and saw three police vehicles racing up the street toward the terrorists' position, one of them apparently a tactical truck. They were just reaching the intersection when a pair of dark SUVs coming from a parallel street beat them to the punch. One of the SUVs performed a sideways power slide and impacted the two squads, driving one into the other. The second SUV jumped to the side and screeched to a halt, whipping into a position parallel with the curb and immediately in front of a minivan. The driver hopped out, went to the driver's side of the minivan and fired a single shot into the window. He then reached inside before returning to the SUV. A moment passed before Encizo witnessed the SUV back into the minivan and push it into the intersection, effectively positioning it in such a way that created a roadblock in concert with the two disabled squad cars.

Encizo watched in amazement as the pair of SUVs then proceeded up the street, engines roaring, in the direction of the terrorists' panel van. There was something about the way the vehicles converged on the enemy position that shot a pang of hope through Encizo's gut like an arrow. When the vehicles stopped and the drivers emerged with SMGs clutched in their hands—pointing their weapons directly at the surprised terrorists—Encizo knew it *had* to be Kwan bringing the cavalry.

Encizo keyed up his headset and spoke into the transmitter. "Sierra Two to Sierra One."

A moment later McCarter's voice came back. "Go, Sierra Two."

"Looks like the Delegate brought some fresh wheels. He's out front but he's outnumbered."

"Received and acknowledged," McCarter said. "See what you can do for him, will you?"

"Copy that," Encizo replied.

The Cuban swung his MP-5 out the window with unbridled glee, sighted down the tube and squeezed the trigger. He delivered each 3-round burst carefully, thankful for the sound suppressor on the SD6 model. The terrorists were using unsuppressed weapons, as were Kwan and his partner, which meant the terrorists likely wouldn't know they were taking fire from above until Encizo had taken down at least a couple. The high ground proved most effective, and Encizo had taken out half of them before they even knew what was happening.

Encizo heard the familiar rattle of MP-5 fire coming

from another direction. Satisfied Hawkins and James had heard his transmission and joined the fray from the second floor, he broke off his engagement and headed back the way they'd originally come. If they could hold off the terrorists long enough for him to reach the first floor, Encizo knew he could help McCarter and Manning by providing flanking fire. He descended the steps two at a time and reached the first floor in about a minute.

Encizo burst through the door and dashed toward the seating area. He knew it wouldn't provide much protection but it might buy McCarter and Manning enough time to charge their position. The Phoenix Force warrior knew it had paid off a moment later when he dropped one of the terrorists under a full-auto salvo and the remaining pair turned in his direction and exposed themselves by opening up on him in response. Encizo evaded their fire as he hit the floor with enough force to drive the air from his lungs.

Bullets burned the air over his head but their action was short-lived as Manning and McCarter took the cue. The pair charged the enemy position and in no time had delivered a volley that cut swathing paths through enemy flesh. The pair of terrorists danced like wild puppets under the assault before collapsing to the dusty floor in puddles of blood left by their comrades.

Encizo climbed slowly to his feet and rubbed his chest, muttering, "That's going to leave one hell of a bruise."

Once reunited with his friends, the trio burst out the front door and found only one surviving terrorist behind the wheel of the panel van, trying to escape. McCarter, Encizo and Manning raised their MP-5s and triggered in a simultaneous blur of combat-honed reaction. The terrorist jerked under the impact of the 9 mm slugs, blood splattering the front and side windows that shattered with the unforgiving force of modern firearm technology.

McCarter keyed his radio. "Sierra Leader, here. You guys are clear to bring out your package. Out!"

Hawkins delivered a roger to confirm they'd received the message and with the trio spread out covering them, they emerged a minute later and dashed for the SUVs, the cover team close on their heels. As they reached the vehicles, McCarter was the first to find Kwan seated behind the front passenger seat of the lead SUV. The neat dark hole in the lower left portion of his gut was no longer visible due to the massive amount of blood seeping from the seams of his hands where they met his abdomen.

It was hot, copious and fairly bright in color.

"Aw, bloody damn," McCarter muttered. He looked over the hood at Encizo and said, "Get Calvin. Looks like an artery."

"No!" Kwan said. "Just go. There is no point in risking the mission."

"Bullshit!" McCarter protested.

Kwan grabbed the Briton's wrist with one hand, his grip surprisingly tight and his eyes pleading. His color had changed even in the moments since McCarter had first seen him. "It'll be too late by the time you can do anything. Please, McMasters…" Kwan moaned and then gritted his teeth. "Please don't f-fucking…waste this."

McCarter realized Kwan was right. He didn't like it but he knew they couldn't remain here—otherwise the entire effort would be in vain.

"You drive!" McCarter said to James. "Manning, you're on shotgun. I'll attend to our man, here."

They all took positions as directed and soon the SUVs were leaving the factory district and headed for the hotel.

They had originally thought about going straight to the airport, but Kwan's man, who took the lead, quickly convinced them the GSF would expect that. At least they could go to the hotel and buy themselves a little time while they waited for the inevitable dragnet to narrow on the immediate area.

McCarter grit his teeth as he pulled a bulky combat dressing from his belt and tried to staunch the flow of blood. It only seemed to make things worse and he wished he'd thought to trade places with James. Not that the team's medic could have done much better at that point. McCarter knew, just as Kwan had known, anything they tried to save the man would be futile.

"Damn it, Hark," McCarter whispered. "Why didn't you keep your head down?"

Kwan forced a smile. "Not my head that got shot."

"Don't get wise with me, mate," McCarter said with a grin of his own.

"Listen…" Kwan gasped for breath and McCarter could actually feel the man's skin begin to grow clammy and cool where he gripped Kwan's arm to keep him as still as possible. "Listen, it's important. I…I filed the flight plans like we talked. I know you're going to the hotel but…don't wait too long. A half hour, no…no more. You understand?"

McCarter nodded. "Yeah, I understand. Hey, mate? You did good—you did real good."

"So did you."

And with those last words on his lips, Hark Kwan died.

CHAPTER NINETEEN

Jack Grimaldi could hardly disguise the warmth that coursed through his body as he witnessed the reunion of mother with son. If nothing else, it was plainly obvious that Meifeng cared greatly for Teng Cai, and she did nothing to hide that fact by the ferocity of embracing him. A shudder seemed to run through her, probably born from relief at her son being delivered alive and well just as McCarter had promised her. This would go a long way in soliciting her cooperation; Grimaldi knew that much.

Hawkins and James moved past the pair, giving Teng and Meifeng a respectful amount of space, as they scooped up the team's equipment and headed for the plane at a nod from the Stony Man pilot. Grimaldi felt a pang of concern at first, but he breathed relief when he saw the remaining team members come through the door a minute later, McCarter trailing the rest. Grimaldi smiled more to himself than any of them, thinking of how much McCarter seemed like a mother duck rounding up her ducklings and keeping them under watchful check.

Grimaldi approached McCarter just as the Phoenix Force leader finished instructing Manning and Encizo in getting all of the gear aboard. The two shook hands and Grimaldi squeezed McCarter's shoulder in a gesture of warm camaraderie coupled with plain relief.

"Glad all of you could join us in one piece."

"Me, too," McCarter replied. "You got our clearance?"

Grimaldi nodded. "Kwan filed the bogus flight plan hours ago. Seems like everything's in order and I've double-checked with flight control. They advised we're clear to leave as soon as we radio in and request departure instructions. I didn't get any sense they thought we were anything other than what we claimed."

"What about customs checks?"

"They didn't indicate there would be any," Grimaldi said. "I guess they figured since everything checked out on our arrival that we're just a private business flight, as declared."

"Or they're just not concerned with anything we might be taking out of the country as illegal."

"May not see it as their problem once we leave Chinese airspace."

"True," McCarter said with a sigh. "Ah, the apathy of government bureaucracy. It can be a beautiful thing, mate. You heard about Kwan?"

"Yeah, I did. Real sorry to hear about that. He was a good man."

"He was at that," McCarter said. "I'm going to *personally* make sure someone's held responsible for that."

Grimaldi inclined his head in the direction of the Cais. "I haven't told them yet."

"I'll take care of it once we're aboard." McCarter checked his watch. "Speaking of which, we'd best see them onto the bird and get wheels up. Lady Luck might be with us at the moment but there's no telling how things might change in the next ten to fifteen minutes once word gets out of what happened. Yan Zhou's got enough bloody weight behind him to suspend all air traffic."

Grimaldi tried not to look worried as he asked, "Is it

possible AF forces might try to engage us once we're in the air?"

"Doubtful," McCarter said, shaking his head. "He wouldn't want to risk killing his boy wonder. If we can get airborne before they're able to shut down the airport, we should be home free."

"Other than they will most likely track us," Grimaldi said. "I can fake the transponder code systems once we're in international airspace, even go dark if we have to. To do it any sooner would cause all kinds of panic on the ground."

"Just ease us out of here nice and normal on the bogus information Kwan planted with the powers that be," McCarter replied. "We'll worry about the rest once we're well away from this place."

Grimaldi replied with a snappy salute, then turned to the task of getting mother and son to collect their things and head for the plane.

McCarter took one last look at the lounge to ensure they'd left nothing behind that might compromise them and then grabbed his gear pack and headed for the plane himself. As he walked across the tarmac, the icy winds brushing at the fatigues where they weren't covered by his blue, wool overcoat, he gave one last thought of respect to Hark Kwan. The guy had paid the ultimate price for the betterment of his country and her people, and that was something McCarter could understand. What Kwan had done he'd done out of duty and honor—his sacrifice would *not* be forgotten by any of the men of Phoenix Force.

And David McCarter swore right at that moment he would return to China soon and do what needed to be done to settle the score.

VICE AIR-MARSHAL Yan Zhou arrived at his office less than an hour after receiving the news the Americans had escaped with Teng Cai.

The team Wen Xiang had hired was to blame for this. Idiots! Zhou couldn't help but wonder why those in charge with the GSF had forced such incompetents on him. He'd provided Xiang's security team with the most advanced equipment and training money could buy, diverted funds from his budget to support their efforts, and they hadn't even been able to oversee the security of one teenage boy and his mother.

Zhou would be the first to admit the special ops unit that had pulled off Teng Cai's defection had been a formidable adversary up to this point, but Zhou could no longer afford these kinds of foul-ups. With Cai now in the hands of the Americans, their plans for using the special missiles to insert GSF forces into the countries of their enemies would now be absolutely useless if Zhou didn't do some damage control. The fact Zhou had called a meeting of Xiang and his associates here at his office attested to Zhou's desire for expediency. Up until now he'd insisted on completely neutral territory for the purposes of being able to disavow any affiliation with the Gold Star Faction if security had ever been compromised. For more than eight years he'd been able to operate without being discovered, but now all that stood to fall apart if he didn't take some sort of decisive action.

The first to arrive was Keqiang Ho Lo, the first advisor to the Minister of Finance, Xuren Xie. Lo was staunchly conservative and had been at odds with military representatives at all levels for a long time—in fact, he'd been Zhou's rival for many years until he'd joined the GSF. Lo had always believed that the People's Republic of China should not work to pursue military superiority above any other country, but rather take precise and subtle measures to consume the wealth and assets of competitors through consumerism and trade practices. While his ideas had gone a long way toward increasing States-held enterprises under the blanket of "economic security" he privately believed that Communist ideals were what had truly brought the trade deficits of the country to less than one percent as of 2012. As a result of his success, he'd become fiercely supportive of the GSF and its views, and his position allowed him to wield great influence in the financial arena.

The second arrival was no less a VIP and a long-time ally. Lei Meng was a high-ranker within the office of the Secretary of Internal Security. He had connections that ran all through the massive PRC cabinet, including the ear of the chief of the MSS. He knew about Wen Xiang and the other "rogue" mercenary units that operated outside the core sphere of internal influence. For the most part he'd opted to turn a blind eye to their activities. However, Zhou also enjoyed a very close personal relationship to Meng and he knew the man wouldn't be so happy when he learned of the failure of the GSF forces to stop the American commandos from stealing Teng Cai and his mother out of the country.

That was why it came as no surprise to Zhou when Meng was the first to question Wen Xiang immediately upon his arrival.

"I trust you have a very good explanation for this," Meng said. "I don't like being dragged from my warm bed at this hour to be given such news. We've paid a terrible price today."

"A price that could cost us untold millions," Lo added.

Zhou smiled. That was Keqiang Ho Lo—always quick

to point out the financial consequences given any opportunity. Zhou quickly recovered when he saw the visible reddening of Xiang's face and realized that if he were to make his move, now would be the time. Among such distinguished men as this, Zhou knew he could score big points by playing the peacemaker. He also had to save Xiang some embarrassment, though, because he still needed the man's resources. Xiang would be the very best at what Yan Zhou had in mind to propose.

"Gentlemen…gentlemen," he said, his tone all buttery warmth. "While I can understand how distressing this is, I think it's wise to point out at this juncture that Mr. Xiang is not the cause for this trouble. It was my decision to move Teng Cai for purposes of security and so I take full responsibility for his falling into the hands of our enemies."

All eyes swung in his direction and Zhou took special note of the surprise in Wen Xiang's. Now to sweeten the pot. "And since there is nothing I can do about that, I feel we must put our focus on how to mitigate the damage."

"And just how do you propose to do that?" Meng asked. "This group that has taken Teng Cai is surely out of the country already. We have no way of tracking them and Cai knows how to defeat the technology you've strived so long to attain."

"That last part you say is quite true," Zhou replied with nonchalance. "But your concerns that we have no way of tracking him are unfounded. In fact, I happen to know *exactly* where they will take young Cai and his mother."

"Then perhaps you could enlighten us."

Zhou cleared his throat and sat back in his chair, pressing his fingertips together with casual air. "We know the prototype we launched was recovered by the U.S. Navy, just as we had predicted, and we also know they believe it to be the work of the North Koreans. It was I who let the information slip to the Korean intelligence about the technology, certain they would send someone to attempt to destroy it. It was all very predictable, you see."

"I'd prefer you skip the melodrama and come to the point, Air Vice-Marshal," Lo interjected. "I've always found your flair for the dramatic somewhat irritating."

"The U.S. scientists assigned to study the prototype have undoubtedly learned by now that the technology could not have been developed by the North Koreans. They will not, however, be able to determine its origin without confirmation from Teng Cai. This buys us the time, you see, to implement the second part of our plan."

"Which is?" Meng asked.

Zhou couldn't help but chuckle with satisfaction at his own ingenuity. "I've arranged for Wen Xiang to implement this phase of our plan. He will go to Alaska, locate Teng Cai and eliminate him and his family should our plan inexplicably fail. He will also carry with him additional evidence, manufactured of course, that will fool the Americans into believing we had nothing to do with it from the start. Evidence that will make it look like the North Koreans have, in fact, been behind the entire deception."

"And just how do you plan to do that?"

"We've employed a highly specialized team that has been training for many months," Zhou said. "Mr. Xiang will travel to Anchorage and rendezvous with the team. They will then eliminate the North Korean cleanup team that we know was sent there and then produce the evidence that disproves our involvement."

"And what about Teng Cai?" Lo asked. "Surely he will

be made to talk, to reveal everything he knows about our activities."

"That will prove to be of no consequence, gentlemen," Zhou replied. "You see, once we've convinced their government of the North Korean involvement, the U.S. will have little choice but to return Teng Cai and the woman, Meifeng, to us. To do otherwise would be an admission of their illegal entry into our country and kidnapping of a Chinese citizen.

"If members in our government were to threaten to go public with such information, this would cause significant embarrassment to the U.S. President and his cabinet. The Americans are entirely too image-conscious to let that happen. They will return Teng Cai to us *voluntarily,* and we will in turn bring him back here to complete his work."

The two men considered this for a time and Zhou left them to it, letting the silence weigh on them as they contemplated his proposal.

"Your plan sounds promising," Meng finally said. "But I have one concern."

Zhou arched his eyebrows. "And what is that?"

"How do we know that your efforts won't be subverted once more, just as they were before."

"Come, my friend. You must understand that this only happened because the Americans had managed to recruit a former agent from your Ministry of State Security to assist them. I believe you're familiar with the name Hark Kwan?"

Something went very sour in Lei Meng's expression. "I will admit that he has been a particularly elusive individual. But that is hardly *our* failing." His eyes shifted to Wen Xiang. "You were supposed to take care of that problem a long time ago."

"Stipulated," Xiang said calmly, although there was obvious venom in his voice. "But as you've said yourself, he was very elusive and there were many sympathetic to his cause."

"Phah! What cause?" Lo said with fury. "Those of us loyal to the Party are not concerned with the petty attempts of subversive incompetents such as Hark Kwan!"

"Despite what you may think," Zhou rebutted, his face taking on a freshly dangerous hue of its own, "Kwan has a significant following. He is also quite adept at covert operations and is well connected among the intelligence communities of a half dozen foreign countries. He is also supplied with funds, the source of which even your financial spies have been unable to discover."

"Frankly, and meaning no disrespect," Xiang said, "this entire point is now moot. Hark Kwan will pose no longer any concern for us. He's *dead*."

This surprised Zhou. "You're certain?"

"Absolutely, Air Vice-Marshal. I eliminated him—personally. He died attempting to cover the foreign operations unit that took Teng Cai. These men were well trained and equipped, not to mention considerably skilled in close-quarters battle techniques. This is why my men were overcome. Their specialty was assassination, and they were trained as such. The black ops team we faced was a military unit of the highest order. We were unprepared for this, just as were the members of your security team in Hebei Province."

"This is why I have hand-selected the team you will lead in the United States," Zhou said, more to allay Lo and Meng's concerns than Xiang's. "They are the very best special operations team the People's Air Force has to offer."

"After what I've seen and heard, they will have to be," Xiang replied.

The remainder of the meeting involved discussing timetables and finances, along with other minor business directly related to the GSF. Once the meeting broke, Zhou was left alone to speak to Wen Xiang.

"Your defense of me and my men was a surprise," Xiang said. "I have to admit that I may have misjudged you."

Yan Zhou dismissed what amounted to Xiang's rhetorical form of an apology with a wave. "I've been a military officer most of my life, Mr. Xiang. As such, I have learned that sometimes one must take responsibility for the actions of those under his command. I was in charge of the operation—therefore your failure is my failure."

Xiang nodded. "I commend you. But of course, in this case, we are not really soldiers. I have always valued my ability to operate autonomously, to work without external interference."

"And I wouldn't have it any other way," Zhou said. "But make no mistake, I wouldn't want a repeat of this incident. That's why nothing must be left to chance. The men you will be leading are not assassins. They are trained soldiers, schooled in the arts of special warfare. You will have to *earn* their respect."

Xiang looked uncertain now. "You seem to have forgotten I have a significant amount of military experience myself."

"I forget nothing, Wen Xiang. So perhaps I can put this in terms that leave you no cause for doubt. I cannot and will not tolerate any more fuck-ups. Go to America, eliminate the North Korean cleanup team at all costs and get the technical schematics I'm sending with you into the hands of the American scientists in possession of the prototype."

"And retrieve Teng Cai, of course."

"Believe me, once they believe the North Koreans have deceived them, they will stop at nothing to hand deliver Teng and Meifeng gift-wrapped to you."

"Understood," Xiang said. "There's just one matter still open that is yet unresolved. What do you wish me to do if we're unsuccessful in accomplishing our mission? This American team is resourceful, and I don't wish to overestimate our chances of success. Certainly you have a contingency plan if we fail to achieve our objectives."

Zhou nodded, his expression grim. "If it should come to that, then you are authorized to eliminate Teng and Meifeng Cai by whatever means at your disposal. If this happens, you will not be able to return here as the government would have to deny any knowledge of your presence in America. You will be written off as a rogue agent who was operating under your own concerns."

"So if you should be forced to officially make such a declaration, may I assume it would be up to me to find my own means to escape from the country?"

"What you do to those ends is your affair," Zhou said. "As long as you do not attempt to compromise the Party or *me* personally. I am somewhat fond of you, Mr. Xiang— or at least fond of your abilities. But if that were to happen, it might be better for you to consider something more honorable. Such as ritual suicide."

"I see," Xiang replied coldly.

"I'm sure that you do," Zhou said, reaching into his desk drawer and handing the forged travel papers to the assassin. "I've checked these personally and they are in order. I wish you every success."

Wen Xiang took the papers and the technical schematics and left without speaking a single word. Zhou took a seat behind his desk and watched with contemplation as Xiang departed. He would be sorry to lose such an important asset, but he knew there could be no remnant of the operation that might be traced back to his office. The chance Xiang actually succeeded only to discover Zhou had betrayed him was a minute one, at best. Yan Zhou was quite satisfied Xiang had just embarked on a mission from which he wasn't scheduled to return.

And Zhou had to admit a certain glimmer of satisfaction at that thought.

CHAPTER TWENTY

Anchorage, Alaska

Able Team sat with Ju Young-Soon in a unmarked sedan—on loan from the base AP security forces responsible for high-profile prisoner transports—just outside the hotel. So far, they hadn't seen anything to support Young-Soon's claim this was where the cleanup team would set up shop. And while he hadn't spoken of his doubts regarding Young-Soon or her wild conjecture to this point, Carl Lyons was finding this whole thing less believable by the minute.

"Well?" Lyons finally said, glancing over his shoulder at Young-Soon.

She sat in the backseat with her hands and feet manacled by a chain run through a steel ring bolted to the floor. They knew immobilizing her posed some risk, since if they encountered any sort of trouble she might be maimed or killed in the process. Lyons had been willing to risk it. Despite her cooperation, she would still fare better in the custody of Able Team or a unit of U.S. Marshals than at the hands of local authorities. Sure, the Anchorage cops were pros all the way—Lyons would've picked a beef with anyone who suggested otherwise—although it wasn't unheard of for cop killers to wind up falling down a few times throughout any period of local incarceration. Blancanales had suggested leaving her in the custody of base police but the Provost Marshal had refused to take responsibility for her without a direct order from the Secretary of the Air Force, and the White House didn't want to show all of their cards yet for fear Young-Soon's capture might leak to the press.

"Yeah," Lyons had grumbled when word came down from on high of the decision. "Let's just put aside national security concerns because it could cause a little bad press."

Lyons waited for Young-Soon but she made no response—she even refused to look him in the eye. He said, "Doesn't look like there's anything to this little killing team with the big plans."

Now Young-Soon met his gaze. "You shouldn't be so quick to judge, American. Don't forget that I'm an expert in the operations of my government."

"What's that supposed to mean?"

"It means that just because you cannot *see* them doesn't mean they aren't present. Do not underestimate them. These men are experts, trained to blend into your society and obscure their activities from experienced agents like me. They will not be so easy to spot."

"Don't bet on it," Blancanales said from his position seated next to her in back.

As if on cue, three Asian men emerged from the hotel entrance and proceeded down the walkway in front of the building to the parking area. Lyons observed they moved with the ease of practiced professionals, but they were clearly watchful as they sauntered to a nondescript sedan parked at the far end of the lot. The car had been backed into its spot, giving it easy access to the parking lot exit. That seemed a bit noteworthy.

"I'd hazard a guess and say that's the crew," remarked Blancanales.

Lyons nodded. "Agreed."

Schwarz reached for the key to crank the engine but Lyons put a restraining hand on his arm. "Wait up a sec. I want to see which way they go." He turned to look at Young-Soon. "Given you're the self-proclaimed expert here, and now that we've confirmed your story, what will their next move be?"

"It depends on how long it's been since they were first activated," Young-Soon replied. "In the first twelve hours, operating procedure requires they attempt to make contact with any surviving agents on the primary mission team."

"Which would be you," Lyons interjected.

Young-Soon nodded. "This is where I was staying. That's how I knew they might come here in an attempt to contact me."

"And you're not here as far as they know," Blancanales said. "So what would be their next move?"

"It's on this I can't be sure."

"Come on, lady!" Lyons said in a huff. "We don't have time to play footsies with this crew. We brought you along at your insistence. If you can't give us any useful information, we'll just turn you over to the—"

The roar of an engine racing past their sedan drowned him out. Four men occupied the late-model Dodge Charger, and from the very brief look Lyons managed to get he could tell immediately they were government types.

"Are those Feds?" Schwarz asked.

"It's a good bet," Blancanales said. "I'm guessing either Homeland Security or FBI."

"What the hell are they doing here?" Lyons growled.

"I'd say getting into trouble," Blancanales said. "Look."

The trio watched helplessly as two more government vehicles joined the first and all converged on the North Koreans' sedan just as it left the parking lot and prepared to make a right turn onto the road, heading away from where Able Team was parked. The sedan braked just as the closest government vehicle rounded the corner, its right wheel jumping the curb in an attempt to pen them in.

In the next moment, a moment that flashed past quicker than a heartbeat, the target sedan rocketed into Reverse and picked up speed. Simultaneously, one of the North Korean agents leaned out the passenger window, leveled an SMG at the nearest federal vehicle and squeezed the trigger. A fusillade of rounds pepper-danced up to the windshield, causing the glass to spiderweb, effectively obfuscating the view of its occupants.

"Aw, shit," Lyons muttered as he gestured for Schwarz to get it in gear.

The Able Team warrior cranked the engine, slapped the gearshift into Drive and tromped the accelerator. He checked his flank and then whipped into traffic, crossing against all lanes at an extreme angle. Seeing no other entry point, he hollered for his passengers to hold fast and then jumped the curb, taking out a couple of low dried bushes before finding purchase on the parking lot. The maneuver put him on a direct intercept course with the North Koreans.

Lyons unleathered his pistol and checked the load, then asked Young-Soon, "Will they be heavily armed?"

"Yes."

Lyons nodded and returned his attention to Schwarz. "They'll run out of parking lot pretty quick. Get as close as possible but pull us up broadside. Pol, unlock her. We're going to have to do this one EVA."

"Unlock her—have you lost your mind?"

"Just do it!"

Blancanales fished the key from his pocket and quickly liberated their prisoner, muttering oaths under his breath as he did so. Young-Soon rubbed at her wrists subconsciously, even though they both knew the cuffs hadn't been that tight. Blancanales gave her one last look, found her expression unreadable, and then turned to checking his own pistol, a 9 mm Browning Double Action. A variant of the Browning Hi-Power, a pistol favored by David McCarter, FN Herstal no longer actively manufactured or sold the weapon, but Blancanales still liked it. The semiautomatic was lightweight and versatile, and manufactured to FN Herstal's highest standards, which meant it was reliable as hell under even the most adverse conditions.

As Lyons had predicted, the sedan ran out of space and the driver was forced to stop. Able Team's vehicle was now the closest and they were the first to overtake the North Koreans. Schwarz had originally planned to put their vehicle broadside to the enemy, but realized such a move would not only put one side or the other in harm's way, but also wouldn't buy them any time to procure the heavier hardware they had stowed in the trunk. As a result, Schwarz slammed on the brakes and kept the nose pointing forward.

"Good thinking," Lyons said as he understood the reason for his teammate's decision.

"Stay here and stay *down!*" Blancanales ordered Young-Soon before going EVA with his friends.

Schwarz popped the trunk and then opened his door.

He took a knee, aimed his Glock pistol at the enemy's vehicle and squeezed the trigger successively. A chorus of autofire resounded, chopping up ground and punching into the body of the sedan door, which, fortunately for Schwarz, had special Kevlar plating to prevent someone from effecting a prisoner escape by taking out the driver with small-arms fire. The unmarked vehicle also had a bullet-resistant front windshield, another reason Able Team had picked the transport sedan for this particular mission.

Lyons had made his own stand, as well, pumping rounds downrange as fast he could pull the trigger. At one point it looked as if he'd hit a backseat passenger because he spotted what appeared to be a spray of blood before the North Korean disappeared from sight. Whether he'd actually hit him or not Lyons would never know, because the next moment his sight was filled by the gaping maw of a rocket launcher. Lyons turned to Schwarz and yelled at him to get Young-Soon clear before he dashed for whatever cover he could find. He glanced to his right and noticed Blancanales with his nose in the trunk. He was about to stop short and retrieve his partner but Blancanales beat him to the punch, moving away from the vehicle with an assault rifle in hand. Lyons paused a heartbeat longer—enough time to verify Schwarz was in the process of pulling Young-Soon clear—before rushing to the shelter of a nearby pickup.

Their sedan went sky-high just seconds after the whoosh and popping report from the rocket launcher. Superheated fiberglass, metal and steel whistled through the air in the wake of the fireball that followed the impact of the rocket-propelled warhead on the sedan. There was definitely nothing short of an Abrams tank that could've repelled such a heavy assault.

Lyons turned to see Blancanales coming up behind in a crouch, the M-16 A-3 held low but at the ready. "Well, looks like Young-Soon told you the truth about them being heavily armed."

"Yeah," Lyons retorted. "But I didn't think that included high explosives and antiarmor weapons."

Blancanales glanced in the direction of the government vehicles and Lyons followed his gaze. The Dodge Charger and its companion sedans were quickly making haste to put distance between themselves and the North Koreans.

"Smart move, under the circumstances," Blancanales said.

Lyons silently agreed with his friend. "Any sign of Gadgets?"

Blancanales scanned the immediate area in a frantic search but finally looked at Lyons and shook his head, a grim set to his features.

"Well, doesn't mean anything," Lyons said. "I'm sure he got clear and he's just keeping his head down. Probably waiting to see what *we* do."

"Don't forget he's also got his hands full with Young-Soon. He might not be able to provide us with much help."

"True enough," Lyons replied. The Able Team warrior sighed. "Well, we can't wait around here all day. Looks like it's up to us to take action before those North Koreans get it in mind to start blasting apart every vehicle in sight."

"Yes, I wouldn't bet against that."

Lyons thought furiously and finally said, "All right, you've got the only AR. I'm going to change position, see if I can flank them."

"Or at least make them *think* that you're flanking them?"

"Right. When I start moving I'll keep moving, so please put on your marksmanship cap and see if you can't take them down a peg."

"I got your six."

Lyons nodded and then burst from cover without ceremony, running a parallel course to the pickup before he cut to the left, keeping as low as he could while weaving between the vehicles for cover. The lot eventually ended, a fact that he knew would force him into exposing his position. Well, that was what he'd have to do if he wanted to give Blancanales a fighting chance to dish out some of what they'd been taking up to this point. Lyons cut around a panel van and came out at a forty-five-degree point approximately twenty-five yards from the enemy vehicle.

One of the North Koreans had taken up a firing position and was searching so intently ahead of him he didn't notice Lyons. The Able Team leader spotted the rocket launcher now lying near the man's feet, obviously discarded, which probably meant they'd only had one disposable launcher and they'd expended it. Lyons raised his pistol, sighted down the slide and squeezed the trigger in one motion. The .45-caliber slug hit on target, punching through the side of the Korean agent's skull and blowing out the other side, splattering the sedan with a grisly montage.

Lyons's action got the attention of the other two agents, who shifted positions and opened up on him, but he got back to the cover of the van before any of their rounds connected. A different chattering interspersed with reports from the enemy's SMGs; clearly reports from an M-16—Blancanales had given them something new to think about. Lyons ducked around cover long enough to see another of the agents near the driver's-side door crumple to the pavement as Blancanales cut him down.

The last one didn't wait for an invitation, instead breaking off and diving into the sedan. He got behind the wheel and dropped the gearshift before Lyons had a chance to draw a bead on him. The sedan tore from its spot in a screech of tires and smoke from burning rubber. The sedan gained speed and soon made enough distance that to continue shooting would've yielded nothing more than wasted ammunition.

Lyons left his position and sprinted back to find Blancanales waiting where he'd left him, joined by Schwarz and Young-Soon.

"This isn't fun," Schwarz said. "I don't want to play anymore."

Lyons turned to see the government vehicles had regrouped and one was headed in their direction while the other two gave chase to the survivor. Lyons wished he had a way to wave them off but he didn't even know who *they* were. If these were federal agents, however, someone in Washington was going to have a lot of explaining to do.

"Black, take Young-Soon over there to the bodies and see if she can identify either of them. I want to get that information before we have to deal with whoever jumped the gun on us."

Schwarz nodded and gestured for Young-Soon to follow him. Lyons had to admit he was a bit surprised to see she was still with them. Not that he didn't trust Schwarz implicitly to keep an eye on her. It was just that she'd cooperated with them at every step and given whatever information they'd asked of her, which had thrown Lyons for a loop. Sure, she hadn't exactly gone out of her way to be forthcoming with intelligence, but then Lyons wouldn't have expected anything else. Young-Soon was a cool customer, no doubt, and skilled at playing her hand with easy detachment.

The government sedan rolled up on them quickly and three men got out, pistols drawn. Lyons thought about protesting at first, but realized in the next moment it didn't matter because he recognized the front-seat passenger. Their eyes locked for a moment before the same look passed over Captain Cronaugher's features. He lowered his pistol slowly and then gestured at the other two men to do the same.

"Norris? What the hell are you doing here?"

"I was just about to ask you the same question," Lyons replied.

IT TOOK MORE than two hours to sort it out, but Lyons eventually got the full story from Cronaugher.

"You assholes," Lyons said. "If you had information like that, why didn't you just call me?"

"Hey, don't give me that crap about *us* being the assholes, Norris," Cronaugher replied. "You bastards shut us completely out of a case involving the murder of two police officers, then we turn around and find you playing nursemaid to the same woman who killed them! And do I need to remind you that it wasn't our idea for us to take custody of Se-Hong Yu? That was all on your people. Everybody knows you guys were just throwing us a bone with Yu anyway."

"All right, gentlemen," Blancanales said with emphasis on the last word. "Let's not cut into each other. It's been a long, hard day for all and we're supposed to be on the same side."

Lyons and Cronaugher stared at each other long and hard, then looked at Blancanales. Always the politician, Blancanales was pleading in silence to be able to intervene on Able Team's behalf at this point. Lyons knew it—he could tell just by the way Blancanales waited, his hands laced pensively in front of him. Finally, Lyons nodded and Blancanales relaxed some with a sigh and a smile. Blancanales knew his friend was taking a chance showing their cards to the local authorities, and if it went wrong it would be Lyons who took all the heat.

Blancanales turned to Cronaugher and said, "Okay, we've discussed it and we're willing to tell you everything we know. But we don't need an audience."

Cronaugher looked at the other men in the room, a couple of uniforms and two detectives who'd been with him, then cocked his head to indicate they should clear out. Once they were gone, Cronaugher took a seat at the head of the conference table and Blancanales sat to his left. For the next twenty minutes, he relayed the events of the past few days with Cronaugher, interrupting him only on occasion to ask a clarifying question or two.

When Blancanales had finished his narrative, Cronaugher leaned back and rubbed his eyes. "Why couldn't I have just been satisfied with some nice cushy job down south? Maybe a sheriff in a one-horse town."

"Because it's not your style," Lyons said.

Cronaugher looked at him. "How would you know?"

"I told you, I used to *be* a big-city cop. You're a certain type—it's in your blood. And you'd go crazy if you had a nice boring job rousting teenagers drinking at a barn party."

"I suppose you're right," Cronaugher finally admitted after taking a moment's pause to reflect on it. "So it just so happens Yu was supplying weapons to this cleanup team, as well as to the woman and her people."

"Right," Blancanales said. "That's how he was able to tell you where to find them."

"And do you know anything about the one who escaped?"

"Only a name…Wee Hum Han. We've got our people looking into him now."

"Hold on a second," Lyons said. "Something's wrong here. Young-Soon told us that the first thing the cleanup team would do is attempt to locate her."

"Right," Blancanales said.

"So how did they know where to look? She's been out of communication with them from the moment she tried to assassinate Yu."

"Maybe Yu told them," Cronaugher said.

"Uh-uh," Lyons said, shaking his head. He stood and began to circle the room, feeling his second wind kick in. "Yu wouldn't have known that. She was in our custody by that time. There wouldn't have been any reason for Han's people to even go to that hotel. They were activated because Young-Soon's handlers figured the mission was already compromised. Since they thought Young-Soon was the only survivor, there wouldn't have been any point in them going to the hotel unless—"

"Unless they went there to meet someone else!" Cronaugher finished.

"Right," Lyons said.

Blancanales shook his head. "So wait a minute, are you saying you think Young-Soon lied about the rest of her team being dead?"

"That's exactly what I'm saying."

"We need to get back to that hotel," Blancanales said evenly.

"Hold on a second here!" Cronaugher interjected. "What are you guys talking about? I thought you said only one guy escaped, this Weenie Ham."

"Wee Hum Han," Blancanales corrected patiently.

Cronaugher waved him off. "Whatever."

"We don't have time to explain," Lyons said. "We'll explain on the way if you'd be so kind as to give us a lift."

"Yes," Blancanales added. "We seem to be fresh out of transportation at the moment."

CHAPTER TWENTY-ONE

"Say that again?" Lyons said.

They were proceeding toward the hotel in Cronaugher's car, the Anchorage police captain driving like a bat out of hell, as Lyons spoke to Stony Man Farm via a secure satellite uplink.

"Phoenix Force has successfully retrieved Teng Cai," Aaron Kurtzman said. "They just cleared into international airspace and should touch down at Elmendorf-Richardson around 0400 hours your time."

"Well, that's outstanding news," Lyons said. "We're getting spread pretty thin here and we could use their help, so tell them they all need to get their beauty rest. Is the chief there?"

"You just missed him. He took off for Wonderland about forty-five minutes ago. And before you ask for Barb, she's finally down for some sleep. Poor girl was up all night and unless it's something that can't wait, I'd prefer not to wake her up."

"No, nothing that can't wait. Just let her know that I had to involve the local authorities in what's happening here and not to worry. We have it under control."

"Oh, I'm sure she'll love hearing *that*."

"And do me a favor?"

"What's that?" Kurtzman asked hesitantly.

"Try to tell her nicely, you know?"

"What do you mean?"

"I don't know," Lyons huffed. "Just…make sure she has her coffee or some hot tea. Maybe a Danish. She likes chocolate, yeah—give her a chocolate Danish. And tell her we send lots of hugs and kisses with the message."

"Are you insane? I'm not telling her that, buddy. You're on your own this time."

"So much for teamwork," Lyons said before he signed off.

"Trouble at home?" Cronaugher said, casting a sideways glance at Lyons before returning his eyes to the road.

"None I haven't been in before. Can't this thing go any faster?"

"I could go code but you said you didn't want to alert this guy."

"Hey, Carl, just how exactly do you plan to find this guy?" Schwarz asked. "It's not like he took out a full-page ad he was staying there."

"And I don't have enough to get you a warrant," Cronaugher said.

"We'll just have to improvise," Lyons replied.

Cronaugher looked askance at the Able Team leader and said, "You're not really with the Office of Naval Intelligence, are you?"

"We are as far as you're concerned," Blancanales interjected before his friend could conjure what he knew would be a more flippant retort. "And don't worry about any repercussions by what we may be about to do. I can personally guarantee they won't fall back on you in any fashion."

"What you may be about to do?" Cronaugher retorted. "Well, gee, I feel better already."

Five minutes later Cronaugher had steered into the

parking lot and pulled up beneath the massive overhang at the front entrance to the hotel.

As Able Team exited the vehicle, Lyons said, "I'm not sure what we're going to be up against so why don't you pull around back and cover the rear entrances."

"Roger that." At the last moment the police captain called after Lyons and held out a radio. "Here, stay in touch."

Lyons almost refused it and then thought better and took the handheld. If they were going to ask Cronaugher to step into potential danger, the least they could do was treat the guy like just another member of the team. The trio assembled at the revolving door and with a nod from Lyons, entered the posh lobby of the hotel. Blancanales and Schwarz immediately fanned out as Lyons strolled to the front desk. As he withdrew his badge he looked conspiratorially in each direction before flipping the credentials onto the desk in front of the youngest of the several attendants.

"Federal agent, miss," he said quietly. "I'm following up on the incident that occurred outside your hotel this morning. We have reason to believe there may be a man wanted in connection with that incident still inside the hotel. However, we believe he had an accomplice that checked him in under an assumed name."

"Really?" the young girl said loudly.

Lyons immediately shushed her and then reverted to a more congenial tone. "I'm sorry, but we don't want to start a panic, now, do we?"

"No, I'm sorry," she said, lowering her voice and looking more properly scared now.

"I don't have a name, all I have is a description," Lyons

said. "He'd be a younger man, early thirties, most likely Korean descent. Do you recall seeing anybody like that?"

She pursed her lips a moment and furrowed her brow. "No, I don't think so…wait. I don't remember seeing a man but I do remember seeing a woman. She was Asian."

"When was this?"

"Yesterday morning."

Bingo, Lyons thought. "What did she look like?"

"Oh, she was very small but really cute. Long dark hair, Asian features, beautiful. I thought maybe she was Chinese but I suppose she could've been Korean."

"Do you remember her name?"

"That much I don't," she said. "But I do recall the room number."

"That will do," Lyons said. "Would you please give it to me?"

"I'm sorry, Agent…?"

"Norris."

"I'm sorry, sir, but I cannot give out any guest information without a warrant."

Lyons looked around to see if a manager or senior attendant was watching but the others that had been there were no longer present, apparently off on other errands or taking a break. He turned back to the girl and smiled, wishing he'd brought Blancanales in to play the part of nice guy.

"Look…Melissa, is it?" Lyons continued, reading her name tag. "Melissa, you did hear about what happened out here this morning?"

"Yes, it's terrible."

"And did you know two people were killed?"

"I heard there was an explosion and some shooting," she replied. "I didn't hear anybody had been killed."

"Well, there were two men killed," Lyons said. "And we now think that one of the men responsible for that tragedy may be upstairs right now, this very moment. And if that's true then he's armed and he poses a significant threat to your customers. So here's what I'm going to do. I promise you won't get into any trouble if you just tell me the room number so we can go up and quietly investigate. Don't you think that would be better than dragging in a whole SWAT team and a bunch of FBI agents, getting the hotel in a big ruckus and perhaps someone else getting hurt? Do you really want all of that to happen? I don't."

"No, no, of course not," she said. She looked around self-consciously to ensure nobody was within earshot and then she punched up something on the terminal in front of her. "Yes, it was a Dr. Soo Yung. She checked into room 518."

"Thank you. Thank you very much, you're a good citizen." Lyons turned on his heel and nodded at his companions.

The three men headed for the elevators but at the last minute Lyons instructed them to go on without him and he'd take the stairwell. He knew Young-Soon's man probably wouldn't be expecting them but he didn't want to take any chances. Lyons doubted that Han's people had killed the guy—that would've been messy and pointless and only serve to call attention to them. That meant either they'd found the guy dead because he'd succumbed to his injuries, or he'd convinced Han's people he still had the situation under control. That meant the North Koreans still posed a threat to the Chinese, and the Gold Star Faction wouldn't leave any stones unturned.

Well, Able Team was about to kick those stones to see just what crawled out from under them.

CHIN NAM SPLASHED his face with cupped hands of cold water a few times and then lifted his head from the washbasin and looked at his reflection. He could hardly believe the face staring at him was his own. His skin looked pale and yellowish in the light, with dark circles below his eyes puffy enough to alter their normal almond shape. Nearly a week's worth of beard stubble now lined his upper lip and jawline.

Pain coursed through his shoulder. He stopped to ease the bandage away and studied the deep wound that would eventually develop into a pucker scar—if he lived long enough for it to fully heal. It was no longer as angry red as at first, and the fever had finally left his body, which meant he was probably out of danger of dying from infection. Had it not been for Ju Young-Soon stealing the painkillers and antibiotics, and her deft if raw surgical skills in removing the bullet, Nam would surely have succumbed to his wounds and died a slow, painful death. After inspection, Nam decided now would be the best time to change the bandage since he didn't know when the opportunity might arise again. As he worked, he considered his current dilemma.

Young-Soon was in the hands of the Americans, and he knew there was little he could do about it. His only bet had been to work with Wee Hum Han in attempting a rescue and destroying the prototype missile—or at least assassinating the scientist charged with discovering its origin. Han had dismissed out of hand any attempt to rescue Young-Soon, insistent that they stick to the mission protocol as defined by their superiors—a mission that included eliminating Young-Soon should she fall into the hands of their enemies. While Nam realized he was expected to submit to Han's authority, he also felt his obligation to Young-Soon as both his superior and the woman who saved his life superseded all of that.

And he was in love with her. It didn't get any simpler than that, though he'd never been able to bring himself to tell her how he felt. He wouldn't have dared—not while they were in the middle of a mission! He'd sworn earlier that morning when Han first arrived with his team, however, that if he got the chance to rescue Young-Soon he wouldn't hesitate to tell her how he felt. All of that assumed he'd get the opportunity to make that rescue attempt, but after his meeting with Han he'd finally drafted a plan that would afford him the opportunity to at least make the attempt while making Han think he was following protocol.

Nam had witnessed the entire violent exchange between Wee Hum Han's team and the American police—he'd also seen that Han was the only one to escape. The two would need each other now more than ever. Han would be desperate to either conclude the mission or to escape alive to exact his revenge another day and redeem himself with their masters in North Korea. What Han didn't realize, and Nam did, was that there was now no going back to their country in any case. They would not be welcome based on their performance, to make no mention there were several probable outcomes at this point.

Nam held no illusions on that account. They were outnumbered, lacking weapons and resources. Their main arms supplier had been incarcerated and most of the primary and cleanup team members were dead. Unless the North Korean Security Ministry decided to send another cleanup team, their chances of evading capture and escaping Alaska were slim. That left Nam with no other options.

Clearing his mind of all the possible scenarios and returning to the moment at hand, Nam completed the bandaging job, swathing the shoulder extra-tightly. He wouldn't want the wound to start bleeding spontaneously and leak through the dressing. He left the bathroom and walked to where a clean shirt lay draped across the bed. He donned and buttoned it, and then slid into the shoulder holster and checked the action on the .380-caliber pistol before securing it. Nam then put on a black silk tie and completed his ensemble with a black leather jacket.

Nam went to the closet where all of his and Ju Young-Soon's spare clothes had been hung neatly. He grabbed two changes of her clothes, and one additional for himself and, stuffed them into his overnight bag. He dumped the rest of the clothes from the closet on the bed. He then proceeded to the wet bar, selected two miniature bottles of clear alcohol and emptied them both onto the clothes. He withdrew a lighter from his pocket and set fire to the pile. The distraction complete, Nam dropped his access cards onto the spreading flames, slung the bag over his good shoulder and left the hotel room.

Strolling casually down the hallway to the elevators, Nam stabbed the down button. When the elevator arrived, he moved aside with a smile to permit a young, giggling couple to exit before he stepped inside and jabbed the button to close the doors. He slipped a key card lifted from a housekeeping cart and swiped it over the magnetic access panel, then pressed the button for the basement. Previous studies of the hotel plans had noted that there was a basement with a subterranean parking garage for staff and deliveries. One of those delivery vans would be leaving shortly.

The button marked B lit to green and Nam smiled with

satisfaction, confident the elevator would go straight to the basement first and not stop to let anyone else on. The bet paid off and within a minute he'd stepped off the elevator and entered an empty corridor. He glanced at a nearby clock and saw it was just after six. It wouldn't be dark for a few hours yet, but that didn't matter since he'd already figured out his plan. As he passed a row of carts, he dropped the access card lanyard onto one of the hooks—they would assume the thing had simply been misplaced.

It only took Nam a minute to then reach the garage and locate a delivery van. Like most hotels, this one shipped out its laundry to an external facility for cleaning. Nam climbed into the back of the delivery van and wriggled his body into the mountain of sealed plastic bags filled with dirty towels, rugs and linen. He then piled some over him to conceal himself fully before settling into the makeshift cushion of the full bags and waiting. He'd seen the vans for the past few days between six-thirty and six forty-five.

Chin Nam wouldn't have long to wait.

WHEN WEE HUM HAN arrived at the small apartment his team had been using as a base of operations, he didn't proceed immediately inside. To panic would be insane. Instead, Han waited for a while in his vehicle parked at a spot about a half block from the building, patiently observing the comings and goings of residents. He didn't see any vehicles parked with occupants who appeared to be casing the building, and he didn't spot any police vehicles making routine passes.

Finally convinced he was clear, Han started his car and proceeded two blocks before parking it in an underground lot that charged only for business days. As this was a weekend, he didn't have to worry about any record of his entering the lot. And by the time anybody got suspicious enough to actually have the police check out the vehicle—something that probably wouldn't happen for days or possibly even weeks—Han would be long gone.

As he hoofed it to the apartment building, Han considered his next move. His team had been all but obliterated and he knew he couldn't trust Chin Nam. Although they had an appointment to rendezvous here within two hours, Han half expected Nam wouldn't show up. He knew of Han's allegiance to Young-Soon and to some degree he understood it. But now wasn't the time to allow themselves to succumb to nostalgia. They had one mission at this point: the elimination of anything that could compromise their country and the destruction of any evidence that might make it appear as if the North Koreans had manufactured the Chinese prototype.

Han pressed his chilled lips together grimly as he slid the key into the lock of the second-floor apartment door and stepped into the darkened interior. The North Korean assassin knew he also had the Chinese secret agencies to worry about. Intelligence from his people had made it clear the Gold Star Faction would send their own assassination team in an attempt to eliminate him and his colleagues. Han wondered how much he could trust that intelligence, frankly. The only way the Chinese could know the North Koreans were here trying to salvage this situation would be if they *knew* about it from the start. That would mean the bogus intel about the prototype had been fed to his people from the start.

So what did it all come down to? Was there a spy within the North Korean Ministry of Security that had been inserted to feed them false intelligence, or were they being observed and their actions reported back to the Chinese? Han didn't find it difficult to believe the GSF had their own people operating inside most of the countries in Asia, his own included, but their counterintelligence services should've been good enough to see a fake like this if they were. The other possibility was that the Chinese had foreseen how this would transpire from the beginning and someone with a lot of smarts had put this plan together based on certain tactical assumptions.

Wee Hum Han simply couldn't accept that latter scenario. No, this had been bogus intelligence fed to his people from the start. The Americans were treating Ju Young-Soon with kid gloves and they had seemed able to predict the moves of his own people right from the beginning. That meant they'd had to see through the deception, as well, and it didn't take a genius to see through the deception. The GSF's leaders would have already figured that out, by now. They *would* send their people to close the loop and the Americans would be eternally grateful, ready to hand over whomever they had or whatever they knew to the Chinese once they were convinced the North Koreans had duped them.

Perhaps Young-Soon's actions here had been the correct ones from the start. Well, that wasn't up to him to decide. Han was a veteran and he'd learned to follow orders. That was the only way to survive in the world of foreign intelligence. The Americans had already demonstrated they weren't afraid to shoot it out with him or his people, and they had the advantage of home territory. That left Han with only one option: he had to make sure Ju Young-Soon was silenced as a liability. If he had to eliminate Chin Nam to see that through, he would do it.

Once he'd closed and secured the door behind him,

Han shrugged out of his heavy coat and bumped up the thermostat a few degrees before putting water on to boil. Some tea would warm his feet and take some of the ache from his bones. While he waited for the kettle to signal, Han set about the task of cleaning the two pistols and the subgun he'd brought. The remainder he'd left in a second rental parked about two miles from the apartment. They would need to make use of that tomorrow morning. It would provide their only means of escape after they completed their mission: the assassination of Ju Young-Soon. And maybe, if the odds were with them, Han hoped he'd get a chance for a rematch with the Americans who had foiled him today.

Even if he died in the attempt, it would prove a fitting and honorable end for both Wee Hum Han and his enemies.

CHAPTER TWENTY-TWO

As soon as Able Team emerged on the floor where they believed Young-Soon's partner was staying, they drew their pistols and converged as a unit. When they reached the door to room 518, Blancanales put his ear close to it and listened for any sounds from inside. He didn't hear anything. He then pressed his palm to the door and pushed to get a sense for how thick it was. Satisfied they could take the thing down on their own, he nodded at.

Lyons returned the nod and then gestured at Schwarz to take a position alongside Blancanales facing the door. With a finger countdown from Lyons, the two each slammed a side-kick to the door, and it busted at the lock and swung inward with practically enough force to take it off its hinges. The pair went in low but immediately reeled back as a gust of dark smoke rushed them along with a terrible heat. Had it not been for their equally swift reactions, the skin on their faces and hands might have been seared off rather than just suffering the singing of hairs on their arms.

"Shit!" Lyons roared as he dived into the hallway.

Schwarz and Lyons began to cough, their lungs nearly overwhelmed by the smoke and heat. Blancanales holstered his pistol and grabbed each of them by an arm, dragging his teammates a decent enough distance they could recover on their own. As they climbed to their feet, Lyons broke into another fit of spasmodic coughing, trying to clear his lungs of the horrific effects of the combustibles.

"Trip that fire alarm, Pol," Lyons finally managed to say, but Blancanales was already on it.

The trio then made their way down the steps and reached the main lobby within a minute. Lyons went to the front desk and advised the clerk, Melissa, to contact the fire department and let them know it wasn't a drill before they made a hasty exit. Schwarz, into whose custody Lyons had entrusted the police radio, had already contacted Cronaugher during their descent in the stairwell. The cop had their vehicle waiting at the curb and as soon as the three were aboard he pulled out of the hotel lot.

"Whew, you guys smell like you've been at a fire," he declared with a wry grin.

"Yeah, you're a regular laugh-riot," Lyons replied.

"Oh, don't be such a sourpuss, Norris. But now I'm left wondering what's next?"

"That's a pretty good question," Schwarz remarked between a few fresh coughs of his own. "What *is* next?"

"Yeah, and the even bigger question is, was Young-Soon's partner actually inside that room and now he's a crispy critter, or was he the one who set the fire?"

Lyons shook his head. "I don't think he was inside that room."

"Why not?" Cronaugher said. "Until the fire department gets here and we get an official report of casualties, we're shooting completely in the dark on this whole international plot you've cooked up."

"'Cooked up'?" Blancanales scoffed from the backseat. "I'd say what happened earlier today with Wee Hum Han and his men pretty much solidifies our theory there are international intelligence agencies involved."

"He's right," Lyons said. "This has become way more than a theory, Cronaugher, and we both know it."

"Okay, I'll give you some heavy shit's definitely gone down the past few days in our relatively quiet town here. Missiles and North Korean killing teams buying guns from black-market arms dealers. But you can't argue with the fact we all but ran this Han character out of town."

"No, *we* ran him out of town," Lyons reminded Cronaugher. "All you guys did was nearly provide cannon fodder for Han. You're not dealing with amateurs here, Cronaugher. These people are first-class professionals who have been trained for this very kind of thing. No amount of annex courses and one week of antiterrorist training you guys have to undergo every couple of years is going to prepare you for stuff like this."

"The dick-flexing aside..." Blancanales interjected, "did you notice anything out of the ordinary when you parked out back?"

"Nope," Cronaugher replied. "All was quiet except for a couple of hotel vans that pulled out of an underground parking garage."

"Vans?"

The cop nodded at Blancanales in the rearview mirror. "Yeah. There's an underground parking facility at the hotel where they make deliveries and such."

"Underground parking garage?" Schwarz's eyebrows arched in a mixed expression of confusion and anger. "Why the hell didn't you tell us?"

"I didn't even remember it until I pulled around back. It's only for employees and delivery people. I doubt your guy could even get access to it, and even if he could—"

"How long after we went in did you see those vans pull out?" Lyons cut in.

"I don't know. What difference does it make?"

"Just *think!*"

"Oh for crissake… Maybe, uh, maybe five or ten minutes?"

"That would've been plenty of time enough for him to set the fire and then get to the basement," Schwarz pointed out.

"But how would he have gained access to the area?" Cronaugher asked. "As I recall, you have to have a special key—a coded access card you swipe in the elevator. I've been down there before on a few occasions, back when I was a patrolman and later as a detective."

"How else?" Lyons growled. "He lifted it off one of the housekeeping staff. I'll bet he knew the schedule of those vans down to practically the minute. Probably hid in one of them and then rode out of the hot zone right under our noses."

Lyons slammed his fist into his palm. "Damn it! We had the guy and we let him skate."

"Maybe not," Blancanales said. "Captain Cronaugher, you said you've been down in that basement before."

"Right."

"Where would those vans be going?"

"Well…probably the laundry facilities if I had to guess. The hotel contracts out those services because the hotel's so massive and they don't have large enough facilities in-house. They take all their internal linens there, as well as any laundry sent out for dry-cleaning by their guests."

"You know where this place is?" Lyons asked.

"Out on the edge of the city."

"Then that's where we need to go," Lyons replied as he checked his watch. "If those vans left when you said they did, we're only about ten minutes behind them. We might be able to catch up to this guy."

"That's a long shot, Norris," Cronaugher retorted.

"Maybe, but it's the only one we got. So step on it."

Ju Young-Soon peered through the bars of the holding cell at the Anchorage police headquarters and looked fixedly at the guard stationed down the hallway. Through the sore muscles that came from her wrestling match with the big blond American to the migrainelike ache in her head from worrying about Chin Nam, Young-Soon found it impossible to sleep. She'd tossed and turned on the thin mattress of the bunk in her isolation cell, the creak and biting of the springs firing the nerves in her back. Neither the mattress nor the ratty wool blanket was able to protect her sufficiently from their torment.

The shouting of criminals and drunks, the slam of cell doors and the regular conversations between bored cops only added to her misery. Finally, Young-Soon sat on the bunk, back to the wall, and tried some form of meditation while staring at the guard at the far end. Eventually the exercises worked and her troubles melted away—she found solace in the memories of her childhood. Certainly life had been simpler then, playing in the park that bordered her school, the evenings at home with her parents.

Young-Soon couldn't remember a time where her entire family hadn't been engaged in government service. It wasn't as much the pro-Communist views of the government officials and political power brokers—merely leftover fodder from another place and time—as it was those members of her family had served the North Korean people out of a sense of duty. It had been a question of honor and dignity, a tradition and way of life for her ancestors, and Young-Soon had always known she would follow in the steps of that tradition. Her father's connections had eventually landed her in a college with a full scholarship; something she'd learned later would come with a significant price.

When her masters in the security service had first approached her about training to become a spy, the young Ju Young-Soon had resisted. She'd fallen deeply in love with a boy while at school and after graduation she'd planned to become an instructor at a military college. Once she'd obtained tenure, she would marry the man she'd met in college—a man to whom she'd given away her heart and virginity—raise beautiful children and have a long and happy life with her family. Her dreams came to a crashing halt when her fiancé suddenly disappeared just prior to her graduation. Shortly thereafter, her parents were killed in a tragic accident that nobody had ever been able to explain fully to her satisfaction.

As a result of those losses, Young-Soon turned to the only other entity she'd known had always taken care of her, always been there when she needed it. Young-Soon immediately enrolled in the NKMFS upon graduation. She excelled while in training, attacking every subject like a leopardess upon unwitting prey. Eventually, she graduated with top honors and was immediately thrown into her first assignment, one that she completed in record time and with very positive results. Her masters were so impressed it wasn't long before she was assigned to lead teams on assignments it would take most other agents years to attain.

That she had bungled this operation so completely disturbed her greatly, and it was while calming herself during meditation that she realized she couldn't do this. She had actually bordered on the betrayal of her country instead of taking appropriate action to prevent the enemies of her country from smearing the pride and heritage of her government. After all, despite the fact the North Korean officials had adamantly refused to back down from their nuclear development was hardly a reason for her to take the guilt of their actions solely upon her shoulders. She'd been given an assignment and she had failed to accomplish it. Despite the fact the Americans had convinced her to give up Wee Hum Han, Young-Soon had managed to hide Nam's existence from them, hoping that he would seize the advantage and get out of America while he could.

Now she'd been led to believe that he would instead attempt to rescue her from them. She couldn't allow that. To wait for Nam to put himself in danger out of some sense of devotion to her was beyond contemptible—the only way to prevent it was to change her operational plan. The military police that'd been guarding her at the airbase had followed every SOP when dealing with her, but the guards here were somewhat lax. She'd spotted on many occasions her ability to overcome them and facilitate an escape, a fact she'd merely noted and filed away for future use if such a time came. That time had come and she proposed to use it. She looked through the bars set into the small window high above her head and estimated the time. Yes, they would be bringing her supper any minute now.

As if on cue, the clang of the main entrance door reverberated down the cavernous corridor of the cell block and the clop of rubber-lugged soles on the painted concrete greeted her ears. Young-Soon waited until the matron who'd brought her meal had reached the cell door before

she opened her eyes slowly, pretending she'd been doz-
ing, squinting like a cat being friendly. Inside, Ju Young-
Soon smiled with how casually the matron opened the
cell door with the key from a ring dangling on her belt
and then pushed it aside with one of her wide hips before
bringing the tray into the cell.

Young-Soon leaped from the bed as the matron turned
her back on her to exit the cell. The woman was broad and
stockier than Young-Soon, but about the same height and
not anywhere near in as good a shape as her opponent.
Young-Soon had snaked a forearm around the matron's
neck and relieved her of the small bulge she'd spotted in
the matron's pocket. None of the guards was supposed
to carry a weapon of any kind, but Young-Soon knew
when she saw someone carrying a weapon. The gaits,
the mannerisms, the faux confidence—all were symp-
toms of someone who was armed but knew they weren't
supposed to be. Most of these untrained boobs had a tell,
each one a bit different and some certainly less obvious
than others, but against the trained eye their dirty little
secrets had no effect. By the time the matron realized she
was under attack it was somewhat too late.

The matron managed to get out a garbled scream, long
enough and loud enough to alert the guard at the desk
down the corridor. The young officer who was fresh-faced
and clearly inexperienced. He had been on duty when
they'd brought Young-Soon to the holding facilities until
the federal agents were finished with Captain Cronaugher
and able to return her to the airbase. He rushed headlong
into the fray, the can of mace appearing in his hand, completely unaware that Young-Soon already had the matron's weapon. The truncheon was the telescopic kind
that extended to approximately three full feet in length.

Young-Soon hadn't used one in some time but she still remembered her training with a number of weapons ranging from unarmed combat to assault rifles, and there were certain principles drilled into her that didn't change whatever the mechanism. Combat was combat, and Young-Soon knew the arts pretty well.

The guard brought the mace to bear but realized he risked exposing the matron, although it was something from which she'd recover. Young-Soon made good use of the guard's momentary hesitation to bring the truncheon into full extension with a flick of her wrist. The next moment she had the weapon in full swing and made contact with the male guard's jaw, the crack of metal on bone echoing through the cavernous hallway. There were shouts of glee mixed with outright cheers from some of the other inmates, but Young-Soon ignored them as well as the periodic pleas to free the prisoners—she would have none of that. They were criminals and drunkards, the worst sort of scum, and she would not have them as allies.

Unless…

The idea came to her in such a flash of insight that Young-Soon could hardly contain her smile. First she would have to deal with the matron, which she did by delivering a palm strike behind the woman's ear. The blow caused the matron's body to go slack as it rendered her unconscious. Young-Soon fished the keys from the matron's belt and quickly walked the cell block until she found what she sought: the three massive gang bikers in leather jackets brought in earlier. She remembered hearing their drunken revelry. She could think of no better allies because while they might have intolerable scruples, she remembered reading that bikers did have a certain moral code among like-minded types.

Young-Soon opened their cell door and stepped into the shadowy interior, keeping part of her senses alert for more guards who might have come to investigate the noise. All three bikers were barely awake, still somewhat intoxicated, one of them even snoring. Young-Soon kicked the bunk of the sleeper and he immediately came awake, wiping the drool from his lips with a meaty palm followed by a furious stream of curses.

"Wake up!" Young-Soon demanded.

As the bikers came to, Young-Soon noticed they'd been placed with a fourth person who clearly did not belong among their rank. The guy was very big, however, and looked considerably mean. She recalled the guards having to fight with this one quite a bit to even get him into the cell, and she wondered how much that had to do with the present company they'd forced upon him in the form of these idiotic, drunken slobs. Whatever else the man might have thought of his biker companions, it was clear he carried somewhat of a newfound lust for the exotic-looking Young-Soon.

The man had dark hair and dark eyes. Those eyes were mean and beady, like the eyes of a rabid dog, and as he rose, the prurient intent in his expression and body language was quite evident to Young-Soon. Good—she'd hoped to use him as a demonstration tool for the bikers.

Young-Soon waited until the man was nearly on top of her before she brought the truncheon that she'd held out of view behind her leg into action. Her first blow caught the man under the point of the chin with the flat, polished ball on the end, applying enough force to cause the weapon to collapse as designed. Young-Soon flicked her wrist to bring it to full extension and delivered a debilitating blow to the outer, bony protuberance of the left knee.

As he folded and collapsed under the blow, Young-Soon rotated the handle and brought it crashing into the top of the man's skull, knocking him completely senseless. For the finish, Young-Soon pivoted into a circular motion, her body flowing quickly and smoothly into a position directly behind her opponent, the metal truncheon now firmly pressed into the man's throat.

Young-Soon gritted her teeth as she pulled, driving the unyielding cold metal into her opponent's windpipe. She pulled strongly and steadily, using the man's shock at her ferocious attack as a point of weakness she fully intended to exploit. It was eerie that he could make no sound, the result of completely having his airway occluded. Although at some point he managed to deliver a whistle, which was the result of crushed bone that penetrated the soft point of his neck and the escape of what little air remained in his starved lungs. Young-Soon waited until the last possible moment before releasing her hold and delivering a front snap kick that drove the man's head into the bars with enough force to crush his skull.

Young-Soon whirled on the three bikers who now sat in stunned silence at what they'd witnessed. They had been in many brawls, certainly, and probably even shared in their own moments of murder and mayhem. What they probably hadn't done, however, was witness the wisp of a woman such as this apply such fierce techniques against a man twice her size with unquestionably brutal if effectively murderous results.

"Listen to me very carefully," Young-Soon said. "I have the option of leaving you here but I believe it would be better for all of us if we worked together. Let us assume I can get you out of here. Is there some place you can take me—perhaps you have transportation?"

"Our rides are probably in the impound lot," one of the bikers stammered.

"And where is that?"

"Out back," the biker who'd been sleeping finally managed to reveal.

Young-Soon nodded curtly. "It is good enough, then. I will strip the woman of her uniform. You will then secure her and the male in the cell. If you betray me—" she pointed at the crumpled corpse of their fellow inmate "—that will be your lot. Do you understand?"

The men all nodded in furious affirmation.

CHAPTER TWENTY-THREE

Able Team and Cronaugher had nearly reached the laundering facilities on the southern edge of Anchorage when the news came through over the radio that Ju Young-Soon had escaped. Lyons was furious when he heard it, but he held off comment until Cronaugher had the opportunity to call in personally to the desk sergeant and get the details of what exactly had transpired. By the time Cronaugher had finished relating the story, Lyons's blood was boiling.

"Some incompetent back at your headquarters needs his head beat in!"

"Hey, we were doing *you* a favor," Cronaugher said.

"Favor or no favor, it's inexcusable," Lyons replied. "This woman killed two of your men and nearly killed *me*. You knew she was dangerous. Didn't you take the proper measures to make sure she remained secure?"

"Look, Norris, I don't think—"

"Men!" Blancanales cut in. "I hate to interrupt this lover's spat, but don't you think maybe we ought to figure out what to do about this and worry about who's to blame and whether proper security measures were implemented later?"

The two fell silent but there was no mistaking the wall of adversity between them. Cronaugher took the first exit off the main road and turned the squad car around.

"What are you doing?" Schwarz inquired.

"Turning around, going back to headquarters. There's

a BOLO out on this Ju Young-Soon and we got every swinging dick coming in to assist in the manhunt. I have to be there to lead one of the squads."

"We need to stop this guy," Blancanales protested, looking at Lyons.

Lyons shook his head. "Sorry, but I have to agree with Cronaugher on this one. Young-Soon poses the greater threat."

"The police can—"

"No, they *can't*. We put her there under their watch, but she's still one hundred percent our responsibility. They're not trained to handle her—we are, and she has to be the greater priority right now."

Cronaugher cleared his throat. "Onc male officer and a matron were found locked up in a cell unconscious—fortunately, both of them will live. Our intelligence squad indicates the woman left with three men from a local biker gang by dressing as a uniformed officer. The bikers probably helped her overpower the guards."

"Don't bet on it," Blancanales interjected. "Chances are better than good she did it all on her own."

"Then she's more dangerous than even our people were led to believe, because she also allegedly murdered a third man, an inmate, without any apparent provocation or motive."

"She had a reason," Lyons said. "It might not have made sense to you but it made sense to her. In fact, I'd bet she did it to send a message to the biker gang in order to solicit their cooperation. You're not dealing with some local yokel here, Cronaugher. This woman is a well-trained espionage agent with the North Koreans, and extremely resourceful. That makes her dangerous and we shouldn't underestimate her capabilities on any point."

"Then why the fuck would you put someone like that in our general holding cells without warning, Norris? If anyone's to blame for this it's you guys for not giving us the full lay of the land."

"We're digressing," Blancanales reminded the pair gently.

"What I don't understand is why she broke out," Schwarz said. "It doesn't make any sense at all. She was cooperative with us from the beginning, never attempted to escape and never resisted at any point. She even provided verifiable information during her interrogation. Why bust out of jail now and risk any deal she might've been able to swing with the federal boys? She has to know this is surely going to land her in Gitmo—that's assuming the Anchorage police don't just blow her away on sight."

"Could you blame them?" Lyons asked, a retort that brought him a surprised look from Cronaugher.

"He is right, though," Blancanales said. "Her move here doesn't make a bit of sense. She was cooperating with us, not to mention she was looking at a pretty good deal from the American government in exchange for her cooperation. Even if the CIA decided to step in and whisk her away somewhere down the line, she at least would've made a decent life for herself. This now definitely makes her Public Enemy Number One in the eyes of all parties involved. She just signed her own death warrant."

"Agreed," Lyons replied. "And for her to do something like this, the stakes have to be *very* high."

Schwarz glanced at his watch. "Well, whatever her reasons, we'd best track her down and do it quickly. David and friends will be landing at the base in just eight short hours, and I don't think they'll be in a terribly good mood if they find out they've stepped into another bad situation."

"They'll adjust as they need to," Lyons said. "You can be sure of that."

"So what's your next move, then?" Cronaugher asked. "We can't just drive around here wasting gasoline."

"I was actually about to ask you the same question," Lyons said.

"Me?"

"Why not? This is your city and I'm guessing with all your years on the job you must have some ideas about where these bikers might take a little lady who just favored them with a good old-fashioned jailbreak. Plus the fact that going back to your headquarters probably won't be the best use of your time."

"Not to mention the three of us aren't going to be a very welcome sight back there," Schwarz said.

Cronaugher scratched at the stubble on his chin and appeared to consider it. "Well, the bikers up here aren't generally known to have one particular hangout. They're a bit scattered and most of them are little more than motorcycle clubs with members that range from blue-collar workers to executives. Hell, they're more yuppies who love bikes, not really hardened criminals.

"But I don't really think that can be said of this group. So if that's the case, these guys are all probably part of the skinhead movement that recently saw a resurgence here. I don't really know where they've set up shop since that hasn't been an area I've had to deal with for a long time. After the Hell's Angels got taken down in the late eighties, most of the gig here has been turned over to the FBI Anchorage office. They've refocused their efforts toward countering international terrorism."

"So where does that leave us?"

"Well, there's a gal I know that works with JTTF here. She specializes in crimes against children, but she used to be part of the Gang Crimes Intelligence unit attached to Anchorage. If anyone knows who's operating in this region and where, she'd be the one."

"Sounds like it's time to go pay the Joint Terrorism Task Force a visit," Carl Lyons replied.

"I REALLY APPRECIATE this, Bernie," Cronaugher said. "I know it's very late."

"It's not *very* late, it's ungodly!" Bernicia Ralston replied. "Do you know what kind of deep, dark hole I'm risking for myself even meeting you down here like this? The information you're asking for is classified, strictly need-to-know. My supervisor would tack my hide to a wall if he discovered I was here giving it out for free."

Ralston paused long enough to cast an appraising gaze at the three men accompanying him. They were federal agents, so they claimed, but they were very rough around the edges. These weren't typical bureaucrats and they weren't Agency. They carried themselves almost like a black-ops team, maybe NSA or DOD. The blond one seemed especially fidgety, and all of them looked tired with nerves frayed at the edges.

Ralston returned her gaze to Cronaugher and then sighed. "Oh, hell, what am I complaining about? You've done lots of favors for me over the years. Least I can do is repay you for that much."

"Thanks, you're a doll," Cronaugher said with a grin.

Ralston pressed her lips together and shook her head with an expression that added a lot more years to her somewhat elegant face than was fair. "I have two ex-husbands who might disagree with you about that, but it's sweet of you to say anyhow."

Ralston wiped her hands on her jeans before taking a seat behind her desk and logging into her computer. As she typed, she said, "I'm going to log into the national database rather than our local office. A lot more requests get funneled through there at all hours, so many that it probably won't even be noticed. And if it is, it'll be weeks or months before anyone inquires why I was inquiring, which will make it more feasible if I simply say, 'Gee, I forget.'"

Ralston paused as she waited for the information to be displayed on her screen, her delicate fingers dancing across the keyboard. At long last she let out a victorious, "Aha," before gesturing for Cronaugher to come around the desk and take a look at the entries.

Cronaugher squinted over her shoulder to see them. "Looks like…hmm. All those entries point to the same address."

"Yeah, the address given by parolees with the Iron Circle Club."

Cronaugher nodded. "I know that address, although I haven't been out that way in years. It used to be the closest thing this city had to an old honky-tonk but I recall it burned down. Wait a minute—are you *kidding* me?"

"What?" Lyons inquired.

Cronaugher looked up from the screen at him with incredulity. "These guys actually applied and were approved as a 501-C organization back in 2005."

Blancanales frowned. "A not-for-profit?"

"Yes," Ralston replied, tapping a couple more keys. "It appears they applied for this status to rebuild and restore homes damaged by fire. They collected quite a bit of money, too, according to the tax records. The IRS audited them the first two years but when they found the books squeaky clean they laid off. They've been in business ever since. And you were right about that place burning down, Cronaugher. One of the first jobs the ICC did was restoring that place as a diner and pub. They even got the deputy mayor of Anchorage to come out for a ribbon-cutting ceremony."

Cronaugher shook his head. "I don't think there's much doubt that's where they took our missing prisoner."

"What's this all about anyway?" Ralston asked, swiveling in her chair to look the cop directly in the eyes.

Cronaugher looked a little uncomfortable and glanced at his associates for help.

What the hell? Lyons thought. What's it going to hurt—the cat's out of the bag anyway. The Able Team leader said, "The Anchorage police were watching a federal prisoner for us. You heard what went down at the hotel this afternoon?"

Ralston nodded. "Yes, and I heard there were automatic weapons involved. My office got a call within an hour of it happening and were told that it was related to a gunrunner taken into custody day before last—a North Korean alien by the name of Se-Hong Yu. Our boss decided not to pursue it since we'd already been advised that the U.S. Marshals and BATF would be taking charge of the case."

"Well, that's not the entire story," Lyons replied. "The woman that escaped just a few hours ago from the holding cell at Anchorage police headquarters is an espionage agent with a North Korean intelligence service. She was sent here to sabotage equipment and assassinate a government scientist."

"And you were sent to stop her?"

"Right," Blancanales said.

"Well, then, I'd guess that you three aren't really from the Office of Naval Intelligence."

"We were actually just sent here to tour the local music circuit," Schwarz said. "We got into all of this secret agent spy stuff as more of a side business. You know, it pays the bills between gigs."

Lyons was about to silence Schwarz but was cut off by Cronaugher.

"Look, just ignore these guys," the police captain said. "They're kind of crazy."

"Noted," Ralston drawled, exchanging glances with each of the Able Team warriors in turn. She gave the computer monitor her full attention. "You know what? I don't really even want to know. I'll give you the address of this place and once you have that you're on your own."

"Story of our lives," Carl Lyons muttered.

EVEN THE DIN of steady conversation and droning of the jukebox feeding unseen speakers couldn't drown the obvious shift in the mood of those occupying the bar upon seeing three of their own enter with a thin, demure Asian at their side. A number of the bikers got out of their chairs and stared at Ju Young-Soon with nothing less than hatred in their eyes. She didn't understand it at first. That was until she spotted the far back wall of the bar, which was covered with a flag from the American Civil War, along with a another flag that was instantly recognizable: a swastika.

Young-Soon hated that symbol—she hated everything it stood for and yet she couldn't fault these men for displaying it. This was their territory and she'd invaded it.

She'd forced herself on the three bikers in that holding cell and demanded they assist her without giving any thought of consequence to her actions. Not that it mattered. She'd made her escape and now it was time to part company with her temporary allies.

That was her plan anyway, although she could tell just from the look on the face of one of the particularly big men now walking toward her that this might not turn out exactly as she'd first planned. She was good, a solid agent who'd been well trained. That didn't make her invincible and it certainly didn't give her any thought she could easily overpower two dozen or so white supremacist bikers who got a collective hard-on just thinking about all the nasty little things they might do to Young-Soon.

The man stopped a few feet short of her and then stared at each of Young-Soon's three escorts. "I don't suppose any of you would mind telling me what you think you were doing bringing this woman into our house."

"Boss, she's here under a white flag," the biggest of the threesome replied. The guy swallowed hard but he managed to keep his voice steady.

"A white flag, huh? Does this look like some kind of welfare office to you, Boyle? You know the rules! Don't bring *nobody* in here unless you got my okay first. And now you make matters worse and pollute this very hallowed ground with some Chinese—"

"I am not Chinese, idiot," Young-Soon declared. "I'm North Korean."

"Shut...*up!*" the boss said. More quietly he added, "I'll get to you in a moment."

"Unfortunately, I don't have time to play these games," Young-Soon said. She turned to Boyle. "I will leave you to attend to your own business. Our partnership has now been terminated. Thank you for honoring our agreement."

"Agreement?" the biker leader echoed. "What the hell agreement did you make?"

"She helped bust us out of jail, Mackey," one of the other guys replied. "And she iced some big-ass dude in our cell. Killed him deader'n shit."

The guy named Mackey raised his eyebrows and folded his muscular forearms, which were snaked with tattoos intertwined in a collage of cobras and dragons. "That right? Well, why don't we all just stand in line to thank her? You dumb mother—"

Young-Soon turned on her heel and headed with purpose toward the entrance. She hoped to get free and clear of the bar before anyone could take further action. Being in the open would at least give her some running room since she didn't have a fighting chance in hell of coming out of this intact any other way.

Unfortunately, Mackey had other ideas because he chased after her and grabbed her arm just as she reached the door. Young-Soon didn't wait to react, having spotted a rack of pool cues in her peripheral vision when she first entered. She reached for the thickest one at the same moment as she twisted inward and drove the heel of her boot onto the key point of Mackey's instep. The guy let out a howl but it was caught up short by the crack of the pool cue against his temple, a blow that opened a wide jagged wound.

Mackey stepped back and released his hold on Young-Soon, but she pressed the attack by immediately following up with a jab to his groin. She delivered a second jab into his chest before whirling and making her exit before any of the other bikers could respond. The entire fight had elapsed in under five seconds.

It was now dark and Young-Soon looked around furiously in search of an escape mechanism. The sudden view of exhaust curling from the tailpipe of a pickup demanded her attention.

Young-Soon raced from the entrance to the run-down bar and across the parking lot until she reached the truck. She peered into the foggy window and saw some sort of movement, then tried the handle to the driver's-side door and found it unlocked. Young-Soon whipped the door open and was greeted with a woman's legs high in the air while a fat, bald slob was humping her for all he was worth. The sudden gust of cold air against the man's bare cheeks alerted him to the presence of an intruder. He turned toward Young-Soon to deliver a flurry of curses but instead bought the broad end of a pool cue into the bridge of his nose. The hooker started screaming as Young-Soon reached in and hauled the man out by his filthy jacket, a feat she managed only because the blow to his nose had temporarily blinded him with pain.

He tumbled to the ground and as Young-Soon jumped into the driver's seat she turned toward the painted woman of the night and ordered her to get out. The hooker immediately complied but she barely cleared the truck, rolling away to avoid serious injury as Young-Soon put the vehicle in gear and tore out of the unpaved lot in a concert of spinning tires, gravel and dust.

Young-Soon remembered the route they'd taken to get here and that down the road just a few miles would be an entrance to the highway. She knew exactly where she had to go. If Nam had agreed to work with Wee Hum Han, the two would arrange to meet at the secret location out of which Han's group had been operating. Young-Soon knew exactly where that meeting place was, although Han had no idea she knew about it. For all that was concerned, Han probably thought she was out of the picture entirely. Well, it would probably come as quite a surprise to him when he discovered she had escaped. It would also mean his mission as it had been assigned to him, mostly like her assassination, would be null and void. The meant either Han would have to work with her and Chin Nam to get them out of the country or she'd be within her rights to do him first.

It was a task she didn't relish but if he provoked her, Ju Young-Soon wouldn't hesitate to destroy him.

CHAPTER TWENTY-FOUR

"There she is!" Cronaugher said.

"Pull over here," Lyons replied.

"What?"

"You heard me," Lyons said. "We don't want her to know we're onto her yet."

"Why the hell not?"

"Zeus, almighty, will you just *pull over?*"

Cronaugher complied although he muttered a half dozen curses under his breath as he did. He sounded like a dog grumbling when ordered by its master to do something it really didn't want to do. He eased the car to the shoulder of the road just shy of the overpass. It wasn't a spot one would wish to get stuck on with mechanical difficulties but at this time of the morning it was the perfect point from which to observe.

Lyons pulled out a pair of IR field glasses, activated a switch and brought them to his eyes. As it turned out there was enough light in the parking lot he didn't really need the infrared so he shut the lighting system down and adjusted the focus. He watched with interest as Ju Young-Soon dashed across the parking lot of the bar, yanked some poor old dude from his pickup and then jumped inside and tore out of the parking lot.

"No question," he said as he passed the field glasses to Cronaugher. "That's definitely our little sweetheart. Looks like your pal Ralston was right on the money."

"She's good at that," Cronaugher replied as he stared through the binocs. He finally dropped them and said, "Why don't you want to take her now? Where is it you're expecting her to lead you?"

It was Blancanales who replied, "To her partner—the one who escaped from the hotel."

"Ah, very crafty. I hadn't even thought of that myself."

"I'm actually betting the farm," Lyons added. "I'm betting that she'll lead us to this Wee Hum Han, as well."

"What makes you think so?"

Lyons snickered. "If we're able to figure out that much, what makes you think she won't?"

"Uh, fellas," Schwarz cut in, "I think those bikers might be intent on sort of ruining our plans. We might want to think about giving that problem a bit of attention."

"Couldn't agree more," Lyons said. He glanced over his shoulder and told his teammates, "Gear up. Looks like we're going to get some action. Cronaugher, put on your driving hat because you're going to have to pull off some pretty tricky moves. Going up against skilled motorcyclists won't necessarily be a walk in the park."

"Particularly considering just how many we're talking about," Blancanales pointed out. "Look."

Blancanales wasn't kidding. The bikers poured from the door of the bar like rats escaping a sinking ship. From that distance they looked much like the rodents they were. There was no disguising the murderous intent in their strides as they rushed to their Hogs, climbed aboard and one by one pulled out of the lot in pursuit of their quarry. Cronaugher waited until the last one pulled out and then eased his car off the shoulder and accelerated smoothly.

"Here we go," Schwarz said.

Ju Young-Soon put the accelerator down hard, brazenly pushing the pickup to its limits. There was little chance she could outrun her pursuers, so she would have to find a way to outwit them—not a terribly difficult task considering the average intelligence between them was probably half that of her own.

Young-Soon wasn't technically a genius but her IQ came pretty close. It was something that had excited her instructors because they were able to push her mental capacities beyond those of most normal agents. There had been standards but the bar hadn't been set particularly high, so Young-Soon had always managed to stand head and shoulders above her fellow recruits. Nearly half of the ministry's candidates failed to graduate and the number-one reason was the lack of ability to think quickly and decisively.

Ju Young-Soon had no such problem and it was probably why she had nearly always succeeded in every task she undertook. This change in her plans was proof enough of that—a chance to redeem herself.

Young-Soon passed an exit sign for a road she knew would take her directly to the airport. There were many open roads out there, which would give her plenty of running room. There was also the hotel room she'd booked, another very purposeful move on her part, where she had a fresh cache of weapons stored. The hotel would put hundreds of bystanders between her and the bikers. Crowds meant distractions and she knew it would be quite packed. There was a convention scheduled at the hotel, and by her estimate the festivities would just be breaking up.

Young-Soon checked her rearview mirror and saw that the bikers were gaining, taking the same exit she had. She was traversing the main road that led to the airport—the same road that passed right by her hotel. Within two minutes she'd reached the hotel, swung into the parking lot and bore down on the entrance to the underground parking garage. Now she had somewhat of a home-turf advantage because she'd made a careful study of the hotel and was much more familiar with the layout than the bikers.

Young-Soon took the first available parking spot she could find as close to the exit as possible. She then dashed from her vehicle to the stairwell, pushed through the heavy metal door and ascended the steps three at a time. She was out of breath by the time she reached her room. She moved straight to the deep chest of drawers, opened the bottom one and withdrew a padlocked leather bag. A quick inventory of its contents satisfied her she could maintain her own against the bikers for quite some time.

She looked out the window and scanned the front lot. At least half a dozen motorcycles were parked in front of the main entrance. Their leader was a gorilla, clumsy and out of shape, but Young-Soon didn't figure he'd risen to his position because he lacked brains. He'd have some of his men cover the front entrance, as well as all of the entry and exit points in the multilevel parking garage. Young-Soon would need a distraction and she thought she knew exactly how to create it.

She yanked open the leather weapons bag, withdrawing a Heckler & Koch UMP-9. The newest offering from HK, this particular model chambered a 9 mm Parabellum cartridge and could fire approximately 650 rounds per minute on single 2-shot and full-auto modes. The weapon was clearly a black market offering since the 9 mm hadn't even been approved for import into the United States—so far only the 40 mm variant had been made available. Once she'd loaded and checked it, Young-

Soon sealed and slung the weapons bag over her shoulder, left the hotel room and headed for the lobby.

"I SENSE DEEP trouble," Schwarz muttered.

"Here?" Cronaugher said. "What the hell would they be doing meeting here?"

"I don't know," Lyons said. "Maybe she's just attempting to divert them."

"It's what I would do," Blancanales added.

Cronaugher looked over his shoulder at the Able Team warrior. "What do you mean?"

"She may be trying to put some bystanders between her and the bikers. If she can stir up enough trouble, it would provide a decent distraction while she made her escape. And look at this parking lot—it's jam-packed."

Lyons shook his head. "We can't wait, boys. There's about to be a whole lot of trouble, and it's the bikers who're going to start it. They'll comb that entire place until they find her, and they won't be too selective about who they mow down to find her if anyone should interfere with them."

"Great," Cronaugher said. "This is just great. You guys are going to be out of a job and I'm going to prison. You know what the life expectancy of an ex-cop is in the joint, friends?"

"Nobody said you were going to live forever," Schwarz replied.

"Let's do it," Lyons said as Cronaugher screeched to a halt in front of the hotel's main entrance.

It was almost like déjà vu for the trio as they went EVA and rushed into the lobby with their pistols at the ready. They spotted one of the bikers leaning over the counter and grabbing a handful of the mousy desk clerk's shirt, shouting at the top of his lungs and threatening him with every form of physical violence.

The clerk couldn't have been more than nineteen or twenty, not big and definitely not capable of defending himself from the massive brute towering over him. Lyons immediately holstered his weapon and headed for the biker but in his peripheral vision he spotted a pair of beefy types, probably wingmen, move into an intercept pattern.

No problem, Lyons thought. He had wingmen of his own and they'd do their jobs.

One of the backup bikers managed to get close enough to reach for Lyons but never actually had the opportunity to make contact—the biker realized a moment too late that he was faced with an equally formidable challenge in the form of Rosario Blancanales. And while Blancanales might have carried a slight paunch and quite a number of years senior to the biker, the warrior also had experience and endurance well beyond most men his age. The biker had never been faced with something like that. A fact that became quite transparent when Blancanales delivered a karate chop to the nerve in the biker's forearm, deflecting the man's attempt to grab Lyons.

The biker turned to Blancanales with surprise and made the mistake of reaching for a punk pistol in his belt, concealed below his shirt, instead of worrying about the old fogey in front of him. Blancanales delivered a rock-solid uppercut that snapped the biker's head back and caused him to drop the pistol. As it clattered to the floor useless, Blancanales followed with a low inside kick to the knee that dislocated ligaments and cracked the shin-bone. The biker dropped to the ground, effectively out of the fight.

The second biker who had originally also been on a

path to head off Lyons realized his partner needed him and changed course to assist. He never got close. Hermann Schwarz took the guy at the waist with a low tackle, his wiry and muscular form twisting at the last moment to grab fistfuls of the biker's bloated leather chaps. Schwarz yanked hard, using the man's legs as levers to act in counterforce to the tackle. The move flipped the biker onto his back and he cracked his skull against the thick carpet that lined the lobby floor.

Lyons had reached the biker assaulting the clerk. He neutralized the situation with a short, straight punch to the man's left kidney. The biker howled in surprise, setting the clerk free with his right hand as his left dipped back to where Lyons had struck. The Able Team leader pressed the assault by grabbing that hand and twisting the arm upward in a single-handed wristlock. Lyons used his other hand to grab the back of the biker's shirt collar and whip him in a circular motion while extending his foot. The biker went down hard and fast, and in the process Lyons's hold neatly dislocated his opponent's shoulder.

Lyons looked at the startled kid, verified he was unharmed and then turned to see how his teammates had fared. As he'd expected, both were upright and grinning, even exchanging a high-five.

Lyons turned at a sign of movement in his periphery and spotted another guy coming toward him. A stream of what looked like dried blood was plastered against the biker's left cheek and he had somewhat of a limp to his gait. Lyons spotted the object in the man's right hand that he held low and close—the reflection of the overhead lights allowed Lyons to estimate the blade had to be a good seven inches or more in length. Just about the right size for the average boot knife.

From the first slash Lyons knew he was dealing with a somewhat experienced knife fighter, although while his technique was good the guy was simply too slow. He was also wounded, recently wounded, and Lyons couldn't help but wonder for a second if he'd acquired his injuries courtesy of Ju Young-Soon. Whatever the case, it didn't seem to be affecting the guy's apparent desire to kill Lyons.

The Able Team commando sidestepped the first slash and pivoted so he was outside the line of attack. He deflected with a Shotokan scissors block and then executed a semicircle while simultaneously directing his opponent's motion upward. At the last possible moment, Lyons reversed direction and turned the arm down, using his enemy's own strength to lock the guy in an arm bar. Lyons then delivered an elbow strike right to the point where the elbow joined the upper arm and turned the cartilage and tendons to mush with an audible snap. The knife sprang from numb fingers and Lyons finished by leaning his weight fully into the man's side and driving him face-first to the floor. Lyons ended the fight with a rabbit punch that knocked the biker out cold.

Before the Able Team warriors could decide what to do for an encore, the reports of automatic weapons fire somewhere in the bowels of the hotel were followed by the screams of many people. In less time than it took Able Team to leave the lobby and head for the direction of the shots, pistols now out and held at the ready, a wall of bystanders rushed them from the massive entrance to a hallway that led to the various conference rooms and event hall.

"Federal agents!" Lyons shouted to the panicked citizens. "Get the hell out of the way!"

But he knew his efforts were futile. He and his teammates were trying to swim upstream against the human tide overpowering them, a virtual wall of bodies that no single human being could navigate. It was pandemonium, utter insanity, and Lyons for one had experienced just about his fill of this situation. To make matters worse, the sounds of more shots echoed down the hall, barely audible above the panicked shouts of men and women alike, but these weren't the same—they were irregular and sounded more like pistols.

Eventually, Able Team managed to get past the crowd, keeping their backs to the walls and thereby saving themselves from being stampeded. The crowd thinned out very quickly and as they moved nearer to one of the conference rooms with its double doors flung wide-open they spotted the source of the shooting. A couple of plainclothes security officers stood just outside those doors, exchanging shots with some unseen enemy inside the room.

They detected the approach of Able Team and turned their weapons in that direction, but Blancanales, who was on point, put up his hands and waved them off. "Whoa, whoa, boys! We're on your side!"

"What's the situation?" Lyons demanded, not one to stand on ceremony.

"Not sure," the one guy said, sweat glistening on his forehead and lip. "Some crazy-ass bitch just walked into the conference room from one of those adjoining doors up front and started shooting up the place."

"Any casualties?" Schwarz asked.

The kid shook his head. "Don't think so. Who are you guys anyway?"

"Federal agents," Blancanales replied.

The man's partner, who looked even younger, said, "Would you maybe mind showing us some kind of identification?"

Lyons scowled. "You're kidding—right?"

He couldn't have been more than twenty-three or twenty-four. A rent-a-cop, nothing more, and hardly experienced at going up against something like this. Ever since the mass shootings that had taken place in America grew in frequency, businesses that catered to large groups of people had felt the need to hire their own security. Unfortunately, they did so on the cheap and they went to corporations who churned out young men and women, many wannabe cops or military flunk-outs, to act as security. A few weeks of training and they were allowed to carry a gun.

"I think we'd best save those details for later," Blancanales replied easily. "Now, why don't you guys head for the front and make sure those people get out safely and we'll deal with this woman."

"I think she just bolted," the older one replied. "You want us to help you run her down?"

"You leave her to us," Lyons ordered. "She's a professional and she's dangerous, and she wouldn't think a moment about cutting both your throats if you gave her the opportunity. Out of your league, so just leave her to us."

"Whatever you say, man," he replied. "I don't get paid enough to be a hero."

"That's funny," Schwarz quipped. "Neither do we."

"Go!" Lyons told the two with a jerk of his thumb, and they went.

"Okay, what's the plan?" Blancanales asked when they were out of earshot.

"She could've killed dozens of people and she didn't," Lyons replied. "She was only looking to create a distraction."

"Well, I'd say she's done a mighty find job of that so far," Schwarz said.

"We need to get back to Cronaugher and have him

bring an army of cops down on this place," Lyons said. "It's too big for us to be able to logically cover it all."

"Why not call him on the radio?" Blancanales asked.

Lyons looked sheepish. "I forgot it."

They realized the impact of his statement only a moment later when they heard the thump of numerous footfalls rushing toward them. Unfortunately, it wasn't their allies—the four bikers were toting pistols and rushing Able Team's position like a first-string defensive line. Unfortunately for them, they weren't going up against a rival gang but against a hardened threesome of urban commandos.

Lyons was the first to reach his belly and he rolled behind a metal garbage can and sighted his first target. Two bullets burned the air above his head, one coming close enough to singe hairs, before Lyons triggered his own pistol twice. Both .45-caliber rounds struck home, ripping through the biker's midsection and driving him to the floor.

Two bikers split off at an angle and tried to fire on Schwarz, but again their inexperience proved fatal. The rounds they fired on the run didn't even come close, and Schwarz, undaunted by their effort, took a knee and returned fire with one shot after another. Before all was done, Schwarz caught one of the bikers with three rounds to the upper body. His partner tumbled to the carpet a moment later, his head smashed open by two rounds that struck him in the jaw and forehead respectively.

Blancanales got the survivor by shooting as he moved at an angle across the hall, timing his shots in rhythm with his breathing and steps. Only an experienced combat shooter could've pulled it off like Blancanales did, his moves as graceful and calculated as a ballet dancer. Blancanales held position, covering the area ahead to give his friends time to regain their feet. When it appeared clear there wouldn't be any further resistance, the three trotted back to the lobby. It was still fairly crowded but now there were uniformed officers coming through the doors and herding people to stand clear.

Lyons quickly recognized one of the officers as Sergeant Moore. The two shouldered their way through the crowd as soon as their eyes locked and, to Lyons's surprise, Moore seemed somewhat more amiable than he had the first time they met.

"Norris, right?" Moore said. When Lyons nodded Morris handed him a cell phone with an open connection. "It's Captain Cronaugher on the phone for you."

"Yeah?" Lyons growled into the phone.

"If you guys are done playing G.I. Joe in there, you might want to know I got your girl in sight."

"Where?"

"She tried to slip out of here in the pandemonium and I immediately recognized her," he said. "She was in the same pickup she brought in."

"That sounds a bit wonky," Lyons replied. "Why would she try to leave in the same vehicle she came in with? Particularly since the owner's probably reported it stolen."

"He has," Cronaugher said. "It just came over the wire."

"You've got eyes on her?"

"Right. She got back on the interstate almost right away. Looks like she may be headed toward a particularly dense residential neighborhood—an area with a lot of low-income housing."

"Okay," Lyons said, locating his teammates and twirling his finger to signal they should form on him. "Tell me how to find you."

CHAPTER TWENTY-FIVE

Joint Base Elmendorf-Richardson

The Bombardier Aerospace Global 5000 touched down several hours earlier than expected, and as the wheels gained purchase and the jet's braking flaps kicked in, all the men of Phoenix Force sighed with relief.

"Ah, terra firma at last!" Hawkins remarked as he peered into the twilight darkness that signaled it was just an hour after midnight in Anchorage.

"I thought you liked to fly," James said tiredly.

"I do," Hawkins said. "But it don't mean I'm not glad to get down in one piece. And especially after *this* mission."

"It was a ball-buster," Rafael Encizo remarked. "I'll grant you that."

As Manning took off his seat belt and moved forward to wake their passengers, McCarter said, "Any of you guys sort of get the impression this was a little *too* easy?"

"You mean, like maybe they *let* us go?" James asked.

McCarter shrugged. "Dunno, mate, but a thought right similar to that had crossed my mind."

"Okay, let's suppose you're right," Encizo said. "Just who would *they* be?"

"Well, we know it was this Wen Xiang's assassins performing security at the docks where we snatched Teng," James said. "But the guys we encountered at the house where we extracted Meifeng and subsequently those in the city were definitely military types."

"Agreed," McCarter replied. "Which is exactly why I'm thinking it was a bit too easy."

"Hark Kwan might disagree with you there, boss," Hawkins said, realizing even as it came out of his mouth that he'd put his foot in it. At the miffed glances from his colleagues he quickly added, "No offense, David."

"Forget it," McCarter said, jabbing his finger at mother and son, groggy at being roused from their slumber. "We should drop this discussion for now anyway."

At that, the men of Phoenix Force gathered their gear and deplaned. There were two squads of Air Force Security Police on the tarmac to greet them, along with a couple of late-model Lincoln Navigators to shuttle them to the hangar facilities. Two Navy corpsmen were on scene to treat any injuries or other medical needs, and to perform blood draws of Meifeng and Teng Cai.

While the Cais submitted to their medical workups, the Phoenix Force warriors made their way up the long corridor to another facility joined to the hangars and labs by an enclosed, transparent walkway. Snow and frost crusted the exterior, which looked to be made from very thick Plexiglas, but the interior of the hall was comparably warm. The transfer from the warmth of the plane to the icy winds of the tarmac back to the warm interior started to weigh heavily on all of the weary commandos.

"I could use a nice, long winter's nap," Manning remarked.

"We can spell each other in an hour or two," McCarter said. "First thing is to get cleaned up, do a full equipment check and then gather for a mission debrief with the Farm."

As they entered the VIP accommodations area, a place set aside to house and feed the parade of scientists, civilian workers and military attachés that rotated nearly year-round through the base, an airman first-class greeted him with a snappy salute that McCarter didn't bother to return with more than a casual wave. They'd been informed on the trip home that they would be treated as a special operations unit of Air Force combat controllers returning from a classified mission. The Farm had figured that would discourage most questions.

"Sir?" the AFC began. "AFC Chandler at your service."

"You can drop the formalities, Chandler," McCarter replied with an easy grin. "Being a master sergeant doesn't rate a salute in Air Force."

"Understood, Master Sergeant. Just a little pumped up, I guess. I was informed to give you a heroes' welcome and—" he looked each of the men over "—frankly we weren't told what for and we *definitely* weren't to ask."

"You know how the Air Force is, son," Hawkins drawled. "They like to be all hush-hush about things like that."

"Okay, Chandler, here's what we can use," McCarter offered. "Some hot showers and a place to store our gear. A bit of hot chow would be nice. We'll also need a secure meeting room with all the latest tech security precautions. You think you can swing it in the next forty-five mikes or so?"

"I can do it sooner than that," Chandler replied with a grin.

"Well, then, lead the way, maestro," Encizo replied.

THEY WERE CLEANED up with hot food in their bellies in thirty minutes flat. They assembled in the meeting room arranged by Chandler, and Hawkins was able to confirm relatively quickly that the security and countermeasures within the facility were top-notch.

Confident with Hawkins's assessment they wouldn't be overheard, McCarter got Stony Man Farm on the horn and immediately ran down their current situation. Brognola and Price listened closely without interrupting until McCarter completed his narrative.

"And just as a side note," McCarter concluded, "there's still a point I want to make that we have some unfinished business with this Yan Zhou. I don't bloody plan to forget it. He needs to answer for not only Kwan's death but his part in helping the GSF."

"We can discuss that at a later time," Brognola confirmed.

"Fine."

"We've already been informed through our contacts that they've finished their medical screening of the Cais," Price said. "Teng's already apparently agreed to work with Dr. Stavros in determining how best to counteract what Stavros has come to christen as the Prodigy Effect."

"Ah, very catchy," Hawkins said.

"Yeah—it's got soul," James added.

"Did you just say soul?" Manning asked. "Really... really? What is this, the 1970s?"

"All right, can it," McCarter said with more irritation than he intended.

When the room fell uncomfortably silent, Price cleared her throat quietly and said, "Our big concern now is how we prepare for a counterresponse to your activities in China."

"What do you mean, Barb?" Encizo asked.

"Well, the Chinese government hasn't taken any official position, but we know the GSF will make some attempt to penetrate the States and kill the Cais."

"You think they'd actually try an assault here on the base?" McCarter inquired.

"They're fanatics," Brognola reminded them. "I wouldn't put it past them to try anything."

"Who would've thunk it?" Hawkins said.

Price replied, "The point is that you men have now operated against the GSF on several occasions. You've seen their capabilities. You know how they think and how they fight, *and* you know how to react to them. The base security police can only do so much, and the Man doesn't want to put all of Elmendorf-Richardson on lockdown."

"Why not?" Manning asked.

"He's worried about it leaking to the press," Brognola said. "And before any of you voices what you're really thinking, I happen to agree with him. First off, we don't want this to turn into another big shit sandwich like the Fort Hood shooting. We also don't want to give other terrorist entities the idea that our military installations can be so easily compromised."

"But surely you think there's more to it than that," McCarter said. "They wouldn't just try this on a whim unless they thought they had some sort of major tactical advantage."

"Very perceptive, David," Price replied.

"Like you said, we've fought them and I think we understand them. So why the concern at your end?"

"There's a good chance they might have a contact on the inside," Price said. "We're assuming that Yan Zhou's behind it, even if he isn't personally leading the charge. He'll probably send Wen Xiang to do his dirty work, and we're pretty certain they have already found a way into the country undetected."

"And how would they pull that off?"

Price tendered a long sigh before going into the full story of Able Team's encounters with the North Korean intelligence service and Stavros's discoveries about the technology behind the prototype. "That's why it's so important for you to get Teng Cai back here quickly."

"But even if he can help Stavros, it may be too late," Brognola added. "We're just going to have to prepare for the worst-case scenario."

"The other item is Able Team's current status," Price continued.

"Yeah, it sounds like our boys have kicked over a few anthills," James remarked.

"They're definitely pushing the envelope. You know they captured a North Korean intelligence agent so I don't need to rehash that. But since we last spoke there have been a number of violent outbreaks involving multiple contacts, and the North Koreans have managed to stay one step ahead of Able Team. It's not for lack of trying, either, believe me."

"So where do things stand?" McCarter asked.

"This agent escaped from police custody. Able's been working with one of their tactical captains to run her down. Everything our profile says about this woman is she's a borderline fanatic. Trained by North Korean security experts and extremely dangerous. So far she's killed two police officers, shot it out with a local hotel security force and allied herself, however briefly, with a fascist biker gang."

"Sounds like a real treat," Hawkins commented.

"She's anything but," Brognola said. "And so far we're

taking somewhat of a black eye because we haven't been able to keep this out of the press. It was only a stroke of good fortune these bikers were involved, because we've now been able to blame just about everything that's happened there as little more than a crime spree. The showdown in the early-morning hours a couple of days ago to bring down Se-Hong Yu, a North Korean black market arms smuggler, was explained away as a traffic accident since there weren't any witnesses."

"And now that Anchorage police have Yu in custody," Price said, "we've at least managed to shut down the flow of illegal weapons to whoever's left in town."

"Well, far be it from me to complain," McCarter said, "but it sounds like Able Team could use our help. I'm not of the mind to just sit here on my bloody arse while they're duking it out with fanatics toting automatic weapons and blowing everything in sight to bloody hell."

"I'm not against any suggestions you may have in assisting them," Price said. "But protection of Teng Cai and his mother is your core mission objective, as well as making sure nothing happens to Dr. Stavros. We don't know when the GSF and Yan Zhou will make their move. But what we do know is they *will* make it in due time."

"Yeah, we have some thoughts about that," McCarter replied.

"Shoot."

"T.J. chatted up Teng Cai quite a bit about the advanced stealth and counterjamming technology he developed. I think I'll let him fill you in."

"Well…" Hawkins said hesitantly, but at a nod from McCarter he paused to collect his thoughts and then pressed on. "Okay, so the way Teng Cai describes it there were two different blueprints. The first of the two chip sets developed was identical to the ones utilized in the prototype missile—according to Cai they had a few vulnerabilities. There are maybe a dozen deployed in planes and missiles of varying type. The second set he claims to have perfected just before we hit the wharf and snatched him out from the GSF. He said there's only one, and he confirmed they couldn't replicate it."

"Why not?" Brognola inquired.

"Well, apparently he's claiming one of the vulnerabilities of the first was the fact that with the right equipment and time, it could be duplicated. The new chip set has a fail-safe, and if anyone attempts to duplicate the architecture it will self-destruct."

"As in how?" James said. "Like it'll blow up?"

Hawkins shook his head. "Nothing quite so dramatic. I'm pretty comfortable with technology but a lot of it was way over my head. I'm betting this Dr. Stavros will be able to understand it much more completely once Cai opens up to her. Apparently, there's a special program built into one of the gates that will scramble all of the EPROM coding—a virus of sorts, from what I can gather."

"And you believe him?" Price asked.

"I didn't get the sense he was deceiving me. He knows cooperating with us at this point is his best bet. Or at least that's what his mother told him. Not to mention we let it slip that Zhou will most likely send Xiang and his goons to try to kill him, and that if he wanted our protection he was going to have to help out when we got here. I think he's being truthful."

"Okay, then, we'll let the brainiacs worry about all the technical stuff," McCarter said. "I think we should consider our operational plan and decide if there's some way we can help out Able Team."

"What did you have in mind?" Brognola asked.

"I'd suggest we split up," McCarter said. "And before you say it, I know it's not a good idea given we have no idea what kind of nastiness Zhou plans to throw our way. But the fact is they won't have much opportunity to put together any sort of real plan, and they could hardly get a force of any decent size into this area quickly. Certainly they won't stand much of a chance of getting past base security, even if they have an op in progress as we speak.

"So what I'm proposing is this. I think it's a pretty safe bet the bastards will try for an airdrop, probably a HALO team of, say, a dozen. If we shore up with the AF Security Police, I'm more than comfortable sparing a couple of Phoenix Force to get to Able Team's location and assist in whatever they have going."

"Makes sense," Price said. She then directed the conversation to Kurtzman. "Bear, how feasible do you think a high altitude low opening airdrop is, given the current satellite weather models and any other factors we haven't considered?"

The familiar clack of keys on Kurtzman's terminal was followed less than a minute later by his response. "Okay, weather wouldn't be a problem. It's plenty clear and the ambient temperature is high enough that it wouldn't affect their equipment in any way provided they're using top-shelf gear."

"What about air traffic patterns?" Brognola asked. "Look at both civilian aviation, passenger and cargo, into Anchorage, as well as the potential for military flights that may be scheduled to land at Elmendorf-Richardson."

"You think they've got that kind of pull?" McCarter asked.

"We have to consider every possibility," Price said. "Remember, we don't know if they have somebody on the inside working with them or not. And if they do plan a HALO jump, we'd have no way of detecting it. That's why we use such tactics ourselves."

"Yeah, but this Wen Xiang's a Chinese MSS gun-for-hire," Manning said. "HALO and black ops like this require many months of highly specialized training. Even if he had it, I doubt any of Zhou's GSF cronies would have undergone such rigorous training."

"Maybe not," McCarter said. "But you're forgetting that Zhou's a vice air-marshal in the PRC's air force. I don't doubt for one second he's got a whole bloody crew of special operators at his disposal. If he says go, they'll go and they won't care where or when or who."

"Okay, so there aren't that many civilian flights," Manning said. "The only one sourced out of China is a Cathay Pacific cargo carrier scheduled to touch down in about two hours for refueling. Then they're on to Toronto. The remaining civilian flights, total of three, are passenger carriers from New York, Washington and Los Angeles."

"None of them would be flying high enough for a HALO jump," McCarter said.

"No, but there's another possibility we haven't considered," Encizo interjected. "What about a low-level marine jump?"

Hawkins furrowed his brow. "Into where?"

"How about the Knik Arm?" McCarter proposed.

Encizo nodded. "It makes sense. Nearly all Asian flights approach the airport by circling in from the north. They could deploy out of a plane on final approach and rendezvous with some type of motor launch. Then it's a short hop to shore, into a road vehicle and they're home free. Short of staging a small army of spotters on the shoreline, there would be no way to detect them."

"That's wicked-crazy at this time of year," Hawkins said. "Water would be freezing."

"But it's doable and we know it," McCarter said.

"Because we've *done* it," Manning added.

McCarter nodded. "Okay, it makes sense that short of a HALO jump from an aircraft, which the NORAD systems could easily detect, a water jump from that Cathay Pacific cargo carrier seems like the best option."

"How do you want to work this then?" Price asked.

"Bear," McCarter replied, "how much time do we have before that ship's scheduled to land?"

"According to the airport's database, you're looking at touchdown in about ninety-eight minutes. And the flight's scheduled to be on time."

"Then we'd best shag our arse. Calvin and Gary, you get Able Team's current location and beat feet over to them. Have Chandler arrange some solid wheels for you. The rest of us will get prepped, get a plan in place and head toward Knik Arm."

"Forgive me for asking, David," Encizo said, "but just exactly how are we supposed to find these guys? Even assuming my guess is right, and they do plan to make this insane jump, we don't have the equipment or manpower to set up a large-scale observation. At least not in the time we have remaining."

"Won't need to, mate," McCarter replied. "Bear in mind we don't have to get out on the surface and search. All we need to do is to look for a boat. And at night, a boat won't be hard to see at all. Set up some thermal imaging and we should be able to pick out heat from any engine on the water. And I sincerely doubt we're going to find too many boats out so early in the morning running dark and silent."

Hawkins nodded. "Yeah, they'll be moving slow and purposeful. And they'll make their landing at the most remote spot on shore they can while still making it easily accessible by vehicle."

"I don't know," Encizo said. "Still seems like a lot of area to cover."

"We'll plot out some likely vectors for you guys at this end," Kurtzman advised. "As you've already concluded, they'll have a pretty small window here. Most likely they'll pick a spot near one of the utility roads that runs along that area. Our dedicated satellite can pinpoint most of that stuff with a negligible margin of error. If in fact this is their plan, we'll find them."

"All I can say is I'm glad we get the warmer job," Manning said. "It's going to be cold and dark out there."

"Yeah," McCarter replied. "For *them*."

CHAPTER TWENTY-SIX

The drive to where Able Team had set up shop took Manning and James less than an hour. After shaking hands with their comrades-in-arms, and making introductions with Captain Cronaugher, Carl Lyons quickly laid it out for the Phoenix Force pair. They had commandeered an unmarked police squad shortly after speaking with Cronaugher and were now positioned behind a convenience store with a relatively decent view of the apartment building a half block up the street.

"And you personally observed her going in there?" James asked Cronaugher.

The police captain nodded. "With my own two eyes."

James looked around and said, "They didn't bring any tactical in on this?"

Lyons shook his head. "Absolutely not. I waved them off. Last thing we need is this place crawling with cops. I'm telling you, guys, these bastards are very sharp and well trained, and they don't give a rat's ass who gets in their way. And Ju Young-Soon, in particular."

"She's the North Korean agent?" Manning asked.

"They all are."

"Do we have a relatively solid number on what 'all' means?"

"We know there are at least three for sure," Blancanales replied. "There could be more but we just don't have enough intelligence to be certain."

"But I got to tell you," Schwarz said, "you guys are a sight for sore eyes. I'm personally going to buy McMasters a steak when we're all through with this."

Knowing he was referring to McCarter, Manning nodded. "We heard you'd been going constant for a while now."

"About twenty-four hours, I'd guess," Lyons confirmed, weariness evident in his voice. "Give or take."

"Okay," James said. "It's your call. How do you want to play it?"

Lyons sighed. "Well, we don't have a blueprint of the building and very little hope of getting it soon even if we asked for one. There's an open-air parking garage but that's it. No underground access and no empty apartments that we know of, so we'll have to come in on the ground floor just like normal folks."

"Through the front door?" Manning asked.

"Already thought about that," Schwarz replied. "It's a no-go. Electronically locked with a speaker system, but we weren't thinking anybody would take kindly to us ringing their buzzer this time of morning."

"And there's one other problem," Lyons said. "Been a bit of traffic in and out of there the past hour. Looks like a party with no sign they're going to stop anytime soon. Only lights on appear to be on the first floor. There may be more but we didn't want to risk checking via the parking lot and being seen by our friends."

"So what's left?" James asked.

"We're thinking we can go through the back door," Lyons said. "It's one of those thick, heavy metal ones, though, and we don't have anything in our bag of tricks powerful enough to open it. It doesn't have an exterior handle, either, so even if we could pick it we'd still not necessarily have any way of easily opening it—maybe a tire iron."

"I've got some pencil detonators and cutting charges with me," Manning said, patting the freshly stocked ordnance satchel at his hip. "Shouldn't be any problem at all."

Lyons grinned. "I'm beginning to side with Black on that steak dinner."

"Aw, shucks," James replied with mock humility. "No need to go for anything fancy."

"So once we get inside," Lyons replied, "we'll be up for a floor-to-floor search. And we'll have to make sure we avoid contact with any of the partiers. They looked like mostly college kids and they were making a heck of a racket, which means they'll probably be drunk and do something stupid."

"Boy, you guys sure don't ask for much," Manning said. "We're going to have our work cut out for us."

"So if we don't know which apartment they're in, how are we going to locate them?"

"Aha!" Blancanales said, raising a finger and looking in Cronaugher's direction. "That's where our police friend comes in. He reached out to a friend at the computer center in their downtown headquarters."

James and Manning looked to Cronaugher for the rest of the explanation, and he grinned sheepishly with a shrug. "I just had him run the address through the DMV database. He came back with a list where registrations referenced apartment numbers. There were only two not on the list—2B and 6D. I don't figure your North Korean bad guys would have vehicles registered to their addresses."

"Nice work!" James said.

"Okay, so now you know the plan. Let's get ready to do the needful," Lyons said.

"And may the Force be with us," Schwarz added.

Blancanales rolled his eyes and shook his head. "You're such a nerd."

WEN XIANG EASED back the cuff of the neoprene-lined glove, secured at his wrist with a waterproofed rubber strap, and glanced at the luminous display on his watch. In just fifteen short minutes they would be deploying for the first phase of their mission. While an attempt like this wouldn't have been his first choice, Xiang had to credit the brilliance of Yan Zhou. He hadn't really held much respect for Zhou, only tolerated the fat and obnoxious prick, but this plan to penetrate the U.S. was a pure stroke of genius. No way would the Americans ever consider an attempt such as this.

He had to temper his thinking because he knew it could also spell doom for him and his men—he'd underestimated the Americans before and it had nearly cost him his life. Of course, they had been up against trained combatants on those previous occasions. This time their greatest two enemies were the elements and time. The water would be shockingly cold, and the heated suits would only offer a very limited amount of protection. If the boat didn't get to them quickly, they would almost certainly die of hypothermia.

If Xiang had been given a choice, he would have opted to travel under forged credentials via a commercial flight, but there hadn't been such an opportunity. The papers Zhou had given him would only be good for facilitating his movement once in the United States, and ultimately to get him out once their mission was complete. In any case, Xiang wouldn't worry about it. He didn't have much experience with something like this, but the trained soldiers accompanying him had made assurances he would be okay if he followed their instructions to the letter.

Xiang would do it—he had no desire to end his life at the cold, dark bottom of American waters, his carcass pecked into oblivion by whatever creatures inhabited those depths. The assassin pushed such morbid thoughts from his mind and concentrated on the job at hand. The minutes seemed to tick by agonizingly slowly, and then suddenly the plane banked sharply and Xiang felt it begin its descent. Another ten minutes crawled by before a small hydraulic door in the belly of the massive cargo liner opened. The first of the twelve-man team went out, and then the next, and finally after the sixth man it was Xiang's turn.

When he hit the water it felt as if every bone in his body had broken, but what he was really feeling were the air bladders conforming to his skin to cushion the impact. As he'd been instructed by the leader of the military unit accompanying him, Xiang had taken a deep breath and held it just before landing. Under normal circumstances, cold water would cause what was known as the Mammalian diving reflex, a condition where the sudden exposure of the head and neck to extremely cold water could slow heart rates and, in some cases, cause cardiac dysrhythmias. Xiang had no desire to find out firsthand. By holding his breath, he would not experience this sudden change in condition, his lungs being filled with warm air to near capacity.

In actuality, Xiang was surprised when he surfaced and realized he wasn't as cold as he'd thought he would be. The thermal properties of his heated suit were doing their job. Xiang immediately donned his warm air exchange and cinched the rubber and neoprene head cover tighter against his skull. He then began to paddle toward the very dim but still visible red-filtered light flashing on the suits of three of the initial jumpers. This gave the others a target to swim toward and provided a triangular beacon for the boat to find.

The team of thirteen men had barely assembled within proximity of each other, close enough to link arms and form a circle, before the faint sound of a boat motor greeted their ears, growing steadily as they bobbed in the icy, fresh-water currents of what the locals has named Knik Arm. Within minutes Xiang felt strong arms help to haul him aboard the boat, and one of his team showed him to an area below where he could get warm and strip out of his specially designed wetsuit.

Xiang took a moment to check his watch again before beginning to strip out of the suit and don the dry, matte-black fatigues packed into the waterproof bag accompanying him. He slipped into combat boots, laced them quickly and completed the ensemble with a utility belt that included a fighting knife, garrote and holstered 9 mm pistol. By the time he'd retrieved the final item from the bag—a Chinese-made QCW-05, a bullpup-style SMG manufactured by Jianshe Industries Group—the boat was once more moving on a course for American shores.

And in just a short time, Xiang would have his chance to redeem his earlier failing and deal death to his most hated enemies.

Ju Young-Soon could tell that her arrival at the rendezvous point had taken both men by such surprise they'd been rendered speechless. By design, she had a key to the apartment and so had seen fit to let herself in. She came through the door so quietly that neither Wee Hum Han nor

Chin Nam heard her at first. When their eyes locked with hers, the two men stood still and gazed on her with awe.

"Wh-what in the name of...Young-Soon!" Nam had finally stammered.

The two hadn't rushed to embrace each other, something that both thought they might have done had it not been for the third, more maniacal presence in the room. Instead, Young-Soon had bowed to Nam and then rendered the same courtesy to Han, who returned the gesture without much enthusiasm.

His face and voice reeked of disrespect when he finally spoke to her. "It is most excellent to see you. I regret to say that we thought our next meeting would not have been an event for celebration."

"I know you were ordered to terminate me if I could not be retrieved," she said. "I didn't start in this business yesterday."

"Which leaves me wondering just exactly how it is you escaped, Young-Soon," Han replied coldly. "I hope for your sake that you've not brought the Americans here. If you've compromised the mission, you must surely know that my original orders to dispense with you would stand."

"You shouldn't be so hasty to kill your own kind, Wee," Young-Soon replied, meeting his gaze without showing the slightest discomfiture. "There are most certainly others of your kind who enjoy such things no less than you. One day our government might send the same kind to end your own life."

"It would be a fitting end."

Young-Soon didn't waver. "Just so. But for now it's only important you know that I *have* escaped and the Americans don't know where I am. I created quite a distraction for them at the hotel near the airport. They will be sorting it out for some time."

"So if you're now free and the police don't know of our whereabouts," Nam said, "what should we do next?"

"Why are you asking her?" Han demanded.

Young-Soon's eyes narrowed and she edged her hand ever closer to the pistol tucked into the small of her back. She'd put it there on the off chance Han opted not to follow protocol and forced her into an alternative action. It wasn't one she *wanted* to take, but Young-Soon wouldn't hesitate if it came down to it.

"He's asking me because I'm still the primary on this mission."

"Ha, that would be laughable if it wasn't so sad!" Han countered with a sneer. "You *have* no mission left, girl. The Americans are convinced more than ever now that we're responsible for firing that missile, and you failed to kill the American scientist."

"I didn't have any reason to kill her," Young-Soon replied.

"No reason? You fool! Those were your orders. You were told to destroy the prototype and kill the American scientist. Instead, you were captured attempting to assassinate Yu, a secondary and relatively unimportant consideration."

"Perhaps that would be true under other circumstances. But what you don't know and I do is that the Americans were already aware that neither the technology nor the missile originated from North Korea. What I decided to do was purposefully allow myself to be captured, to find out what they *did* know, and then to decide what course of action to take. It was then that I realized exactly what had happened."

Chin Nam's eyes narrowed. "What do you mean?"

Young-Soon gazed at him only a moment, intent on not taking her eyes off Wee Hum Han for more than a second. "There was no way that our people could have known what the Chinese had planned unless it had been fed to them. Our intelligence network isn't that good, frankly." Young-Soon looked back at Han. "When I heard what the Americans had to say, I realized that someone had allowed that information to reach us. They were expecting us to react to it, and we played straight into their hands. And once those individuals discovered what it was I planned to do, they put *you* into action. Isn't that right?"

"It's standard procedure," Han replied with a frosty grin.

"And is it also procedure to betray your government and your own people for the cause of a terrorist organization?"

"What?" Nam interjected. "Young-Soon, what are you talking about? *What terrorist organization?* You're not making any sense."

"Oh, it all makes perfect sense to me now. You see, Han is actually part of the Gold Star Faction."

"What? That's insane!"

"It is also a very serious accusation," Han said, all mocking gone from his tone, which had now taken on a much darker tenor—just as his face. "The GSF is a myth, at best. And anyway, they are a Chinese terror group."

"They are much more than that, Wee, and you know it because you are a part of them. The reach of the GSF is extensive. Chinese, Japanese, Koreans…and yes, even Americans are part of their ranks. They are not confined to the spread of Chinese power. Their very nature suggests hardline Communism that they believe should be forced upon the whole world. Such a doctrine would mean the end of peace and security in our country. So please stop pretending your ignorance. You are a terrorist and a murderer. And more despicable, you are a fucking traitor to North Korea."

"And you are *dead!*" Han shouted.

Ju Young-Soon had expected Han to try something but she couldn't have been ready for what happened next. She heard the first signs of trouble from behind and while she kept her pistol pointed in Han's direction she risked a glance over her left shoulder. From the bedroom door just off the main hallway she saw the two men emerge with SMGs held low and ready.

Young-Soon heard Nam's shout of warning just a heartbeat before she turned, dropped to her knees and leveled her pistol in the direction of her enemies.

ABLE TEAM, MANNING and James were all bejeweled with various weapons of war dangling from holsters, sheaths and in some cases their hands. To an observer they were like five ghosts of death as they moved up the sidewalk toward the apartment building. They reached the front, unobserved by anyone but Cronaugher, who waited in his squad car a safe distance—he had orders to call in the cavalry as soon as he got their signal—and scanned their flanks before they rounded the far side of the building and moved in cover-and-run patterns along the edge of the parking area.

At one point, Lyons looked up long enough to spot the lights in the sixth-floor window and he wondered for a moment if that wasn't their location. What is it Cronaugher had said? Apartments 2B and 6D? Yeah, that *had* to be the place because the lights were all out on the second floor and they knew enough to know that the 2B unit was on this same side that faced onto the parking lot.

The five warriors reached the rear door within a minute, and Manning went to work with his magic bag. He lined the keyed lock mounted just above the plate that was bolted in place where the handle would've been on most other doors with the special cutting explosives. He then withdrew a pencil detonator, primed it by yanking back on a timed fuse and then ordered everyone to stand clear. The cutting charge made more noise than Lyons would've preferred but there wasn't anything he could do about it now. Only a red-hot, smoking pattern was left where the lock had once been.

As James withdrew a Ka-bar and used it to clear what remained of the bolt from the frame, Manning told Lyons, "Don't you just love it?"

"Makes my nipples hard," Schwarz said.

Lyons blanched. *"T-M-I."*

"Let's *go* already," Blancanales whispered fiercely.

The five entered the door as one coordinated unit and immediately headed up the stairs. They had planned to try the sixth floor first, confident that if they hit the jackpot on the first go the terrorists wouldn't be able to escape. To maximize their resources, Manning and James had agreed to hold position at the second floor in the event the terrorists were occupying both units. While the possibilities of such an arrangement were unlikely, the team didn't plan to leave anything to chance. Their enemies were resourceful, and underestimating that resourcefulness was a really good way to end up being carried out of the area of operation feet first.

At the second-floor landing, James and Manning entered the hallway and fanned out to take position in the deepest shadows of the dimly lit hallway.

From the appearance of the walls and floors, Lyons could tell why this had been deemed a low-income area. He could hear the steady thump of the music, the raucous voices and drunken laughter still, even as they rounded the corner of the stairs to begin heading to the third floor. But it wasn't until they got the fifth floor that they all heard the steady and distant sounds of autofire and realized they had chosen wisely.

Another party of its own had obviously just gotten started, and Able Team was hellfire bent on crashing it.

Young-Soon took the first gunner with three shots to the chest, the 9 mm pistol barking in steady rhythm as the rounds tore away flesh and bone before puncturing the guy's lungs. A pink spray erupted from the man's mouth even as his corpse was already tumbling to the floor. The second man aligned his sights on Young-Soon, but she managed to get a shot off that somehow happened to strike the stock of the SMG and drive the initial volley of rounds spitting from the muzzle off course. It was the only break she got because the man, obviously an experienced combatant, continued to charge and sprawled on top of her. The move surprised her and the pistol was knocked from her grip.

Chin Nam stood frozen in place for only a few seconds before training took over and he reacted with blazing speed. His own pistol came into play and he whipped it in Han's direction, now confident that every word his beloved had spoken was true. Han didn't look that surprised and this caused Nam a moment's hesitation. Han dropped from view and rolled out of Nam's immediate sight picture. Nam followed, rounding the tall bar separating the main living area from the kitchenette, but Wee Hum Han was nowhere to be found.

Nam then realized his mistake and turned toward the overstuffed recliner to his immediate right. His moment of insight couldn't save him before Han managed to gain the upper hand by driving a short punch into Nam's injured shoulder. White-hot lances of pain cut through to the bone and Nam let out a scream, only remaining conscious because the heavy bandaging served to cushion the blow a bit. But it was a distraction and more than enough time for Han to draw his gun and shoot Nam in the belly at point-blank range.

Nam's pistol clattered from numbed fingers as his eyes went wide with shock. He cast one last, hopeless look at Han, who now grinned sadistically in his face, and then he collapsed in a heap to the floor. Han kicked the pistol out of Nam's reach, considered putting another round into the man's head, but then he refrained in preference to letting Nam die slowly and painfully. It was a much more fitting end.

Han turned to the commotion at hand and saw that Young-Soon had somehow managed to get the upper hand against her enemy. She was straddling his chest now, punching him repeatedly in the face, her hands bloody with the pulp that had become her opponent's nose. Han crossed the distance in two strides, pointed the pistol at the back of Young-Soon's head and squeezed the trigger. Her body lurched forward, her head smashing against the wall, leaving a gory streak as she slid grotesquely to a point where her belly covered the face of the man she'd bested.

Han thought about leaving the weakling behind but

he realized that loyalty commanded loyalty, so he shoved Young-Soon's corpse aside with his foot and dragged the man to his feet. He could barely see, his face a mask of blood and his nose clearly broken. All the same, Han grunted before turning the man and shoving him out ahead of him. It was time to leave—the shooting would surely result in a police response.

There was nothing more he could do here—he'd accomplished the mission Yan Zhou had sent him to undertake.

THE MEN OF Able Team didn't expect company to emerge from apartment 6D as they alighted on the sixth-floor landing. They especially weren't expecting trouble to come in the form of only two men, one armed and the other with blood streaming down his face. The injured man was obviously being helped, if only in a subtle way, by another man as he staggered into the hall like a zombie. The guy accompanying him, a pistol in his right hand, turned to see the three Able Team warriors and a mixed expression of shock and recognition crossed his face.

Both men realized they were faced with enemies and they raised their weapons in a purely reactionary course. It didn't pan out for either of them as Able Team unloaded with a furious barrage of pistol fire, the muzzles of their weapons flashing in concert to their very violent and effective response. The pair of terrorists danced and jerked under the assault, Mash-Face being the first to fall under a merciless hail of slugs to his belly and chest. The other man followed him a moment later as two rounds caught him in the face simultaneously, the pressure from the dual impact splitting his skull wide-open and depositing his brains all over the nearby walls. His virtually headless body seemed to teeter for a moment before falling prone to the dirty, cracked linoleum.

Able Team held position and waited for more trouble but after a reasonable time they realized it had ended much more quickly than it had begun. They moved quickly and proficiently up the hall until they entered the apartment and found a sight they hardly expected. One man who'd been toting a machine gun lay on his back at the far end of the hall, motionless. A second body faced down closer to the front door, a pool of fresh blood obscuring the back of her head and her neck cocked at a rather odd angle.

In the profile of the dim light, they recognized the body as that of Ju Young-Soon. They heard a groan and something that sounded like someone dragging a club foot, and as they moved cautiously into the apartment they spotted another man, one they didn't recognize, dragging himself with everything he had toward Young-Soon. Upon seeing the men of Able Team, he reached one hand out and pointed to her, dredging up a deep, mournful wail from somewhere deep in his bowels.

"Jesus..." Blancanales whispered.

"Tell Cronaugher we need medical here," Lyons said.

Then his tactical radio buzzed for attention and when he answered it he heard Manning's voice come through crisp and clear. "Sit-rep?"

"We're done here," Lyons replied. "No bad guys left. You?"

"All clear and no trouble from this apartment down here."

"Good."

"David just checked in, too. Says if we got the time, he could sure as hell use us."

"Understood. Hang tight and we'll join you in a minute."

IT WAS JUST before dawn when Phoenix Force sighted the enemy courtesy of the eagle-eyed T. J. Hawkins.

"That's good work, T.J.," McCarter said when Hawkins informed him.

"He's just younger," Encizo remarked. "Better eyesight then us old fogeys."

"Or lucky," McCarter quipped.

"No luck," Hawkins objected. "Just a heaping pile of skill."

"Oh, it's a bloody heaping pile of somethin'."

With that, Phoenix Force left their observation spot. They'd managed to secure an elevated site that gave them a fairly decent view of the shoreline. True to his word, Kurtzman had managed to pinpoint the location of a remote heat signature—about the size of a half-ton motor launch—which they then got a USAF spy drone from Elmendorf-Richardson to confirm. They'd even managed to get an exact count of the enemy force—thirteen bodies in all.

"A baker's dozen," Hawkins had remarked.

Now McCarter said, "Time to go turn up the heat on that baker's dozen."

The three men returned to the Hummer on loan from the base security police and climbed aboard. As Encizo cranked the engine and put it in gear, the cell phone on McCarter's belt demanded attention.

He held up his hand toward Encizo. "Hold here a moment, mate. Yeah?"

"It's your friendly neighborhood cavalry," Lyons's voice replied, hoarse but surprisingly upbeat.

McCarter couldn't resist grinning at his friend's gibe. "About time you got off your sorry duffs and did something."

"Hey, it's supposed to be a cushy government job, ain't it?"

"Depends who's in charge. Where away?"

"Close. According to your GPS signal we're within five minutes of your position."

"Well, then, keep on us," McCarter said. "We've spotted the target and we need to intercept ASAP. So shag your arse and get to us as soon as you can. When we get in the thick of it, I'll be call-sign Vanilla."

"Cute, very original."

"Came up with it myself. Out."

McCarter nodded at Encizo, who put the Hummer in gear, performed a one-eighty and then accelerated smoothly down the service road. Eventually, they left the hardball and continued on crush-refined, the vibration of the Hummer enough to rattle their teeth.

"Obviously they haven't graded this in a while," McCarter noted over the bone-jarring ride.

Encizo kept his hands locked steadily on the wheel, adjusting his speed as the turns in the road demanded. It wouldn't have done for them to rush to meet their enemy only to never arrive because they wound up in the ditch. In reality, they didn't have much of a plan for this engagement anyway. Time was fast running out, and they knew that if even one of their enemies was allowed to escape it could have dire consequences for Teng Cai and his mother. It only took one assassin's bullet hitting its mark, and the show was over for the young prodigy. Not to mention the threat to the civilian populace at large. No, hitting these foreign invaders hard and fast and without mercy *was* their only option at this point. At least out here in this bleak, rugged Alaskan wilderness Phoenix Force and Able Team could wage their private little war without it landing in the papers.

If they did the job right, nobody would ever even know.

Up ahead they caught the brief glimmer of headlights on a switchback below their own piece of road. Encizo immediately killed his own lights and slowed considerably, letting their eyes adjust as they scanned either side for an opportune location to conceal their vehicle and still provide them a good point from which to launch an ambush. They found it a minute later at a turn in the road, and Encizo eased the vehicle between two massive pine trees, the base of their trunks shrouded with tall patches of dried brush. All three men immediately went EVA, convening at the back of the Hummer, where Hawkins handed out squad-based weapons.

Encizo took an M-60 A-3 machine gun and immediately charged away to set up the optimal field of fire. McCarter opted for a MINIMI 7.62 × 51mm NATO machine gun manufactured by the incomparable FN Herstal. Hawkins then brought out his own preferred peacemaker, an M-16/M-203 combo and a good supply of 40 mm HE grenades. The team spread out and took up firing positions, careful to ensure none of them would cross outside the boundaries of the road when the shooting started. Too many times soldiers had been killed in situations just like this as a result of friendly fire—the Stony Man teams had trained to make sure nothing like that *ever* happened among their ranks.

Time seemed to tick by like someone had tossed the world into a bowl of honey, where seconds seemed to pass like minutes. Slowly, the Phoenix Force ambushers could hear the sound of an approaching engine...and then two... three. So, a total of three vehicles, which probably meant cars. What in fact came around the corner was a pickup in the lead, followed by a van and trailed by a late-model four-door coupe.

McCarter and Encizo waited without fidgeting, ignoring the ice-cold ground that cut through their guts and threatened to suck the very breath from them. They would have to wait for Hawkins to make the first move since he was packing the explosives, and the delivery of the first grenade was meant to be the signal to engage. At last it came in the form of crack, perhaps a little louder than a shotgun, followed by the eruption of dirt and gravel from the road in the wake of an orange fireball.

The grenade didn't hit any of the vehicles, just as planned, because they'd first wanted to ensure they had a verifiable enemy. To have unilaterally blown up a group of hunters or college kids out having a good time wasn't something anyone on the team wanted for their conscience. There was enough blood on their respective hands, and adding to it with the blood of innocents was a much harder pill than any of them cared to swallow.

As they'd hoped, the parties in the vehicle responded in just a way that left no doubt they were the enemies Phoenix Force sought. The lead vehicle immediately dodged to the side and pulled over, several faces peering out of the windows at the remnants of the grenade Hawkins had delivered spot-on between the pickup and van. The van fishtailed and skidded out of control until it came to a nose-grinding halt in a deep ditch.

The coupe stopped in the center of the road and four men bailed from it, automatic weapons leveled and sweeping the trees immediately to their left with autofire. None of them had been able to tell from where exactly the grenade had been launched, a testament to Hawkins's skill, but they responded nonetheless with commendable swiftness. Too bad it wasn't in the right direction.

Upon seeing these first targets ripe for the picking, McCarter and Encizo opened up on full volume with the machine guns, hammering the first of the combatants in a deadly crossfire. At the same moment, the van's rear door flipped open and six more men spilled out, branching away from the carnage and searching for cover and concealment among the nearby foliage.

McCarter eased off the trigger long enough to see the men try to escape the assault. But they had barely reached cover when they started to topple.

McCarter realized that Lyons had arrived and was engaging the targets from the opposite side of the road, probably realizing beforehand that if he was going to pick the ideal ambush spot he would've gone with McCarter's choice. Great minds, the Briton thought before putting his cheek back to the stock and swinging the muzzle of the FN MINIMI to acquire his next target.

RAFAEL ENCIZO WAS a veteran combatant with more firefights under his belt than even the majority of his teammates. In all that time, though, he'd never seen a veritable slaughter like this one—the enemy had fallen into the trap of overconfidence and now Phoenix Force and Able Team were teaching them the error of their ways. Encizo had brought down two of the four from the coupe with headshots before he saw the three in the pickup bail and take up firing positions in the wrong direction. The terrorists were shooting *up* the road.

Like McCarter, Encizo realized they now had their enemy caught in a furious gauntlet. All the past few days of violence and murder, with their opponents somehow keeping one step ahead of them, was culminating into a victory for the good guys. And Encizo, for one, was glad to be a part of it. He triggered his weapon and took another terrorist down, this one from the van. The three near the pickup folded under the pinpoint accuracy of Manning, James and the hot shots of Able Team. The party only got more interesting when Hawkins's next grenade landed in the center of the bed of the pickup. Metal, glass and melted rubber combined to propel dangerous flaming missiles in every direction, cutting through those close enough to succumb to its effects while it lit the night in a fantastic blaze of retribution.

Within minutes, the battled ended as the last terrorist collapsed under a fusillade of heavy-caliber slugs. When the echoes of battle finally died away, all that remained to comfort the victors was the crackle of flames from the three wrecked vehicles. And somewhere in the distant and bitter cold of dawn, a coyote howled—proof that even in the wake of violent and ugly death life did go on. And yet somehow, it didn't bring peace to the men of Phoenix Force and Able Team. Instead, it left them only with the melancholy sense they had kept their commitment—their solid oath to fight alongside their brothers and defend freedom for America.

CHAPTER TWENTY-SEVEN

"Distance to target?" the man asked.

"About one-hundred-twenty meters," David McCarter replied. "Windage is northwest, two at an angle of about eight-zero-five."

"Good. Now all we have to do is wait. Shouldn't be more than a minute or two."

"If that intel I got you was good," McCarter said.

The man took his eye from the high-powered sniper scope mounted above a Heckler & Koch PSG-1 and pinned McCarter with his cold, blue gaze. "I'd trust your intel over most anybody else's I know, David."

McCarter looked sheepish and then returned his attention to the spotter scope. "I appreciate you letting me come along on this one."

"I would've been plenty happy to let you do it yourself, if you'd chosen."

"Nah," McCarter replied, not taking his eyes from the scope. "This is your area of expertise more than mine."

"You're good with a rifle."

Now McCarter looked at his friend. "Maybe so. But I'm *not* you, mate."

The man grinned. "Some would consider that a stroke of good luck."

"I'm just glad I was able to book you for this trip."

"It's no sweat," the man said, the creases in his forehead betraying the burden he wore on his ever-troubled brow. "Hark Kwan didn't deserve what he got. But he went down living large and now we have to make sure this doesn't happen again."

"You're bloody right on about that." McCarter checked the spotter scope again and said, "Okay, here we go."

The sniper put his eye back to the scope and made a minor adjustment before his body settled into a position so still it appeared he'd just died. McCarter knew better—he couldn't have chosen a finer friend or colleague to join him for this venture. And while a part of him would've wished to pull the trigger himself, he knew the man alongside him was equal to the job. McCarter wanted a guarantee and this was the guy who could give it to him, no doubt about it.

"Target's in sight," McCarter said.

"Confirm identity?" came the reply.

McCarter hesitated a moment, lifted his head long enough to wipe a speck of dust in his eye, then returned to his position. After a long moment he said, "Target is confirmed—the target *is* Vice Air-Marshal Yan Zhou."

And with that, the Executioner squeezed the trigger.

* * * * *

The Executioner

Don Pendleton's

REBEL BLAST

American scientists are held hostage when Chechen rebels take control of a town....

A rebel group has taken control of a town in Chechnya, threatening the lives of a group of American mining surveyors trapped there. To stop them, the Russian military plans to annihilate the terrorists by destroying the town and everyone living there—including the American civilians. Flying in under the radar, Mack Bolan, along with a makeshift team of mercenaries, has less than 24 hours to find the surveyors and get them out alive before all hell breaks loose.

GOLD
EAGLE®

Available November wherever books and ebooks are sold.

TAKE 'EM FREE

2 action-packed novels plus a mystery bonus

NO RISK

NO OBLIGATION TO BUY

Don Pendleton's Mack Bolan®

GROUND ZERO

Within striking range of America...

The kidnapping of a high-ranking U.S. intelligence official by Somali pirates requires a quick and dirty extraction, and Bolan is tapped for the mission. But when its successful completion red-flags covert data, indicating an imminent attack on U.S. soil, the situation turns hard and deadly. The trail leads back to Iran and Bolan must go undercover in Tehran. Here, seconds count as he races to eliminate the power behind the threat and stop an enemy taking aim at America's heart with intent to kill.

Available December wherever books and ebooks are sold.